APL, Ever AFTER

Chrissie Harrison

Valericain
Press

For Zoë, my happy ever after

Chapter One

B eth offered her cheek, sidelining his attempted kiss.

'Thanks for a lovely evening,' said Number 33.

'It was really nice to meet you,' she fibbed.

'How are you fixed for next weekend?' he asked, fishy breath tickling her nostrils. Yes, he'd had the salmon, but the odour had been there when he arrived.

Way to make a good impression, 33... I mean Callum.

'Busy jumping naked into a pit of spikes,' Beth wanted to say.

'I'll have to check my diary,' she replied.

Hopefully, he'd understand that was universal code for "I have no intention of seeing you again". The guy surely knew that not all first dates led to second dates. Her conversion ratio was 20%. Third dates? 5%.

It's a numbers game, 33. Please read the room.

He gave a resigned smile. 'Okay.'

He *did* have a nice smile, but the problem was all the other stuff. Well, not *all* the other stuff. Some stuff. The inability to take an interest in her life—not just her chest—was a turn-off, especially as his profile used the word "empathetic". And she hadn't been thrilled by his 47-minute discourse on voting constituency boundary changes.

She *had* checked her watch. Subtly.

Still, standing outside Winchester's finest seafood restaurant, she realised she was being hard on Callum. Perhaps first date nerves had caused his verbal diarrhoea. Perhaps he simply loved his job. Perhaps he was trying to stop *her* from talking about the world of venture capital. Perhaps he wanted an excuse to gaze into her eyes. He had been. She'd gazed into his. A mistake, given the attempted kiss. He must have thought things had gone well. And they had—more or less.

He'd arrived on time. He'd courteously paid for dinner. He'd opened the door for her. All big ticks. But there was the breath thing. And his incessant eyebrow tugging. And his Apple Watch face was the Mickey Mouse one. Fine if you're ten, not if you're thirty-seven.

Some people might call Beth picky. No: she was merely being careful. Once bitten, twice shy.

'Where are you parked?' he asked.

'I came on the bus.' She pointed across the road to a bus stop that was mercifully close but not, technically, hers.

'Want a lift?'

'Um... no, thanks.'

Disappointment pursed his lips. 'Okay. I'm this way.' He waved her to the pedestrian crossing.

At least he's being a gent. And he's already tried the kiss thing, so hopefully no more of that in a mo.

At the wrong bus stop, they shook hands.

'Thanks for walking me over,' she said. 'Drive safe.'

'Take it easy, Beth. I'll wait to hear from you.'

'Absolutely.' She flashed a smile and parked her backside on the sloping slab of plastic that constituted a seat under the bus shelter.

Mercifully, he took that to mean "End of the evening. Now please sod off", and duly strolled away.

A bus glided to a halt with a hiss of air brakes.

Her stomach tensed.

Please don't look over your shoulder.

He looked over his shoulder.

She glanced at the matrix display under the canopy's roof. This stop only served one route.

Shit.

So she stepped aboard and almost made it to the solitary vacant seat before the bus pulled away. Almost.

The lurch threw her sideways. She grabbed for the rail. Missed. Toppled into an older woman in a purple beret, who shot Beth the evils.

'Sorry,' Beth said, grimacing. Then, propelled by the vehicle's acceleration and a desperation to escape the scene of the crime, she blundered up to the back row, whacking her head on the low ceiling, and thumped down onto the seat.

Fucking fuckety fuck.

Rubbing her head, she took out her phone to check the route, see where she was being unwittingly taken. The bus slowed.

In every crisis, there is opportunity.

She sprang up, keeping her head bowed, let the vehicle's momentum carry her to the doors, then stepped gratefully back into the cool June dusk.

Glancing nervously around—just her luck that Callum would still be strolling past—she crossed the road and secreted herself in another shelter, ready to head back to her *actual* destination.

Fifteen minutes later, she arrived at her suburban semi.

In the hallway, she tugged off her low heels and put them on the small rack. As Callum was a six-footer, she'd added an extra inch onto her 5'7", on the off-chance they'd get into a smooch. As it was, she wouldn't be kissing him again.

Best to rip the plaster off quickly.

She pulled out her phone, thumbed the dating app, located his profile, and sent a brief but polite note saying she didn't want to take things any further.

Closing her eyes, she let out a breath of relief.

Sorry, 33. You were not my lucky number.

The lights were on in the living room. Beth didn't like coming home to darkness—not out of fear, only to give some sense of warmth and comfort. Crusading naysayers like Wilson (number 20) would have accused her of single-handedly killing the planet by keeping three bulbs on unnecessarily. However, she didn't care what Wilson Joseph thought, because he'd sneezed without covering his nose, reckoned women weren't cut out for football, and had his bloody name the wrong way round.

She glanced at the trio of whisky bottles on the side cupboard.

It was Saturday night, and after the evening's failure, she deserved a tot. To her credit, she hadn't had a drink following *every* bad date. She'd be a raging alcoholic by now. Instead, she'd maintained the mantra that it was a numbers game and she merely needed to kiss a few more frogs. Ideally, metaphorically. But the game was becoming tedious and disenchanting.

She poured a finger of Glenfarclas 15yo into one of a pair of cut-glass tumblers. Some wedding presents were too nice to throw away. Or let Leon have.

A corner of the room squawked.

She wandered over and opened the cage door. 'Hey, Quincunx.' She lifted the parrot onto her shoulder. 'Anything to say for yourself tonight?'

'Squawk.'

In nine months, the parrot hadn't said a single bloody word. She'd considered asking the rehoming centre for a refund, especially as the bird was there because its previous owner had become fed up with its constant chatter. It was a hell of a relationship litmus test that she couldn't even find a pet that was on her wavelength. She'd had better conversation with Jeremy (number 7) and his sparkling repartee had opened with "What's your favourite type of bread?"

She sank into the sofa's welcome embrace. Quincunx nuzzled at her hair.

She'd bought the bird for company, something to fill the house that felt very empty when Leon moved out. A companion who didn't complain at almost every VAR decision on Match Of The Day. Yet Beth didn't resent her soon-to-be ex-husband for watching football. She might as well have been annoyed about the toilet seat being left up or him falling asleep immediately after sex. Unfair if the sex was excellent. And Leon's was.

She sipped the whisky. Its smooth warmth slipped down her throat.

Leon never appreciated whisky. That wasn't why they split. No single thing was, truthfully. They simply reached the end of the road.

He wasn't a parrot person either. When they'd hooked up, twelve years ago, age 22, he'd mocked her collection of parrot paraphernalia. Later, when they'd moved into this, the marital household, her colourful array of sketches, trinkets and figurines was banished to the loft.

She still hadn't retrieved the keepsakes. Perhaps tomorrow.

Give Quincunx some avian company, after a fashion.

She stroked his white feathers.

What had caused the sulphur-crested cockatoo to fall silent? Was it the environment? The tension of divorce in the air? His cage? Did the little guy hate his name?

Is it me, buddy, not you? I give as much love as I can.

Well, there was no way she was sticking with "Cocky", the name when she acquired him. Yes, it's sweet when a child names a pet, but if she'd introduced him to friends as "Cocky the cockatoo", they might have rushed out and bought her a doll's house or some loom bands.

Besides, "Quincunx" was nicely maths-y, as well as sounding a bit rude. If she found a bloke worthy of bringing home—Ben (number 26) was the only one so far—and he knew the word meant the pattern of five dots on dice, she was onto a good thing. Mr Right needed to have a smart head on his shoulders... and fulfil other criteria.

Many, admittedly.

Too many, apparently.

How come that with thousands of eligible men in the country, plenty of ways to meet them, and a range of apps to facilitate the dating game, she'd struck out with quite magnificent consistency?

Is it me, not them?

She swiped to the second screen of her phone, held a thumb to the chosen icon, and, when they all jiggled, she tapped the tiny minus sign.

"Delete App"?

You betcha.

Tap.

If love truly was a numbers game, Beth Moore was fed up with counting.

Chapter Two

After Saturday morning's early bike ride around the Hampshire countryside—punctuated by a coffee and pastry stop—Sam Carter luxuriated in the shower, considering the weekend ahead.

How to stay away from his ageing laptop, avoid being sucked into work? A year ago, he'd have kept busy, doing some coding for a client, crushing deadlines, exceeding their expectations. Now, the projects were too humdrum. Nothing excited him. Why give more than a pound of flesh?

He towelled down.

A little voice said it was time to move on, branch out. Even take a leap of faith and set up on his own. But there were bills to pay, and nobody to lean on. No flatmate, no girlfriend. On the plus side, if he did work weekends, there'd be nobody to frown at him, lecture about work-life balance.

He looked in the mirror.

Lecturing would be okay if the lecturer was a foxy brunette, her head screwed on, her idiosyncrasies adorable, and with a penchant for 32-year-old full-stack software developers who can't name a single Taylor Swift song but make a decent beef wellington.

Oh, and providing we'd met in Paris.

He pulled on a T-shirt and joggers, made his hair "indoor presentable" rather than "going out smart", and began all the house-y things he avoided during the week.

Yeah, she'd have to be happy with that, too.

Mid-afternoon, he was reclining on the sofa, Casablanca—one of his favourites—on the TV, when his mobile rang. It was a FaceTime call.

He propped the phone on the coffee table. 'Hi, sis. Happy birthdaversary.'

Elodie's face broke into a smile, as it did when he used the dumb, made-up word. 'Hi, bro. Just calling to say thanks for my present.'

Another face dipped into the frame. 'Thanks, buddy,' said Warren. 'Happy -aversary, mate.'

Elodie eye-rolled. 'Promise me that one day you'll grow up?'

'We can't all be as sad, sensible and settled down as you.'

Sam loved telling people that his sister met hubby Warren on a school trip. Sometimes he'd pretend they were 9, eyes met across a coach aisle. Sometimes he'd say she was 9 and he was a teacher. The expressions of disgust and disbelief were worth the stress of trying to keep a straight face.

Actually, both were teachers from different schools who were visiting Bayeux on the same day. Later, in the hotel, they'd bonded over much-needed drinks. Despite living an hour apart in the UK and working like dogs, this was no barrier to true love.

Elodie spoke fluent French. Sam was jealous. He'd been learning for five years... slowly. Languages didn't come naturally. But imagine meeting the hot Parisian girl of your dreams and being unable to understand a word she said;

"Take me to bed immediately, big sexy English man." (whatever that was in French)

"Huh?"

"Au revoir." (He knew that much).

Must do more Duolingo!

Elodie and Warren were hoping for one or more ankle biters of their own. Being around hundreds of kids, day in and day out, somehow hadn't soured them to the prospect. Coming home every evening would be a breeze—herding one cat instead of twenty-five.

So they were "trying". Sam never asked for progress updates. Picturing your sister and brother-in-law *going at it* could put a guy right off his Pret lunch. Instead, he awaited the gleeful phone call or a WhatsApp picture of an indistinct black-and-white blob overlaid with heart and champagne emojis.

This wasn't that call, meaning they were still at the aubergine emoji stage.

Don't get an image, don't get an image...

Elodie's wedding was on her birthday, so Sam usually bought her a birthday present incorporating the relevant anniversary motif. This year, the theme was wool or copper. He'd chosen a toy woollen sheep. Firstly, Elodie had liked sheep since she was a youngster. Secondly—and he'd never known whether any coincidence was involved—she'd become Mrs Ramsbottom. The sheep thing was an in-joke. She'd probably have preferred an Amazon voucher, but hid it well.

'I know I sound like a stuck record, but it's pretty sad that I'm the person in your life who gets these well-thought-out gifts.'

'I still have the receipt. Post it back and I'll get a refund. I could use some new trainers.'

'That's not what I mean, and you know it!' Her brow furrowed in fake indignation. 'You have a lot of love to give, Sam. You're the most romantic guy I know.'

'Don't let Warren hear you say that.'

'Stop deflecting. When are you going to channel all that love into the future Mrs Carter?'

'Er, when I meet her? Come on, El, I don't need you on my case, too. If a romantic meet-cute in Paris worked for Mum and Dad, why not me? I'd love to be still going strong fifty years later, like they are.'

She closed her eyes. 'Yeah. Sorry. Judgemental. And it's not *really* a chore that my baby brother gets me nice things. Especially after all the punishment I dished out when we were kids.' She frowned. 'So long as this isn't a lame "living through us" thing. Because I *so* don't need the pressure.'

He laughed. 'God, no. I mean, yes to the happy ever after, but I'd rather live vicariously through someone with more money and better taste in music.'

She poked out her tongue. He responded in kind.

She took a deep breath. 'Look, I know your "destiny in Paris" dream comes from a good place. It would be brilliant, not to mention hilarious, if you had some kind of... genetic predisposition for it.'

'Because of the whole "conceived in the 4th Arrondissement" thing—'

'Which is hearsay, but still. It's sweet that they—'

He raised a hand. 'Please. Don't make me get an image.'

Mum and Dad's 10th wedding anniversary weekend in Paris—a return to the city where they met—may or may not have created Sam, but it was a romantic notion. Had they tried extra hard to give Elodie a sibling? It didn't matter—he still joked that she was merely a trial run for the child Mum and Dad *actually* wanted. However, the *rehearsal* offspring was the one who would be presenting them with grandchildren.

'Okay, okay,' Elodie replied. 'What I mean is, don't let your life disappear. Finding your person is the *best* thing, and I want the most for you.' A grin cracked her face. 'Besides, the sooner you hook up, move in, get hitched, the less likely that your wedding ceremony will be interrupted by whatever squealing rascals pop out of my vagina in the next couple of years.'

Oh God, El, please don't mention your vagina.

'Your concern for the ambience of my potential nuptials is touching.'

'Well, I want to be able to stay on until midnight and get leathered, rather than have to take two toddlers back to the hotel at six.'

'You old romantic, sis.'

Chapter Three

Beth woke at seven. The alarm was usually redundant, as her body had become used to the routine. Eighteen months ago, she'd seen an article saying it was healthier to keep to a schedule, and at the time, she embraced anything to feel some form of renewal, of upswing.

She'd not long told Leon they were kidding themselves that things were all rosy in the garden. He'd reluctantly agreed. So, having grabbed the marital bull by the horns, she'd started making positive changes. The first was to move into the spare room. It was lonelier and starker, but she could set the 7 a.m. alarm without disturbing Leon's lazy weekend mornings. Plus, the mattress was almost box-fresh, not pummelled by a decade of marital relations.

Well, maybe six years. Things had tailed off in the last few.

Finally, mercifully, he'd moved out. She suspected he had a new *friend* to move in with. There was no malice: she was happy if he found love again. She was certainly doing her darndest to.

If only he'd been as keen to deal with the divorce admin as he had to get laid.

You can't talk, Missy. Or Mrs, for the time being.

She didn't use "Ms". Didn't like it. Although having struck out with 33 different guys, Ms might soon be an ideal moniker. How ironic that she'd tried even harder than he to get laid.

No, not get laid. Find another special person. Besides, I'm dealing with my side of the paperwork. Whilst having a full-on job, learning to rattle around in this house, and casting aside most of the eligible men in Hampshire.

She spread out in the bed, starfish pose.

It was great to be back in the marital bedroom. After tossing out the old linen, she'd hoovered and cleaned meticulously. Under the bed, she'd found a single sock, the long-lost Gladiator DVD, and enough dust to give half of Winchester asthma.

She enjoyed having the ensuite again. Months of using the main bathroom had got tiresome. As had cramming barely half her clothes into the spare room's single IKEA wardrobe with two dowels missing. Still, First World problems.

Things had grown worse, clothing-wise, recently. The shopping sprees weren't purely triggered by her wallowing in the marital failure. It was also wallowing in more than a year's worth of failed dates. Often, she blamed the outfit, but this was easily rectified by buying something else.

Of course, this smacked of the problem being her, when it was, of course, them. Nobody said it was easy to find a "happy ever after".

She lingered in the shower, had breakfast, then walked a mile to the Sainsbury's Local. After a yoga session in the living room, she gave Quincunx an hour of play and stimulation.

I was going to bring those things down from the loft.

However, lunch with Eve was looming, leaving no time to ascend the wobbly Ladder Of Doom. Fixing the loft ladder was one of many things that had never risen high enough on Leon's DIY list.

She stroked the parrot's plumage. Quin responded with a squawk.
'Yeah, some blabbermouth you are,' she scoffed.

On the day she brought Quincunx home, she'd lain awake thinking of amusing phrases to teach him. "To infinity and beyond" was a favourite. Or responding "Who's there" to "Knock knock". "Fuck off" would be obvious yet hilarious, especially if her parents were to visit. However, those self-indulgent plans were sad—ironic because she'd bought the parrot to add levity to her forlorn, mired in slo-mo breakup, life. The only amusing thing about the whole enterprise was that the bloody bird hadn't even mustered "Hello".

I mean, "Loser bitch" would be a start. Or even "Pieces of eight".

She fed Quin a treat, wondering what would arrive first: avian dialogue, a new bloke in her life, or HS2.

Eve, perennially early, was already at The White Hart.

Beth had never arrived at the office before her. She'd once suspected Eve was shagging Nigel, the early-shift security guard. However, her friend would never do that because he was a security guard, six inches shorter than her, wore white socks, and was called Nigel.

In any case, Eve was dating a guy called Taylor. Great bod, rugby fan, egg allergy.

'Hi, Annie.' Eve had once joked that because Beth shortened her name from Bethany, the "any" part—which sounded like "Annie", the famous orphan—had been orphaned.

'Hey, Beanie,' Beth replied. It was hardly an original nickname for an accountant.

Beth sipped the white wine Eve had bought her. 'How's Taylor?'

i.e. "If you're not still together, can I have him?"
No, I don't mean that. Judging by looks isn't the answer.
'We're... good.'

Beth frowned. 'That sounds ripe for discussion.'

Eve shot an undecipherable look. 'Not now, okay? Let's do you. How was number thirty-three?'

'I didn't realise you were counting too.'

'Aha! So you *are* counting.'

Beth swatted a hand. 'You make me sound cold and analytical. It's *so* not like work.'

'No "business plan" for Mr Right?' Eve joked.

Beth snarled and swept up the menu. The jibe cut unusually deep, due to her introspection, the strike-out rate, her low ebb. Thirty-three was a *lot*, undeniably. And she *hadn't* been counting... until recently. Now she regretted totting up the diary entries.

Eve sighed, went to the bar and ordered their food.

When she returned, her tone was conciliatory. 'It's only concern, you know that? After what happened with Declan.'

Beth scoffed. 'It's okay. He's long gone. I deleted that app.'

'You shouldn't have given him your number.'

'I know. Lesson learned.'

Declan hadn't taken no for an answer. When she'd refused sex on the third date, he'd taken offence but not understood that she wanted to call it quits. His barrage of texts was, if not stalkery, certainly persistent. She'd blocked his number. Thankfully, there had been no fallout.

Eve drank. 'What number was he?'

'Eleven.' She glowered. 'Wait, are you still mocking me?'

'Tell me you don't have a spreadsheet.'

'I do not have a fucking spreadsheet. What, you think I'm collecting dates like football stickers or Pokémon?' She snorted. 'For starters, I don't have time to wait for one to *evolve* into the right guy. I don't want a project. I'm not looking to change him.'

Eve laid a hand on Beth's. 'Honestly, it's a relief you're still searching. I'd have given up long before now. Thirty-three? That's stamina.'

She took a long slurp of wine. 'I have to believe. But it's tough.' A big breath left her. 'Not sure I'm not cut out for apps. Maybe I have unrealistic expectations of how well they'll work.'

'Unrealistic? Nah. You're just disappointed.'

'Hmm.' Beth fiddled with her paper napkin, folding it into the shape of a bird. 'Do you think I'm difficult to live with?'

'Er, I don't live with you.'

'Share an office. Same thing.'

Eve spluttered a laugh. 'It is *so* not the same thing. There's no way you're as alpha at home. Or if you are, Leon was a brave man.'

'I am not alpha!'

'You are a *bit*.'

'VC is a man's world. Anyway, quit avoiding the question. Am I hard work?'

Eve stirred her cocktail for a fortnight or so. 'You're being careful. Maybe over-careful.'

Beth calmed the hackles which jumped to attention. It was one thing to ask for honest feedback, but another to receive the answer you didn't want.

'So you don't think it's a numbers game? I mean, numbers are your trade, Beanie. What are the chances? One in a million of meeting Mr Right. Even dating ten people doesn't dent those astronomical odds.'

Eve waggled her head. 'True, but your approach is hardly *improving* the odds. And you're being too analytical. What happened to love?'

Beth's eyes narrowed. 'This *is* about love. It's about not screwing it up a second time. I'm just doing all the... due diligence upfront, rather than during the sodding marriage!'

Eve hooted. '"Due diligence"? Geek much?'

'You know what I mean. Research the guy. We're all statistics on one side of the divorce line. I want to be on the *right* side next time. It's worth the hard work *now* to give myself, and him, the best chance.'

'But it's not supposed to be a chore, babe. It's meant to be an enjoyable dance, falling in love.'

Beth swirled the wine in her glass. 'And that's what I miss. The romance. Apps don't have the "eyes met across a crowded room" thing.'

'So why try them?'

'Because science. Because numbers. Let the software kiss the frogs so I don't have to. But you know what the problem is? You can create a perfect profile, be as honest as the day is long, but that's only half the story. The guy before last turned up half an hour late without any decent excuse. Was tardiness on his profile? Was it bollocks.' She necked the wine. 'Where's the question about punctuality? Or whether someone has freckles? Or whether you're still in love with your ex... who clearly dumped you for always being late, treating serving staff like navel lint, or having "Do Ya Think I'm Sexy?" as your text tone.'

'This does all sound a *bit* picky.'

'So you're saying I should fall in love at first sight again? Not work through all the things... okay, sometimes the *little* things... which matter? The *real-life* stuff. Coexisting. Cohabiting. Being a team.' She winced. 'Ow. That sounds very work-y.'

Eve's brow knit. 'You're not *in* a team, Annie. Not really. You fly solo. Find the businesses seeking investment, vet them, get a proposal together, run it by the suits—'

Beth's palm came up. 'Except there's a new sheriff in town.' Her shoulders fell. Due to a company reshuffle—along with a few redundancies—her amenable boss had been given the boot.

Eve grinned with deliberate cruelty. 'Yeah, *another* man to convince that you're the right stuff.'

Beth fake stabbed her friend's hand with the fork. 'Thanks for pointing that out. Sod's Law that they recruited externally. I'll be starting from scratch with this new boss man. Assuming it's a man.' She frowned. 'Why have they been so tight-lipped about him?'

Eve shrugged. 'To avoid pissing off the people they've let go. Or reshuffled.'

Beth upended her wine glass. It yielded only three drops. 'Whoever it is will see my recent record. I need a winner, babe. I've gotta find an investment that pays out. Quincunx doesn't contribute to the mortgage anything *like* Leon used to.'

'Then stop going through dates like a hot knife through butter. Snag one that'll rent a room for a few months.'

Beth held up the fork. 'Don't make me stab you properly. Or I'll have to hope for a mixed-sex prison. Hook up with a nice murderer or something.'

'Probably better with an embezzler. Then when you both get out, you'll be on easy street.'

'I am not dating *any* man for money. I want to spend the rest of my life with someone because they are utterly perfect. Okay, *Beanie*?'

Eve raised a hand. 'Hundred percent. I mean, you'll need a Matron of Honour, won't you?'

Beth shook her head. 'You're impossible.'

'Maybe. But at least *I'm* not too impossible to get laid.'

Chapter Four

S am peered across the dim, bustling space at the two people sitting in the faux American diner area. His smile was instinctive.

Fly, my little birdies.

He could do no more than make the introduction. Becoming emotionally invested in their journey was a waste of time and energy. He wasn't *adopting* these people.

Above the background chatter and thump of music, the space rang with whacks and clangs of balls on clubs and obstacles.

Every conversation, every new friendship, needs an icebreaker. Whilst it was ridiculous to expect two people to bond over something as trivial as a love of the circus, it had happened. Of course, Sam had booked the circus-themed course of the junkyard golf venue for exactly this reason.

During the first 9 holes, Maddy and Ian—the two singles he'd invited—chatted and laughed like longtime friends. Now, they'd grabbed a bite to eat and were getting properly acquainted. They'd return for the second 9 holes... assuming they didn't link hands, hail a cab, and dash to one of their homes to get down to business. Sam doubted it. He'd done his prep. His Spidey sense had tingled. His odd, inexplicable, matchmaking brain indicated a good chance of Cupid's arrow finding its target.

A heavy hand gripped his shoulder. 'What's up? Worried about unlucky thirteen?'

Sam faced his best friend, Paul. 'Actually, I hadn't considered that part. Why? Are you trying to put the mockers on them?'

Paul laughed. 'No way. I want them to get what Lena and I have. Can't argue with your track record, mate.'

'Says the guy who laughed at my explanation for this.' He indicated the two figures hunched over mediocre, overpriced burgers and fries.

'I know. Sorry. Should have faith, shouldn't I? I'm the living proof of what you do... however and why ever you do it.' Paul tapped Sam's forehead. 'Christ knows what's in there. But looks like it's worked out for Maddy and Ian.'

'Don't get carried away, mate. I can only lead the horses to water. Can't make them drink.'

'Or jump into bed. Or get married.' Paul thumbed at the 7th hole. 'Anyway, let's go. We're holding up the group behind.'

Paul's wife Lena, their mutual friend George, and Rhianna—a work colleague of Lena—were shaking their heads in fake impatience. They weren't actually frustrated—everyone knew this occasion was about the fledgling couple. The five had subtly let Maddy and Ian get ahead on the course, so they had more time to bond over refreshments.

'Admiring your handiwork, mate?' George asked.

'Yeah,' Sam said. 'See, sometimes it's the little things. Like circus clowns, okay?'

'Sometimes it's everything.' Lena pulled Paul close. He smiled nervously.

Rhianna laughed. 'Sometimes they just need to save your life!'

Sam grinned. Not even he could invent an introduction so crazy, fanciful and, frankly, impulsive. No research. No pondering whether the traits, views, preferences and lifestyles of the two protagonists were ingredients for a Happy Ever After... or at least a Happy For Now.

Rhianna was a graphic designer at an agency in town. A 5'6" blonde who liked beaches, rum, and cryptic crosswords. Her girlfriend, Amy, was a firefighter. A 5'11", raven-haired, directly spoken, motorbike-riding Amazonian from the Welsh Valleys. And she'd run into a burning building, hoisted Rhianna out in a fireman's—*fireperson's*—lift, and given her the kiss of life.

Four months on, and the kisses were all recreational.

'Not everyone can have an amazing origin story,' Paul said.

'But God, you two have to get married,' Lena suggested. 'What a tale for the kids.'

'Plus, we're the only people in Hampshire that Sam hasn't set up,' Rhianna added.

Sam growled.

'I'm still waiting,' George said.

'You're undateable,' Sam replied.

'History would argue with that.'

That was true enough. George, a Winchester College alumnus, had the particular brand of annoyingly self-confident swagger created by a public school education. The matinee idol looks didn't hurt. George, whilst not quite earning the "playboy" tag—and he certainly wasn't a dickhead, never needed Sam's matchmaking services. Still, it hadn't yielded a relationship longer than about a year, so as soon as a potential long-term partner appeared in Sam's peripheral vision, an introduction would be made.

'Look, are we gonna play?' Paul tapped his putter on the ground.

'It's your turn, honey.' Lena's eyebrows arched.

George slapped Paul's back. 'Numpty.'

Paul shook it off, put his ball on the start line, sighted the crazy obstacle, then delivered his shot. He never mentioned that he used to play *real* golf off a 12 handicap.

'You coming to that comedy night?' George asked.

Sam frowned. 'What comedy night?'

Rhianna sipped her Coke. 'Amy bagged a handful of comp tickets. Her mate's doing a set at The Laugh Club in a couple of weeks.'

'Is she any good?'

Rhianna beamed. 'Hannah? Hilarious. She's with a talent agency and everything.'

'So?' George nudged Sam. 'You wanna come? Better still, you know anyone who's into comedy clubs? Blonde, stacked, likes a fast car?'

George had impressively pigeonholed himself, and his preferred date, in one sentence.

'If I did, you'd already have met her,' Sam replied.

'What *is* it about you and getting people together?' Rhianna asked.

'If I knew, I'd be a millionaire.' He took a slug of beer.

Lena whacked her ball. It cannoned off an obstacle and rebounded to six feet away. She growled in frustration. Paul laughed. She slapped his arm. He winced perceptibly.

Sam filed that away. It was unheard of for the iconically happy couple to spat in public.

George pointed his bottle at Sam. 'I mean... You *could* make a million.'

Sam chuckled. 'What, by charging people for introductions? I *have* a job. I don't want to run a sodding dating agency.'

Lena tapped his shoulder. 'Your go, hon.'

Sam took his shot. He wasn't a golfer—badminton was his game—but he made a decent fist of things on the "short form" of the game.

Rhianna popped her ball on the tee. 'I think George means an app.'

'Absolutely,' Paul said. 'An app. Perfect. Don't know why we didn't think of it before.'

'Because it's bollocks?' Sam suggested.

'You're kidding,' George said. 'Building apps is your *job*.'

'Which is hardly a thrill-a-minute, okay?'

'Exactly,' Paul replied. 'You've been joking about leaving VentaTech. Moaning about how it's a sausage machine, cloning productivity and booking apps. So go solo. Here's your first project.'

Sam shivered. 'Thanks but no thanks.'

'Why? Your brain seems to be wired up for creating dates. Why not turn it into an app? You have plenty of free time. Especially as you refuse to date anyone. And I won't point out the crushing irony of that.'

'Alright,' Sam said, desperate to move on from this familiar and wearisome topic. 'What do you expect me to do? Stick a USB cable in my ear and download my brain?'

Lena eyed him with almost maternal frustration. 'Your work is turning a written specification into code. This is right in your wheelhouse.'

'Newsflash for you, there *are* dating apps already. Tons of them.'

'Yeah,' George said. 'I've tried three. And do you see a ring on this finger?'

Sam didn't point out that George was the least likely person in the group, possibly the whole venue, to embody the C-word. Commitment.

He held up both hands. 'This is all very noble and kind and everything, but really? You can't app-ify what I have. It's too... intangible.'

'So you're saying you're not a good enough software engineer?' Paul suggested.

'No, I just—'

'You don't believe you have a gift,' Lena said.

'Well, I mean—'

'You've put twelve sets of people together. They all lasted months, years,' George said.

Lena took Paul's hand. 'Exhibit A.'

'Okay. Let's chill out here,' Sam said. 'It's a crowded market. To even get an app off the ground, something which needs big numbers to make the algorithm work, requires a lot of effort. Marketing. Money.' He gulped his beer. 'Plus, things like emotion, observation, the personal touch, they're not the same as code.' He shot Paul a glower. 'And I *am* good enough, thanks very much.'

Rhianna stepped in. 'Look, Sam, I've only known you for a few weeks. And I agree the idea is crazy. But so is your ability to do... whatever it is you do. An app is just matching a set of questions. Criteria. You use criteria. You must be running some kind of database in there.' She tapped his forehead. 'Why not write it up?'

'It's... I can't...'

'There's a limit to your generosity of spirit?' Lena asked.

'Maybe he doesn't want to retire to a desert island in five years,' George said.

'Paris, more like.' Paul rolled his eyes.

Sam didn't rise to that. Yet his friends were looking at him expectantly. Supportively.

I guess it does make sense... kind of.

He sighed hard. 'I'll think about it.'

Lena's eyes became saucers. She grabbed his wrist. 'I know someone. The perfect person for this. Beth. She's in venture capital.'

Sam arched back. 'I'm not jumping into a Dragon's Den thing.'

'Nothing like that. You wanted money, marketing. Find an investor. She'll do the work. If she reckons the project is a goer, you're sorted. Paul and I'll advocate for you on the matchmaking thing. Your work skills, too.' She beamed. 'And I'll tell you what. Another thing about Beth. She is all over the dating app market. She is your *ideal* customer.'

'Lena, I don't have an ideal customer. I'm just me. With no app. Or anything. One minute this is a crazy idea, next minute you'll all have me at a million downloads on the App Store.'

Paul patted Sam's shoulder. 'Take a chance, mate. Meet this... Beth woman. If she thinks it's all tilting at windmills, you'll be able to say "Told you so".'

George's voice was low and oddly heartfelt. 'You should get something back from the universe for all the happy dates you've created. Look at it as a passion project. A way of showing your skills. A kind of... CV, if you ever move jobs. Go on. Take a meeting. You're used to that, right?'

Sam glanced back and forth. His heart thudded. 'This is *so* harebrained.'

'Let Beth decide that,' Paul said.

Sam's neck hairs prickled. 'This better not be a setup.'

'Says the king of setups,' George pointed out.

Sam eyed Paul. 'If your wife is trying to get me a date by stealth, you're both off my Christmas list.'

Paul shook his head. 'She'd never muscle in on your territory. Territory we're only suggesting you try to make money from. And possibly a new career. And, ideally, happiness.'

Sam's mind whorled, pulse rattled. Was it nerves that this was all a poorly-veiled romantic setup, worry that the whole thing was a big joke, or excitement that maybe there was a route out of his workplace drudgery?

'Okay. I'll meet her for lunch. A public place. And this is a *business* meeting.'

If this matchmaking malarkey were a job, instead of merely an odd and inexplicable knack, it would be a damn sight more fun than the stuff at work.

"Would be"? It already was. Witnessing friends, workmates, even friends of friends, find an emotional bond was immensely satisfying. Without his own Miss Right, he basked in reflected love. Coding was *dry*. Making people happy was *nourishing*.

Love made the world go round.

Chapter Five

B eth took an Uber to the café for her lunchtime meeting with the guy Lena had texted about.

Monday was a work-from-home day—she was only required in the office twice a week, and some weeks she didn't manage that, what with meetings and travel—so she'd researched Sam Carter on LinkedIn, and been stopped dead by his headshot. The half-smile oozed a suave moodiness, with brown eyes she wanted to dive into. Thick brown hair and casual, not curated, stubble. Eyebrows that needed thinning—

Stop. This is a business meeting. And what happened to not wanting a man-as-a-project?

She'd shaken off the ridiculous, girlish, fancy-at-first-sight thing, having made that mistake with Leon, getting swept up on a tidal wave of impulsive desire. Instead, she browsed Sam's work history, impressed. Oddly, they'd attended the same Uni, but she didn't recall ever seeing him.

Throughout the taxi ride, she worked hard to subdue unfamiliar nerves. They weren't caused by foolish romantic notions, but by a professional apprehension. According to Lena, Sam had an uncanny knack for matchmaking and was considering a dating app "with a difference". It was a perfect time for this to fall in Beth's lap. A project to get emotionally invested in, one not requiring much seed capital, and with potential mass-market uptake... leading to investor returns and a fat bonus for her.

If, and only if, it wasn't some flight of fancy. Lena was a smart cookie, and whilst she'd bigged up Sam, she wouldn't do it to placate an idiot's ridiculous invention. Still, Beth needed to vet both the person and the business idea. If Sam had his head screwed on, was a decent software engineer, and his spooky flair for connecting couples was *a thing*, could they brew up a success story?

The taxi pulled up outside the Italian bistro at 12:25.

Five minutes early. Good.

Inside, she paused at the unattended Please Wait To Be Seated sign. Then, to her left, someone stood up from a table. Recognising Sam from his profile picture—though he was taller than expected, shading six feet—she walked over.

He stuck out a hand. 'Beth?'

She shook. His grip was firm and warm. 'Good to meet you, Sam.'

He gestured to a seat. 'Shall we?'

What a gent.

As an icebreaker, she mentioned Uni, and they had a chuckle. Nevertheless, underneath Sam's easy-going exterior was a stiffness, a nervousness—possibly he was unfamiliar with pitching business ideas. Still, he'd dressed appropriately: chinos, open-necked shirt, jacket. Yet her attention was drawn to everything *above* the neckline.

I'm here for a meeting. Not a date.

They chatted about how both knew Lena, and he revealed that he'd set up Paul and Lena on their first date almost a decade ago. It was his greatest success story. This segued nicely into the reason for the meeting. Still, something Lena said made Beth nervous.

She fingered a knot in the wooden tabletop, then met his eye. 'Sorry, Sam, but I need to ask. Are you actually serious about this?'

He looked mildly offended. 'Which part? That I'm some freaky matchmaker with a curiously long winning streak, or believing it can be the basis of a new app?'

'I suppose... the second part. I can't argue with all the dates you've facilitated, can I? Why would you, or Lena, make up something like that?'

'They wouldn't. But I can see why you're sceptical.' He fiddled with his cutlery. 'On one hand, you have my brain, and on the other hand, there's putting those nuances into code. And convincing people it works. People who already have a hundred dating apps to choose from.'

'You have experience with those?'

He half laughed. 'No. Dating apps are not my thing.' He raised a defensive palm. 'Not to say that should prejudice me as a potential client. But I understand if it does.'

She frowned. 'Oh. I thought this came from seeing a gap in the market. Dissatisfaction with what's out there, that kind of thing.'

He shook his head. 'No. Sorry. I'm not in the dating game. Is that a dealbreaker?'

'No. No. I don't mean to pry. It's part of... due diligence. For work.' She pursed her lips. 'Being honest, Lena said you and dating was "complex". I took it to mean you'd had as much bad luck as me.'

His brow arched. 'You have?'

She chuckled sadly. 'Thirty-three and counting.'

'Thirty-three boyfriends?' He winced hard. 'Sorry. Awful thing to say. None of my business.' He tapped the table. 'Unlike this, which is *supposed* to be business.'

She put a hand near his. 'It's okay, Sam. We're discussing a dating app, and your history with creating relationships, and the industry, and working out whether we're a good fit as business partners—'

'Partners?'

'What? Did you think this was like a bank loan or something?'

'I... I don't know.' He sighed. 'Look, this is my first rodeo, and you're right, it is a punt. I only came here to get my friends off my back.'

'But they believe in you. As a matchmaker. And a programmer. And they think the idea has legs.'

'Of course. This isn't some practical joke. Or I hope not. Wasting your time coming here. It's not that, is it, Beth? Lena's not having a laugh?' His expression was plaintive, concerned.

'No. This is what I do. I look for business ideas, get them funding, we take a stake in the company, and, for some ventures, I mentor them through the initial phase.'

At that moment, the food arrived, and they dug in. She tucked the linen napkin into her collar, not wanting to get the crisp white shirt covered in sauce blowback.

Sam's eyes were busy as he processed the last fifteen minutes. 'Lena was matchmaking too, wasn't she? In a way.'

'Professionally? I think so.'

He angled his head. 'She does owe me for the introduction to her future husband.'

'I'm curious. How does it work? Do you know within five minutes of meeting someone who to introduce them to?'

'Almost never. Yes, Paul and Lena got married, but it took months to see they belonged together.' He laid his fork in the dish. 'I need to get to *know* a person before I can see if they are a good fit. With deeper knowledge, there's a better chance of a match. Occasionally, one aspect of a person makes an introduction obvious, but it's no "thunderbolt of love" thing. Slow burn is always safer in the long run.'

'Amen to that.' Having rushed into marrying Leon, perhaps another way was better.

Rushed? We dated for over a year. Perhaps the problem was sleeping with him on the second encounter. God, he turned me on...

'The problem is that people expect an app to deliver instant gratification. Decisions based on swiping.' His expression was sober. 'That's not how I work. And I don't want any favours. Lena will understand.'

She pushed her plate aside, interlacing her fingers on the table. 'It sounds like you try to build real connections, not just put people together who will fancy each other.'

'Absolutely. I reckon what kills relationships is the day-to-day grind, the arguments over things that never get put on dating profiles because companies don't ask. *That's* the point of difference.'

Instinctively, she nodded. Yes, she and Leon had described the last few years as "growing apart"—a handy catch-all—but in truth, it was all the stuff around coexisting, living life, knowing who you are and what you want, and what you want from a partner. *That's* where the mismatches were.

She checked her watch. Time had flown. 'Look, Sam, I'm on the clock, but I think we... I mean you... *have* something here. I want to hear more. Then I'll be able to put a proposal together, run it past the boss, and get you some money.'

He eased back. 'You think this is a goer?'

'It's not a slam dunk, but I have to admit I'm personally invested in putting the magic in your brain into some... formula.' She shook her head. 'Still, it's not about me. I don't hold the purse strings. But I do have a big advantage in this niche. All the stuff for the suits, yes, that has to be by the book. Costs, market research, business plan, all that... box-ticking. But this app is about *people*, isn't it?'

'One hundred percent.'

'Then, for starters, I can give you thirty-three things that turn people off potential partners, or create mismatches. You said you're not into dating apps? Isn't it best to work with someone who *is*... or was?' She shrugged. 'Assuming you want to go ahead. We're not the only game in town. And I'm not the only one at the firm. You need to pick someone you want to work with. Who believes in you.'

She pulled her handbag off the chair. It swung forward and smacked into her plate, sending the cutlery clattering to the floor.

'Fuck,' she exclaimed under her breath.

Sam sniggered and looked away. Her face reddened.

Way to make a good impression.

She cleared her throat. 'And, if you want, pick a VC who's clumsy and swears too much.'

'That feels like something to put on your dating profile.' He smirked.

Best not to say that I'd pretty much given up on them. Hardly likely to win his business—or respect.

'Hmm.' She fumbled in her bag for a business card.

I can't wait to get new cards printed up.

Company CEO, Allen, despite working in an industry where millions of pounds were sloshed around, was a penny-pincher. In any case, she hadn't wanted to do any of the post-divorce admin—like changing her name on countless apps, websites and sundry services—until the ink was dry on the decree absolute.

Sam had crouched by her side, collected the errant cutlery and laid it gently on her plate. She was touched again by his courtesy. As he stood, their eyes met.

She tendered the card. He scrutinised it. 'You really believe this could work?'

'Don't be swayed by my opinion, but honestly, yes. I get *such* dry stuff across my desk. Literally investing in *love*? Hell, I'd give you the money myself if I had it.'

The warmest smile broke on his lips. He reached out. 'Then that's a tentative Yes.'

She clasped his hand. 'Great.'

Could Sam Carter be the answer to her prayers, professionally *and* personally?

Chapter Six

Sam had trouble focusing on work that afternoon.

A crazy notion about his inexplicable gift had somehow morphed into a fledgling business idea. Still, the nagging sense that it was all designed to trap him into a date wasn't helped by his penchant for brunettes in crisp white shirts.

Beth hadn't laughed him out of the brasserie. In fact, she'd suggested they meet again to thrash out the details, understand his "process". Except he didn't have "a process". He had feelings. A sixth sense. And how the hell do you put that into ones and zeros?

But it would be churlish not to give it a go. After all, as he took the lift down to Reception at six o'clock, the relative drudgery of life pressed in on him. The job was decent and the pay competitive, but it never gave the sense of accomplishment that a successful double date did. His current project was a loyalty app for a small restaurant chain across the South East. Hardly thrilling stuff.

He crossed the foyer of the faceless office building. Ten companies inhabited the thirteen floors, and arguably his was the least exciting.

The only talking points were when one of the lifts broke or the death-defying window cleaners came down on their cradle. A TV company, Park Productions, monopolised the gossip. The CEO was arrested for sexual harassment, and one of the employees had amusingly lit up the foyer with a tirade about her BAFTA.

Sam's most memorable day at VentaTech was when the new coffee machine arrived.

George's hot hatch was waiting in the car park, exhaust growling.

Sam tossed his sports bag into the back, and sank into the passenger seat. The door was barely closed before George accelerated enthusiastically towards the exit. Sam grasped the seat bolster.

'How did it go?' George asked.

'It went well,' he replied noncommittally.

'Did you get her number?'

Sam frowned. 'Of course.'

George grinned. 'Wahey! And Lena said she's *fit as*.' He gunned the car away from the lights.

'I got her *business card*. This was a *meeting*. Unless I've been stitched up?'

George settled down to 47 miles per hour in a 40 zone. 'How come for you it's being "stitched up" but for all the people you put together it's a "public service"?'

'Because this is "Do as I say, not as I do". I'm the lucky one here. I know my destiny. Some people need a little push. So if this meeting was you lot trying to crowbar me into a date, I'm going to be *really* unimpressed.' Sam winced as they buzzed through an amber light. 'And I'm not posting bail for you, either.'

George fluttered a hand. 'Fifteen years, no points, never been stopped.'

'Hmm.' Sam didn't mention that there were other ways to get a criminal conviction—as his friend knew all too well.

'I'm interested in your project, okay? How did the *meeting* go?'

Sam gave him the rundown, which lasted five minutes until they reached the sports centre.

They grabbed their bags and strolled to the changing room. The weekly badminton session hardly constituted a fitness regime, but it was a step in the right direction. When Dad had a non-fatal heart attack last year, his doctor blamed an inactive lifestyle. Sam, who sat behind a desk five days a week, saw a vision of the future.

George invariably won their games, but he was good company—despite his driving style, shallow relationships, and ridicule of men who drink white wine. He was also a bright sod.

'Mate, you always say your dating setups are only planting the seed? Well, this app is like that. I can't *make* you do it. But none of us wants to see you fail.' He patted Sam's shoulder. 'All we can do is say thanks for these matchmakes, and buy you a beer. This app could mean real *money*.'

'If it works. I need to set up a business, appear legitimate. That's pretty scary.'

George waved it away. 'Easy. I'll give you a hand. You should do it anyway. Future proofing. You're bored at work, as you keep saying.'

'Yeah, but this app is a big commitment of time. Researching, planning, designing it. Coming up with the logic, the permutations.' He shot a sober glance. 'All with no guarantee of success.'

'Absolutely. There *are* no guarantees in life. But your winning streak says it's worth a shot.'

Winning streak? That reminds me...

He grabbed George's arm and brought them to a halt. 'Did you notice anything on Sunday? Between Paul and Lena?'

'No. Like what?'

'They seemed... off. Like they'd had a fight.'

George laughed. 'So? Shit happens. Married life can't be rainbows and unicorns every day, not even for the relationships *you* create.' He shot a concerned, sympathetic expression. 'I hope *you're* not expecting that when you find the right person.'

What to say? Mum and Dad had the perfect relationship. So did Elodie and Warren. Was it too ridiculous to expect the same? Especially if he followed their France-themed hookups? The City of Love had earned its title for a reason.

Sam painted on a smile. 'No. I need to let go. They're grown-ups.'

'And proof that you're good at this matchmaking lark.'

They entered the locker room.

Sam opened a cubbyhole. 'Yeah. Ian messaged me yesterday. He says Maddy's the best thing since sliced bread.'

'Ideal proof for Beth, then. All these dates will feed into the algorithm.'

'Like... proof of concept?' Sam laced his trainers. 'I suppose.' He gazed at a spot in space. A penny dropped. 'You know what? When you're not being a dick, you do have moments of brilliance.'

That was a big understatement. Whilst George worked as a high-street insurance broker, he had a profitable sideline trading shares. He'd taught himself, wanting to escape from his parents' shadow and not be mocked for living off them. If Sam needed a cheerleader, someone who'd add objectivity and brain power to the project, George was ideal.

They headed into the sports hall, which rang with the squeak of trainers on wood and the thwack of shuttlecocks on strings.

George pointed his racket towards the vacant Court 2. 'You should invite Beth along to one of these dates, let her see the master in action.'

'I'm sure she doesn't work evenings and weekends. Doesn't need to, in that line of work. Bet she's bonused up to the eyeballs.'

'Who cares? She's interested in the project, and sounds like she's been spending *months* doing the evenings and weekend dating thing for pleasure anyway. Get her to ride shotgun.'

Sam grimaced. This sounded a lot like inviting Beth out. Crossing a line between business and pleasure.

George stopped walking. 'You still think this is all some brilliant scheme, don't you? Get your head out of your arse. Are you telling me that you're happy to work with Beth, take her company's money and support, use her guidance, but you won't let her into your process? I may not be one to talk, but if she's shot thirty-three guys down in flames, which is probably some world record, then even if this *was* a sneaky attempt to get you and her together, it hasn't got a snowball in hell's chance.'

Sam's shoulders relaxed. 'You're right. She's Miss Undateable.'

Chapter Seven

B eth walked out of the lunch meeting feeling buoyed and excited.

Sam had brought something exciting to the table: an old-school romanticism to the way he understood and paired people. Could this skill truly be transformed into a tool for thousands of people to find their soulmate, their One?

Still, despite being invested in a silver bullet to cure her losing streak, she needed to remain objective, not become emotionally involved in the project. Yet in some self-torturing way, she was keen to revisit her failures, to document the dating experience and use it to help with the criteria. She was an ideal beta tester.

Beth Moore was *made* for this project.

And then she arrived at the office...

Across the aisle from her desk was a small breakout room. Behind the glass partition sat three people. Two were her teammates. The third caused a double-take.

'Shit,' she murmured, chest tightening.

At that moment, he looked across. His mouth curled upwards knowingly, almost a sneer.

Stomach roiling, she dashed to the Ladies to regain her composure... without making it too apparent that she was dashing. She gazed at her reflection in the wide mirror. Her cheeks were red with frustration and embarrassment.

Declan. Why the fuck did it have to be Declan?

When she got back to her desk, he was there. Waiting. Like a Venus flytrap. Previously, he'd attempted to snare her romantically. Now he was her boss. She'd be chewed up. Maybe spat out.

Do Venus flytraps spit things out? Flies they want revenge on?

He offered a hand. 'Beth Moore?'

She painted on a smile. 'Yes.'

His double-handed grip was over-firm, the flytrap's lobes clasping its prey. 'Declan Black. Great to meet you. Sorry it's taken so long. Busy touring our European offices.'

'No problem.' She showed the full set of pearly whites, desperate to kill him with kindness. After all, wasn't it possible that he didn't remember her? Their first date. Their second date. His nagging texts.

He waved her to the breakout room. 'Want to run me through what you're working on at the moment?' Butter wouldn't melt.

She forced the smile to her eyes. 'Absolutely.'

She followed him into what would surely be a torture chamber.

That evening, Beth sat on the sofa, reflecting.

'What a day.'

She stroked Quincunx's plumage, eliciting a mournful squawk.

Parrots sensed low mood. It had been an ideal pet to buy following the split with Leon.

In her year off after Uni—seeking space before joining the capitalist world of 7 a.m. commutes, glass ceilings, and middle-aged white men trying to peer down her blouse—Beth had travelled.

In Brazil, she'd slept with a guy who owned a parrot. Marco. That was the parrot's name. She couldn't remember the guy's name. Did it matter? No. She didn't remember the sex either, so both were probably unremarkable.

Parrot Guy had taught the bird to respond to "Marco" with "Polo". Hilarious. She'd hoped for similar repartee with Quincunx, but no dice. Still, its empathic qualities were very welcome tonight.

'What a day,' she repeated.

Declan Black was a world-class piece of work. Nothing like a carnivorous plant; more like a chess grand master. The meeting, while it simmered with tension, never strayed into sneers and snipes. If he was overbearing as a date, he was cool as a cucumber at work. She'd questioned whether it was the same guy—then spied his pinkie ring with the scorpion motif and realised that, yes, life had shat in her kettle.

She hadn't mentioned Sam's dating app. Firstly, the project was barely off the ground. Secondly, at the mention of dating, Declan might have vaulted the table and left a scorpion imprint on her face.

As it was, she smelt a hard time ahead. If he wasn't the forgiving type, he could make her life hell—at the precise moment she needed a winner. Plus, she wanted Sam's dating app to be the answer to many people's prayers, hers included. Even the research process might show where she was going wrong.

'I'm hardly Miss Undateable, am I?' she beseeched Quincunx.

He crooned sympathetically.

'Well, maybe this new app will give me the answer.'

The following day, Sam texted. A matchmake date was coming up, and he suggested she come along.

Hence, on Sunday night, she arrived at the venue in good spirits. The large pub was quiet, with the most obvious activity being the quizmaster—who looked like a roadie—setting up in the back room.

It was billed as a double date. Sam's original teammate, Lena, had bowed out to make room for Operation App Research. Beth wanted proof that his talent for putting two people together translated into the seed for romance. She needed to prove in her business plan, which would go to Declan Slimebag Black, that her client had a viable proposition.

Unfortunately, Beth wasn't a quiz night person. Cocktails? Yes. A movie night in? Yes. This? No.

It wasn't an *intellectual* issue. She knew stuff. She'd done quizzes at Uni—Thursday nights at the Half Moon down the road from the halls of residence. Music was her specialist subject. And making eyes at Josh Waterstone. Then, when sex with Josh turned out to be a tedious three-minute event, and Zoe "I am a music encyclopaedia" Andrews joined the team, Beth bailed.

Tonight, however, things were different. She wasn't there for the quiz. She was there for work, including a meeting with Sam beforehand. Added to that, Jon and Rachel—the twosome that Sam had set up to meet—would undoubtedly outscore Beth on more topics than Boyzone and Beyoncé.

Also, she had no plans to have three-minute sex with Sam. Nor Jon, as that would undermine the grand plan. However, if the plan went spectacularly wrong, and Jon was *her* Mr Right, she'd be silly not to take advantage. She hoped that wouldn't happen. Firstly, it would subvert the date. Secondly, it would show cracks in Sam's method. Thirdly, if she did find love, it would make her much less invested in seeing the app work out.

Sam was already at the bar, looking as appealing as she remembered. The lush hair she wanted to run her fingers through, excellent dress sense, and an adorable dimple in his chin.

'Hi Beth. How are you?'

They shook hands. 'Good. Apprehensive, maybe. And it's been an... odd week.'

'Well, let's have a drink and you can tell me about it.'

They went to a secluded table, and she outlined the Declan situation. It was crucial that Sam knew the project could be dead in the water if her boss was holding a grudge. How ironic that her unsuccessful date might prevent a dating app from getting off the ground.

As she recounted the tale, he listened intently, showing why he was good at assessing people.

'So,' she said, 'If you know anyone wanting to go out with a dickhead, give me a shout. Perhaps if we get Declan loved up, he'll be a pushover when it comes to approving the project.' She sighed. 'Shame this couldn't have happened a few weeks ago. My last boss *was* a pushover.'

Sam smiled sympathetically. 'Honestly, don't put yourself in a difficult position for me. It sounds like work will be toxic enough anyway.'

She played with the swizzle stick in her G&T. 'I have to suck it up. Maybe I've got it wrong. Maybe it'll be fine. I hope so. I need to show they were right to keep me on after the reorganisation. I certainly won't give Declan the satisfaction of letting him emotionally force me out because I refused to date him.'

'What was the issue? Why didn't it work out? I don't mean the pestering, but before that.'

'Other than he couldn't keep his eyes off my chest?' She arched her brow.

Sam's professional, courteous approach cracked. A hairline fracture, a brief glance downwards. That hadn't been her aim—she didn't want to attract the type of man who considered tits the most important selection criteria.

'I mean, that's plenty, right?' he said.

'There's other stuff, but,' she fluttered a hand, 'let's not spoil the evening with it.'

He raised his glass. 'Deal.'

She chinked. 'Deal.'

Chapter Eight

'Look, Beth, you realise that by offering to spill the dirt on all your dating... *non-starters*... you're baring your soul quite a lot. And we have only just met.'

She reached towards him, stopping short. 'Isn't dating *about* opening up to a stranger? And as I seem to be *really* bad at making it work, I need to go over my life, my hangups, with a fine-tooth comb.' She shot a sober expression. 'Otherwise, maybe I'm kidding myself that I'll find someone. Which I do want.' She sipped her drink, eying the table. 'And you do... right?'

He coughed, a hot flush on his neck. 'Yes. Absolutely. Subject to... criteria.'

'Same as all of us.' She checked her watch: the quiz started in fifteen minutes. 'So. Criteria. What kinds of things do you see, look for? What causes you to think two people are compatible? Jon and Rachel, for instance.'

He took a steadying gulp of beer. He shuffled his chair closer. She put her elbows on the table. He noted with curiosity that her mobile phone case had a parrot design. Their gazes met. She had nice eyes. Yet the eyes, the chairs, and the table *weren't* in Paris. And Beth Moore was his... *backer*. Hopefully.

'Jon and Rachel. Okay. They both like quizzes, that's an easy one. They're quite socially reserved. They've each lost a parent. I know Rachel from work, and I've seen the way she looks at one of the guys there. A married one, sadly for her. I've overheard them chat. I know her politics, that she hates cooking, that she wants three kids.' He pictured Paul's stag do; the first time he'd met Jon, one of the groom's old friends. 'Jon loves cooking. His politics fit. He has an older sister and loves looking after her kids. Want any more?'

'No.' Beth was inspecting his face. 'You're very observant, aren't you? Empathic. An old romantic?'

'Definitely. But romance isn't everyone's cup of tea.'

'Sometimes I get the feeling that romance is dead,' she mourned.

'No, it isn't. Although maybe it's plugged into one of those machines that go *beep*.' He winked.

She laughed, unabashed. 'Are you exclusively a matchmaker for the romantic type?'

'No. If there is a common theme, it's a desire for commitment. If someone wants to fool around, there are apps for that. For them, compatibility at a deep... *soulmate* level isn't necessary.'

Her head dipped. 'No. And maybe expecting that to come from a profile picture and ten bullet points is why I failed.'

'Hey. Don't beat yourself up. This is a numbers game. Like VC, right?'

'Absolutely. But I get enough numbers from nine til five. After that, I'd rather cut to the chase. Hence why we're here.'

He looked around. 'Doing pub quizzes with strangers? That doesn't seem like your thing.'

'Well spotted. It isn't. But it's quality research time. Besides, if dating apps and I aren't a workable thing, doing the legwork might be the answer. We're all busy. There are legions of apps because there's a need. There'll be a market for your product, especially if it has a USP.' She raised her glass, eyes twinkling. 'But wouldn't it be hilariously ironic if it wasn't your skills, or our app, but all this research that created *my* moment? If my ideal man was sitting in a place like this. During one of our meetings, planning sessions, date fix-ups. If he was here *right now* and I didn't even know it?'

'I suppose so. It would be nice to think that, in some way, even accidentally, I helped break your losing streak.'

She drew her shoulders up, chest out, and offered her hand. 'So, subject to contract, is this a *firm* yes?'

He shook. Her grip was firm, yet warm and genuine. 'Let's do this.'

A grin cracked her face. 'You can't imagine how happy that makes me.'

'Maybe wait a while before you say that. If I'm a nightmare to work with, at least you won't have to get down on your knees and beg Declan to approve the funding.'

She grimaced, shuddering. 'Thanks for that image. On my knees in front of Declan? Yuk.'

'Sorry. I didn't invite you here to dredge up the past.'

'Except on the History round, of course.' She winked.

'True. So let's refresh our drinks, find a table, and invent a ridiculous team name.'

Chapter Nine

B eth followed Sam to the bar, maintaining sufficient distance to watch his fine backside.

While hanging on his every word, she'd been speculating what *Sam's* criteria were. Because no app was necessary to validate how many of *her* boxes he ticked. However, she'd made dating judgments quickly before, and fallen at the first or second hurdle. No point in making the mistake again.

They found a table.

'One-two. One-two. One-two-three. Three-two-one.' The quizmaster was doing a lengthy and utterly redundant mic check.

A girl walked up. Petite, uncooperative hair, chunky heels. Introductions were made. This was swiftly followed by Jon's arrival. He was a broad-shouldered blond with an earring and a West Country burr.

Sam marshalled them onto the table: Beth opposite him, and next to Jon, who faced Rachel. This way, the presumptive couple could gaze at each other, but Jon could chat to Beth if he wished... or if he wasn't *feeling it* with Rachel. Beth had no problem with that, but a date wasn't on the cards. Earrings weren't her thing. Nor a Cornish accent.

Still, the four-way conversation was free-flowing, peppered by laughter. Jon's eyes regularly sought Rachel's, despite a glimpse of cleavage being an alternative site for attention.

Love is when you want the eyes. Lust is when you want the body.

When Jon and Rachel went to the bar, Beth angled her head towards them. 'What do you think?'

'I'm hopeful,' Sam replied. 'But the quiz will tell us a lot. It's a team game.' A light went on in his head. 'Hypothetically, if you *know* you have the correct answer, but I'm sticking to my guns on *my* answer, what do you do? Fight tooth and nail to get your answer submitted, or let me have my way and enjoy the self-satisfaction when I'm wrong?'

She pondered. 'What if *I'm* wrong? If my bolshy overconfidence becomes an embarrassing failure?'

'You mean, would I gloat? Hypothetically?'

'Yeah.'

He bit the inside of his cheek. On some people, this was unattractive. Not Sam.

'Depends. On a date? I'd either have conceded ground or be magnanimous.' A smile hit him. 'Because it's a team game, and the win is important.'

'Very politically correct.'

He did a mock bow. 'It's also about love, which is why we're here.'

Beth had a fine time. It was like rolling back the years. Between the rounds, Sam effortlessly kept the conversation flowing, seeding topics for the wannabe lovebirds to run with.

During the quizzing, the atmosphere was hushed and solemn. Jon and Rachel were seasoned pros, the right side of nerdy. At the halfway point, team Cunning Linguists was in third place. Beth was surprised that Sam came up with the name. Whilst he was affable, there was a distance, like he was holding something back. A fear of letting go, of bonding. It piqued her curiosity.

Round Six was the inflexion point. Question Four.

'What is the currency of Albania?' came the too-loud voice over the portable PA.

Jon's face was a blank. Rachel stared at the ceiling.

'The lev,' Sam murmured. His expression was almost lofty.

She shook her head. 'The lek.'

His frown was deep. 'No. Lev.'

She checked their companions, who shrugged in unison. Rachel tittered. Jon's hand inched closer to hers.

Beth leant in further. 'It's lek.' Her pen hovered over the paper.

'I'm pretty sure—'

'Question five,' said the quizmaster.

She gazed intently into Sam's eyes, whose brows were knit in resistance. Her pulse raced.

Come on, mate. I don't want to fall out before we've even begun this journey. If we do fall out eventually, fine. After the app is done. And, ideally, it'll be a bed that we fall out of.

'Hundred percent?' he asked.

'Ninety-nine. You?'

Sam glanced at Jon and Rachel, who were already discussing the next question. Beth sensed the cogs whirring behind his forehead.

He tapped the paper. 'Put "lek".'

'Sure?'

'*One* of us has to be wrong.'

'Or both of us,' she suggested.

'I'd rather be wrong about this but right about... the other thing.' He angled his head minutely towards Rachel.

'Hear, hear!' Beth whispered.

She wrote down the answer. One she was sure was correct. Later, she might tell Sam that Besjana in the office was Albanian. Or she might not.

An hour later, the Cunning Linguists came second, three points behind The Brians Trust, who deserved the win on the merit of the team name alone, notwithstanding that two of the guys looked like they were called Brian, even if they weren't.

There were mutual congratulations over the table, with Jon and Rachel's handshake lasting a few beats longer than the others.

Rachel checked her phone, saying she needed an early night. Jon offered to escort her to the car park. Beth noticed the tic of happiness in the corner of Sam's eye. His joy was so sweet that it was infectious. A feel-good factor jangled her bones. Perhaps if her own hookup was still months away, she could survive off the glows from other radiant hearts?

Thanks and goodbyes were said. Beth didn't explicitly say she'd be up for next Sunday's quiz, but it sure beat an overnight hotel in Chatham ahead of a Monday morning meeting about a price comparison website for ethically sourced fava beans or whatever.

She pulled out a chair. 'Well?'

Sam sat. 'Those two?'

'Or we can discuss the lev versus lek thing?' She fluttered her lashes.

'I think they have a good chance.'

She took that to mean he didn't want to admit defeat on the currency question. She didn't care. This wasn't a point-scoring thing.

Except for the point-scoring aspect, of course. It wasn't about the quiz. It was about the evening. And she'd had a great time.

She swilled the last of her drink around the glass. 'You realise you'll never hit a hundred percent? Fourteen couples out of fourteen dates is impressive, but we can't expect fourteen *hundred* to all work. Fourteen *thousand*.'

'I'm not naïve, if that's what you mean. I'm not perfect. No app is. Our strapline won't be "Guaranteed Love" or some crap like that. It'll be that we... come at things from a new angle. It's the differences that cause problems, not the common ground.'

'That's hardly saying much.'

A tic of frustration zipped across his face.

She touched his arm. 'Sorry. I meant...' She pushed at her hair. 'I realise we're still in the... discovery phase, you and me. And I'll need some meat on the bone. Yes, I've seen the proof tonight—'

'Assuming they last a while.'

'Assuming that, yes. But Declan will want to know the USP. We won't be asking for millions in funding, maybe only five figures at first, but we have to do this by the book.' She sat up straighter. 'Pitch it to me. The Why.'

Sam tapped the tabletop. 'Sometimes it's the little things that kill a relationship. Music tastes. Not taking the bins out. Sometimes it's the bigger things, and not the bigger things that normally get put on dating profiles.'

'But there have to be a million questions. Are you suggesting we cover *all* bases? Because a profile setup time of two weeks would be a *big* turnoff, believe me.'

Ouch, that sounded catty.

But he didn't comment. 'We have to do the normal stuff about physical appearance, wanting kids, indoorsy or outdoorsy, etcetera.' He drank another inch of his third beer. 'But it's *character* we want to get into. Views, values, trust ethic. Look, here's a hypothetical. This is for the guys. Let's say your girlfriend is out for the night with her mates. What are you *primarily* thinking about?'

She grinned. 'I'd assume you were wondering who was going to win whatever football match you were watching on the TV.'

'Lovely stereotype. Thanks for that.'

She tapped his arm. 'Kidding. Sorry, go on.'

'I'd say you're thinking one of three things. One, you want her to have a good time. Two, you hope she comes home safely. Three, you worry she'll cop off with another guy.'

Beth leant back. 'Really?'

'Absolutely. Years ago, my girlfriend was on a night out and there was a police incident nearby. I couldn't get hold of her. I was in bits. Then she called. She was fine.'

'I'm pleased to hear it.'

He flashed that lovely smile. 'Thanks. The point is, how someone answers this question is a character insight. My answer is A or B. If your answer is C, it's possible that you're a jealous or possessive type. *Possible.* The main thing is knowing your partner's views. It's about honesty and trust. I'm not saying every woman needs *protecting.*' He glanced at her arms. 'I bet you have a decent left hook.'

'Let's hope you don't find out.'

'Which is why the currency question was your call.' He beamed. 'Anyway. I'm not sure whether that qualifies as a pitch, but you get the idea. Long-term relationships hinge on compatibility in the day-to-day stuff. Some people want to do everything with their partner. Others are happy with separate lives under the same roof. Or a middle ground.'

'Hmm.' She toyed with the stem of her glass. 'So what split you and this girl up? Clearly, you didn't have Sam's Magic Touch back then.'

'No. But it was a lesson in give and take. I got invited to a friend's wedding. It was a small affair, no kids and only partners of relatives. My girlfriend wasn't invited.'

Beth shrugged. 'Fair enough. It's *their* day.'

'Apparently not. My girlfriend said it was an injustice. She insisted that if she couldn't go, I should boycott the wedding.'

Beth's mouth fell open.

Sam nodded. 'Exactly. We cooled off for a few weeks. I went to the wedding. Then we met up again. She couldn't believe I'd gone. I dumped her. If the reverse had happened, I'd have let her go along.'

'Of course. You're the king of wanting other people to be happy.'

'Yeah. The point of the app is to head off any surprises. To ask the questions, even the hypothetical ones, that reveal who someone *is*. I agree it's not a cast-iron guarantee of success, but it's something new in the market.' He tossed up his hands. 'It's a punt. I'm doing this in my spare time. It sounds like you're judged on these projects. Don't do this for the *romance* of it. Do it because you believe.'

She clasped his wrist. 'You change lives, Sam.' An impish grin broke. 'Heaven knows how, but I can't wait to find out.'

'Does that mean you want to be the subject of the next dating experiment? Couple number fifteen?'

A shiver crackled across her shoulders. 'No, thanks.'

'But if I find you Mr Right in the next couple of weeks, it'll prove tonight wasn't a one-off.'

'And it will also mean I have no free time.' She perked her eyebrows. 'What with all the high quality sex I'll be having with the man of my dreams.'

Sam pretended to write on his palm. '"Requires high quality sex". Thanks. That's the Beth data up and running.'

She slapped his hand playfully. 'I meant that my free time is limited, and it needs to be reserved for us. I mean, us working through the specification, your huge list of insightful criteria, a marketing plan, and a million other things.' She met his gaze. 'So don't *you* enter into this lightly either. As well as thirty-three men, I've had spats with plenty of friends and colleagues. I'm far from perfect, that much is becoming clear.'

'We're all flawed.'

She wasn't convinced. She hadn't spotted anything about Sam that warned her off a working relationship, a friendship... or something more profound. Perhaps the coming weeks would uncover why he was single. There had to be a reason.

And if there wasn't? It would be hard not to let business and pleasure mix.

"High quality" pleasure.

Chapter Ten

S am lay his head against the sofa backrest and looked at the living
room ceiling.

Oh yeah. Need to change that bulb.

It was past eleven, but there was no point in heading up to bed yet.
His brain was boiling.

Had his odd gift put him on the precipice of a business venture?
It was scary and exciting in equal measure. Despite the opportunity
to strike out on his own, a little voice at the base of his skull, a tiny
flashing amber light, a niggling concern, said VentaTech wouldn't
be thrilled to discover this off-piste enterprise. An app creator
discovering a business opportunity and going solo? Not to mention
that one of the company's products, one of its clients, was a dating
app.

The label underneath the flashing light read "Conflict of Interest".

Sam pressed fingers against his eyelids. He'd not long shaken off
the "Dr No" nickname.

'That's Sam,' friends jibed. '"No" to jumping ship to a different company. "No" to any woman he didn't meet in Paris. "No" to even a *fling* while he waits for destiny to knock on his door.'

'At least you got the "Doctor" part right,' he once joked. Sam Carter, BEng, PhD Computer Science.

Still, he had to follow his instinct, and it wasn't true that he hadn't dated *at all*. Still, it had been a few years... years more keenly focused on other people's matchups. And the result? Was he unhappy and shy? No. Was he working on something that could change his life? Yes.

He'd have to moonlight on this project. Keep it as secret as humanly possible. None of his mates would squeal. Nor Beth.

That lifted his mood, replaying the evening. How well Jon and Rachel had hit it off. How well all four had worked together on the quiz team. What good company Beth was.

He picked his phone off the sofa cushion and opened WhatsApp.

Rachel hadn't messaged. No problem. There would be thanks soon enough.

Nothing from Beth either, though he hadn't expected a message. He was merely her next client. In any case, he didn't want gratitude—nothing had happened yet. If, in a year or two, she bought him dinner as thanks for producing a winning app—thereby delivering her a performance bonus—then fine. Even better if she invited him over to meet her fiancé, a man that the app had found.

It was funny how George had painted her as Miss Undateable. She didn't come across like that. Perhaps, as she let layers peel back, offering insights into an extraordinary string of "No, I don't want to see you again" dates, Sam would discover why she was a complete nightmare.

So long as she was okay to work with.

Thanks, Lena. You're pretty good at matchmaking, too.

He tapped Lena's picture, ready to send a message.

The ringtone blared.

'Fuck!' He almost dropped the phone. He thumbed the green circle. 'What's up? Can't sleep?'

Paul's booming laugh reverberated in Sam's ear. 'No. Waiting for the old ball and chain to finish her three-hour evening skincare routine.'

Paul used the "ball and chain" line ironically, although Lena *was* a stickler for a beauty regimen. Still, Sam's curiosity was piqued, especially given the hint of frostiness he'd noticed at the golf venue. But he couldn't exactly pile in with "How's the marriage working out these days?"

'So is this a social call at,' he checked his watch, 'Eleven fourteen on a Sunday night? I mean, it's nice to be loved, but...'

'How was it with Beth?'

Here we go. Shown your true colours now, mate.

'Is that a leading question?'

'I mean as a potential account manager,' Paul said.

'Really? Or is Lena hovering close by, so that when I tell you Beth and I have been at it like rabbits since we got home from the quiz, wifey can let out a squeal of delight because her subversive plan worked?'

That laugh again. 'No, you bellend. Do you think I'd let her stitch you up?'

'Says Mr Butter Wouldn't Melt. Even on the stag do, you were trying to fix me up with that girl in the hotel bar.'

'I was drunk, and I hadn't had years of lectures about how nobody's allowed to put the mockers on your Paris destiny hangup. Anyway, if Lena *had* put you with Beth out of some... subversive... *love* thing, don't you think she'd tell me? After all, we want you to find someone. Mostly so I can shave one of *your* eyebrows on the stag do. At this rate, they'll be grey and bushy before you have a date, let alone a fiancée.'

'So you rang to take the piss? Again.'

'No. I rang because Jon texted a pic of him and Rachel outside the pub. Man, you didn't tell me how hot she is.'

Sam frowned hard. 'Small point here, mate. You know that woman who's hogging the ensuite? She's your *wife*. And this is *precisely* the wrong time to be lusting after Rachel, given the successful date.'

'I'm kidding. I mean, Jon's done well. Assuming it goes the distance. The point about the app is the long-term angle. I get it. I'm Exhibit A. Oh, hang on. Mrs Exhibit A has finished. Now I can take a dump.'

Sam winced. 'Thanks for the image.'

'So you and Beth are going ahead? As business partners, before you give me grief.'

That word spiked his nerves. 'Partners? I hope this company of hers doesn't shaft me. Make me sign some unfathomable paperwork that leaves me with a five percent share as soon as things take off. Assuming they *do* take off.'

'And does Beth seem like the type who'd smile to your face while stabbing you in the back?'

The geography of that didn't compute. 'I'm not sure her arms would reach.'

Paul laughed. 'Does that mean you're picturing how she'd get her arms around you, eh? *Now* who's trying to subvert this business relationship?'

'Get lost. Tell Jon I'm happy he had a good evening. And when I see Rachel at the office, I'll mention that this creepy, married mate of mine thinks she has nice tits.'

'I did not mention her tits! That's you extrapolating. And what does *that* say? Shit. Look what you've done. Lena is growling at me.'

His voice went distant. 'No, love, I was *not* talking about anyone's tits. I think Sam has a thing for Rachel. Which is pretty stupid, right, after she hooked up with Jon. It's just him living vicariously through—'

'I am not living vicariously through anyone!' Sam bawled down the phone, loud enough for his neighbours, and probably Paul's, to hear.

Paul guffawed. 'You're so touchy. Look, before I go, there's a guy at work you should meet. Mark. His last girlfriend turned into a psycho hose beast. He could use your services. I'll text you his deets. Okay?'

Sam couldn't hear any undercurrent in that. 'Sure. Now go and make up with wifey. And say thanks for the intro. I owe her a drink.'

'Will do. Oh, she says, "Nothing less than Bollinger". Anyway, see you around.'

'Yeah, sure, night.' He hung up and flopped back on the sofa.

Mark.

Another name to add to the roster. If the successes kept coming, new singletons had to appear on his radar. More research was critical if the app was to succeed. He needed happy customers, people to spread the word, suggest new users.

He, like Beth, knew it was a numbers game.

Chapter Eleven

T he bus lolled along one of Winchester's arterial roads.

Beth needed coffee. She hadn't slept well.

The evening with Sam, Jon and Rachel had worried her. Viewing it as a double date was a slippery slope. She wasn't working on this project to *date*. Hell, no. Not after the last few months. Yet why meet Sam—a guy who lived and breathed matchmaking, who wanted to create a dating app—if she was sworn off finding love?

Because this was different. This was avoiding the insanity trap of doing the same thing over and over and expecting a different result. She was shaking things up, moving away from methods that didn't suit her, towards something which did—Sam's new app.

As a by-product, the research and specification phase would cast a million-watt lamp on her love life, illuminating the dark nooks and crannies where her hangups and shortcomings lived. As Sam would wisely suggest, it's better to know what makes you tick than wait for someone else to find out... especially months and years into a relationship.

Crucially, with her VC head on, she needed to back a winner. Doubly so in the eyes of Declan, who might have it in for her from day one.

And yet...

These noble ideals were overshadowed by one simple fact: Sam Carter was wonderful.

The bus flew past the Shell petrol station.

Shit.

She jabbed the bell. The bus stop glided past the window.

Daydreamer.

She grabbed the handrail and bustled down the swaying stairs.

"Friars Lane", the nameless female voice announced. The bus slowed to a halt. Beth darted out of the doors and trudged down the pavement in the direction they'd come.

Looks like I'll get my steps in today.

She spent the morning on the proposal. A good business case, underpinned by Sam's track record in both coding and matchmaking, was vital.

She pondered whether Declan would be onside with the whole idea, given that a dating app had matched him with this impossible bitch called Beth Moore. Yet surely he wanted love, too? What irony if Sam's app worked better for Declan than for her?

At least it would get him off my back.

Returning from the lunch break, she found Declan scrutinising her laptop screen.

Her teeth clenched.

'Interesting,' he said, in a tone that was as snide as it was curious.

'It's a proposal for a dating app,' she replied brightly. 'A new client I've picked up.'

'*Potential* client,' he said patronisingly.

'Yes. But it's a strong idea.'

He perched on the desk. 'What's the USP? Is this a dating app for picky and judgmental people?'

She bit her tongue. 'Does it matter, as long as it makes money?'

'It's a crowded market.'

'This is different. I wouldn't be wasting my time otherwise. Dating apps aren't my cup of tea anymore.'

His eyebrows raised. 'Oh, really? Bad experiences?'

She swallowed hard. 'One or two. But you have to kiss a lot of frogs in this world.'

'If they'll *let* you kiss them, sure.' He frowned. 'What's the female equivalent of frogs? I never know. Women are always saying that all the ghastly men they meet, the apparent swathes of them across the country, are frogs. What about the unpalatable ladies that *men* have to sift through to find their princess?' He leant in slightly. 'Is there a term for those? Crones? Witches? Something worse?'

She put her shoulders back. 'Frogs, I think. They have female ones of those, don't they?'

'Shall we say toads? Let's agree on that.'

'Absolutely. I have a *huge* problem with warts. And in the *worst* areas.'

His lip curled slightly, which delighted her.

Yeah, froggy boss man, that wart-free zone you'll never get to see.

He coughed. 'I look forward to seeing the proposal.'

'And I look forward to your swift sign-off, Declan. So we can save plenty of men from all those witches. And put a nice sum in the company's bank account over the next few years.'

His eyes narrowed. 'I'm sure you'll be able to *convince* me about this project. I'm here late tonight, so maybe pop into my office at six.'

She glanced at the corner cubicle. Six p.m. An empty floor, the blinds on his office partition closed, an implication that the convincing might involve *further* after-hours sessions.

'Sorry, but I have to get away on time today. Tomorrow afternoon?'

His nose wrinkled. 'I'll check my diary.' He waved loosely at her laptop. 'I'll let you get on.'

She sank into her seat, concerned about how far she'd have to go to get this thing approved. She texted Lena about a drink. Not a "Six cocktails, drown my sorrows because my new boss is a bitter scumbag" evening, merely a "What have I got myself into?" chat.

The friends had met four years ago on a First Aiders course that their respective companies had sent them on. They'd hit it off immediately, including over cocktails and tapas during the overnight stay. Beth's mouth-to-mouth practice the following morning had probably blown gin vapour into the CPR manikin's plastic lungs...

That evening, having succeeded in disembarking at the correct bus stop, she headed to the wine bar, bought Lena and herself mocktails—it was a work night, and they found a secluded table.

Lena stirred the virgin colada. 'Paul said last night went well.'

'Yeah. We've really got the beginnings of something.'

'The project, you mean?'

'What else?' Beth's heart pounded. 'Or what did I miss? Was this all a ruse to fix me up with Sam?'

'Hell no. I wouldn't dare.'

Beth waved her cocktail umbrella. 'I mean, go ahead, honey. If you can work a miracle with my love life, like he does with other people's, bring it on.'

'No. *Of course* I'd intro you to anyone suitable. But not Sam. Anyone but Sam.'

Beth leant back. 'What have you done?' she breathed.

Lena's hand shot across the table and grabbed Beth's wrist. 'Oh God. Don't get the wrong idea.' She shook her head. 'I only mean that he's not the right sort. For dating.'

'Whyyyy?'

'Like I said before, it's complex.'

'How complex? Like... ex-offender complex? Married-but-hides-it complex? Please don't say he's aromantic, because that would make his performance Oscar-worthy.'

Thankfully, Lena smiled. 'No. Sam just doesn't date. Well, won't date. He has a... plan.'

Beth's mind swirled. 'A plan. Internet bride? Waiting for Zendaya to get a surprise divorce? Ooh! Hang on. Is it one of those pacts? You know, there's someone from school, or Uni, and they were best friends but never had the courage to hump each other ragged, then one night they drunkenly agreed that if they hadn't found The One,' she used air quotes, 'by age forty, they'd get hitched, rather than face a life alone?'

Lena laughed in her typically throaty, almost dirty fashion. 'No. I mean, that has a kind of romance to it, right? In a sad, yearning, "settling" kind of way.'

'Yeah, but Sam doesn't seem like the settling type.'

'Far from it. And there's the rub. His romantic ideal is so OTT, so beyond sweet, that it's, being honest, a bit blinkered.'

Beth sipped her drink. 'Come on. Spill.'

Lena took a deep breath. 'Now, please remember that this comes from a good place, because I love Sam. We all do—'

'But...?'

'He believes, no, he *knows*, that he'll meet his true love in Paris.' She shrugged faintly. 'Set eyes on, date, marry, two kids, happy ever after.'

Beth blinked a few times, tapping the side of her glass. 'Wow.' Her mouth hung open.

'It's some dream, huh? Romance dialled up to eleven. A side order of cheese, perhaps, but even *thinking* like that is enough to get some women wet.'

Beth's stomach butterflied, but the feeling went no lower. 'The girl of his dreams is in Paris.' She said it as neither a statement nor a question, neither impressed nor saddened. Disappointed, perhaps.

'His parents met there. Dated, married, two kids, happy ever after. His sister met her husband in France, and they honeymooned there too.' Lena's eyes widened. 'Wait a minute. So did you.'

Beth snorted. 'Yeah. Don't remind me.'

'What? You told me it was dreamy.'

She scrunched her hair. 'I suppose. No. It was. I... You mention that, I think about Leon, about the marriage, about how we screwed it up.' She drank, shaking her head. 'One swallow doesn't make a summer. The City of Love doesn't guarantee a forever.' She chuckled, irony like a piledriver in her chest. 'Sam wants that? If he knew my history, he'd reframe his expectations. Sam, of all people. The man who's conceiving a "guaranteed long-term love" app. I'm walking proof that satin sheets, four-posters, views of the Eiffel Tower and croissants a-go-go for a week is not a slam dunk. Investments in love can go down as well as up.'

'I hear you. But he feels that his parents' meeting, and their future, is a sign. He loves films set in the city. Casablanca, for one. "We'll always have Paris", you know? But it's not superficial. Sam would never milk the honeymoon, consider his romantic gestures complete, then lie on the sofa for the next thirty years, watching rugby, casually tossing twenties your way so you can pop down to the lingerie department.'

'Neither did Leon,' she pointed out.

Lena took Beth's hand. 'Things end, hon. Please stop beating yourself up. I know you're not *really* down on love, once bitten, twice shy. Sam has a heart of gold. And he's brilliant at what he does. He's *such* a people person. And, okay, he's putting *his* love life on hold for some perfect eyes-met-across-a-moonlit-table-by-the-Seine dream, but he's also putting himself *out* to help other people find togetherness... in much more humdrum ways.'

'Pub quiz, for one.' Beth sighed. 'I should live and let live.'

'It's all we can do. I thought you should know, that's all. Not to try anything on. Not to expect that working with Sam will... go anywhere.'

'You're acting like it's an absolute certainty that I'd *want* to go out with him in the first place. There are other fish in the sea.'

Lena fake grimaced. 'Unless the remaining ones saw thirty-three of their fishy friends being hooked and gutted by you, and are now hiding in secret sea caves, then, yeah.'

'I mean, pretty harsh, but let's see whether Sam's single-minded devotion to his cause, or my inability to find literally *anyone* compatible, leads to marriage first.' She chuckled. 'The race is on.'

'Or the two of you could agree on a pact? Give it 'til you're both forty and desperate, then settle.'

Beth gave her friend the finger.

Lena responded by offering to buy the next drink. While she was at the bar, Beth reflected.

What a state of affairs.

She'd embarked on dates with a string of guys based on significantly less information than she already had about Sam. Yet the *one* person she'd date in a heartbeat wasn't going to be interested in her.

Or maybe, as they worked together over the coming weeks, Sam's resistance would crumble? Ultimately, he'd know whether they stood a chance, wouldn't he? He was the *expert*. He could spot compatibility from a mile away.

And if it *was* there, and he didn't spot it, it would show he was fallible. Very fallible.

And the app would be dead in the water. As would her job.

Wish I'd ordered a double whisky.

Chapter Twelve

S am's pen hovered over the signature box.

This was impossible. Hateful. How could the company do this to him? Now, of all the times?

The angel and demon on his shoulder were going at it hammer and tongs. Or harp and trident. But he couldn't *not* sign. This was his employment contract. If he kicked up a fuss, it would look suspicious—who reads T&Cs anyway? *He* did, because reviewing specifications and fine print was part of his job—translating a client's demands into code, examining logic, and validating usability.

Six years ago, he'd read his employment contract and been thrilled to sign. A new dawn for Sam Carter. A business on the up, ripe with interesting projects.

Now, one paragraph stood out. The "no conflict of interest" clause. He was forbidden from stealing clients or setting up a business in direct competition with VentaTech.

One small problem: CarterSoft, his two-day-old company, created as a vehicle for the app. He'd walked taller, having taken control of both the opportunity and his career. He was investing in himself. Hopefully, Beth's company would invest in him, too.

The pen still hovered.

Hang on.

CarterSoft wasn't *competing*. It wasn't *stealing* clients. The project was *his*. True, he could have taken the idea to the suits at VentaTech, but why should he? What they didn't know couldn't hurt them. He wasn't planning to fake endless sick days to work on the project. He wasn't trying to kick VentaTech's dating app client out of the industry.

'Sod it,' he murmured.

He signed.

After lunch, the day took a huge upswing. He was buzzing as he emerged from the team meeting. His colleague David shot an expression that spoke volumes, so Sam made a "T" gesture.

They rendezvoused in the building's airy lobby and headed to the café across the square.

'Very interesting,' David said.

'Don't jinx it,' Sam replied. 'Mergers are about cost-cutting. Wouldn't that be the biggest irony? We join up with this French firm, and six weeks later, I'm on the redundancy list.'

'But it's a gift. An end to this celibacy of yours—'

'I am not bloody celibate,' Sam hissed as they joined the counter queue.

At one year's office Christmas party, when David and Sam were trading notes on new PA Mari-Denise—beautiful eyes, iffy dress sense—they'd got onto the subject of Sam's dating life. He'd glossed over the details, saying only that he was holding out for the right girl, and that the "City of Love" tag originated for a reason.

'Alright, keep your hair on. The point is, you wanted a chance to get to Paris, and here you are. Maybe you'll meet a nice French maid.'

'We'll see,' Sam said.

They shuffled past the café's noticeboard.

David tapped a flyer. 'You going to this? Apparently, she's hilarious.'

Sam read the promo for the comedy night, headlined by Hannah Thomas. 'Oh, yeah. Friend of mine said we should go.'

'She works in our building. For that production company. *Well* fit.'

'So you're planning to sit in the front row with a boner—'

'What can I get you?' the wide-eyed barista asked.

They sat on the bench outside, sipping from takeaway cups, watching the pigeons fight for pastry crumbs.

'So will you do some research?' David asked.

'On that company in Paris? No.'

David shook his head. 'I don't get you. The future Mrs Carter is a Eurostar and a romantic dinner away, and you're just going to let it *happen*?'

'Yes. If I was that desperate, I'd be taking every one of my twenty-five days' annual leave wandering the streets over there.' He jabbed a finger. 'But there's no point in explaining that to a man whose seduction technique was grinding up against someone on a sticky dancefloor.'

'Actually, Kira was doing the grinding.' David had met his long-term partner in a nightclub.

'Thanks for the image. The point is, yes, I am going to let it happen. Destiny finds us in different ways.'

David frowned hard. 'You do see the crushing irony? That the best exponent of careful research, understanding how people tick, vetting them, then introducing them, is throwing all that out the window when it comes to organising his *own* date. Is this a "Do as I say, not as I do" thing?'

'Exactly.'

Yet David, for his faults, had a point. Would that change anything? Hell no. Why did it need to? VentaTech might have handed Sam his dream.

The remainder of the week was less eventful, but continued a hopeful theme.

He and Beth exchanged regular texts. She'd sent through the skeleton of a business proposal, and he'd fleshed it out. The document focused on market, USP, timeline, costs—dry stuff that was designed to answer the question, "When are we going to start coining it in?".

Seeing the idea in black and white spurred Sam to action. The magic in his brain wasn't miraculously going to morph into a piece of software: he needed a technical framework, a database of sorts—hell, even a spreadsheet was a start. As Rhianna had said, the lynchpin was a list of criteria, and he wasn't inventing this from scratch; he had years of experience—twelve successful couples. This was enough for a first draft. At worst, it would prove to Beth that his skill *could* be app-ified.

On a whim, he took Thursday as annual leave and spent the day at home, his hands a blur over the laptop. Even though the first steps were back-of-the-fag-packet stuff, it was clear where to begin: Paul and Lena. Theirs was the relationship he'd known for the longest, and not only could he remember the reasons he'd initially set them up, he'd also observed how their marriage developed. There were a ton of preferences, values, opinions and facts with which to populate this draftiest of draft versions.

When that was complete, at past ten thirty in the evening, he created two "users" called Paul and Lena—column titles on the spreadsheet—and ran something approximating a "matching formula".

Unsurprisingly, the couple had a 94% compatibility rating. Yes, it wasn't gospel, and there were hundreds more criteria to add, but it proved the theory. His gut feelings, observations, and enquiring mind had, nine years earlier, put the two singletons together, believing they had a long and happy future together.

And now, computer said YES.

On Friday, he spent an evening in the pub with Paul and Mark, his workmate seeking a date. Mark was a lanky, red-haired guy with a fondness for the outdoors, jazz, and humanitarian causes.

Paul asked how the app and the VC funding were coming along. Sam said it was early days. All he had were criteria for *successful* relationships. Beth would provide the other side of the story. Anyhow, that was in the future. This get-together was about Mark, understanding what he wanted from love and life.

As Sam walked the mile home, streetlights breaking up the navy blue sky of twilight, he mulled the situation, mentally scrolling through female workmates, friends, friends-of-friends, and assorted acquaintances.

Anna.

He'd met Anna, a neighbour from six doors down, at a street party for the Queen's 95th. She'd organised the event, and it was a predictably modest, polite gathering... apart from the hordes of screaming kids, the godawful jazz trio she'd booked, and two blokes from the dilapidated house at the end of the road getting wasted on Aldi own-brand lager.

Anna was pretty, gregarious, principled, and had spent the last nine months walking the South West Coast Path, one weekend at a time. Sam sensed a compatibility with Mark—providing the guy found her attractive, so he scrolled through his photos and found the selfie he'd taken with Anna at the street party. He forwarded it to Mark, who replied with a string of emojis.

Fifteen minutes later, sitting on the sofa while the TV played a millionth repeat of QI, he checked the weekend's weather and sent separate messages to Mark, Anna, and Beth.

Chapter Thirteen

As Beth headed to the picnic on Saturday, she was worrying about the silliest, most *British* thing: how to say hello.

The chat with Lena had created a quandary. Sam's dating approach was counter to their raison d'être—finding simple ways to put compatible people together. It was easy for Beth to be enthusiastic about the project, hard to understand what made him tick, harder still to rein in her hormones.

As she pulled into the gravelled rural car park, Sam was getting out of his car nearby. He'd dressed outdoorsy but stylish, his hair was on point, and he appeared taller, more rugged.

Her heart pattered, double time.

Get a grip, Beth.

This was ostensibly a business meeting, a coffee before Mark and Anna arrived. In the back seat of her car was a cooler bag of a few things she'd picked up in M&S Food, and a deeply unfashionable picnic blanket that hadn't been used in years. When she'd retrieved it from the cupboard under the stairs, a memory had hit.

2018. A deserted spot in a woodland in the Ardennes. Leon had barely finished setting up the lunch spread when the light caught his face perfectly, and she couldn't help herself. Within a minute, their trousers were off, and she astride him. It was their only split-second mutual orgasm, such that as they lay there afterwards, she was thinking, "We made a baby. Must have."

They hadn't. Mercifully, in hindsight.

She wondered whether today's trio had brought rugs with similar provenance. Sam, she doubted.

He strolled over. 'Morning.'

'Perfect day for it,' she said, gazing at the azure sky.

And then, that hesitation as both thought, "Where do we go from here? Who are we to each other?"

Sod it.

She stepped in and gave him a loose clench. He smelled clean and fresh.

They walked to the cabin-like coffee shop, which had National Trust vibes but with fewer septuagenarian customers. Each chose coffee and a cake, and they sat at an outside bench table carved with various initials, and sporting a glass containing one centimetre of flat Coke and a dead wasp.

She stirred her cappuccino. He was eyeing the slightly un-tanned indent on the third finger of her left hand. The marriage might be almost gone, but the evidence clung on.

'Ah. Mr Observant.'

He grimaced gently. 'Sorry. None of my business.'

'Really? I think it absolutely is. You're not the only one with "It's complex" in their dating profile.'

He looked down, sheepish. 'So Lena told you.'

'Were you going to keep it a secret? Not ideal for a good working relationship.'

'It's hardly a secret. It's not like I'm ashamed or anything.'

'No, but kind of funny, right? Of all the people to invent a dating app, it's the man who won't date.'

'I will,' he said firmly. 'But only when the timing's perfect.'

'You make it sound so *ordinary*. What are the chances that, among all the criteria and preferences we come up with, "Believes he is destined to meet his future wife in Paris" will make it into the release version?'

His jaw hardened. 'If this is a problem, we should call it a day. Save you a lot of problems with the boss.' He pushed his chair back.

She grabbed his arm, then pulled away. 'Sorry.'

He looked at her hand. She put it in her lap, as if concealing a weapon.

They mentally circled each other.

She glanced around, fearing she'd created A Scene. Five minutes into this theoretically idyllic date-slash-meeting, and she'd fucked it up. Why be snippy about his destiny? Forget the Paris fixation, why jeopardise the project by chasing Sam? Business and pleasure are seldom good bedfellows. Imagine he *was* available, and they did hit it off romantically. What if it came crashing down and they still had to work together? Awkward.

All the same, she wanted to skip the coffee, head onto the Downs, lay out the blanket, and give it another good rucking.

She was figuring out how to rescue the morning when,

'Beth?'

'Yeah?'

'Did your boss, Declan, sign off the proposal yet?'

She shook her head. 'No. Maybe next week.'

He gestured loosely. 'Yet here you are. This is over and above, isn't it?' He leant forwards. 'Let me ask you. What if the answer from the suits is No? What then?'

'You mean, is this app dead in the water? You *can* take it elsewhere. Reuse the proposal if you want. Minus our company logo, of course.' She forced a smile.

The smile he returned faded, his shoulders drooping, head shaking. With a sigh, he tipped his chin up, gaze to the heavens. He leant back, seeking the comfort of a backrest.

And back. And back. And his fingers scrabbled for the tabletop, missing, as his knees thwacked the underside of the table and he toppled onto the grass, limbs flailing.

'Fuck!'

The only two OAPs in the entire outside space, seated nearby, tutted.

Beth clapped her hand over a laugh, unthreaded her legs, went to the ungainly heap of gorgeous manhood, and knelt.

'This Parisian woman better have a thing for amateur stuntmen.'

The glower in his eyes gave way to a glint. 'Definitely. Perhaps "Useless idiot" should be on our criteria list.'

She hauled him upright. They almost bumped together.

'It's actually a very endearing quality,' she said.

'Less so the unnecessary antagonism towards the person who holds the keys to my future. Sorry.'

'No. It was my fault. Let's... go out and come in again, okay?'

'Deal.' He offered a hand.

She angled her head at the building. 'Washroom's on the left. Don't want you handling pork pies and cherry tomatoes with those grubby mitts.'

He frowned. 'How did you know I brought those?'

'I didn't. Just what I'd bring. And did, actually. And you're not touching those either, *Tom Cruise*.'

He cracked a grin, holding a hand to his waist, indicating height. 'Into short guys, are you?'

'Absolutely not.' She cocked a thumb. 'Hurry up, or I'll eat your cake too.'

Chapter Fourteen

S am returned to find his slice of cake gone, the plate bearing only crumbs. Beth was gazing out across the view, brown hair caressing her shoulders, the sun accentuating her cheekbones.

With a shrug verging on coquettish, she picked up a fork, ready to dive into her untouched chocolate cake.

He calmly switched the two plates and dug in. 'So what if your company aren't interested?'

She put away a smirk. 'It's your call. Go it alone if you can. Of course, you'll have to fund the marketing, server costs, and any R&D you can't handle. I don't know your financial situation. Like I said before, I'd give you the money myself if I had it. Best I can offer is my time. Tag team. Inside information from someone who *is* in the market.' She touched her forehead. 'Sorry.'

He calmed his hackles. 'Ah, my "stupid" dream.'

'It isn't stupid. It's noble. Romantic. I can't imagine anything *more* romantic.'

'But...?' He sipped his coffee.

'You're missing out on a lot in the meantime.'

'That's one view. The flip side is that *because* I have this gut feeling, I have to honour it. Gut feelings are part of these matchups. If I went out with a girl in the meantime, waiting for the France hookup to happen, isn't it shitty to dump her as soon as I find someone better? Especially if that was the plan all along? I don't want a stopgap. It's not fair on her, whoever she is.'

Beth put her elbows on the table and laid her chin in cupped hands. 'So even if there *was* someone suitable in your catalogue of singletons, you'd pass them up?'

'Moot point. There isn't anyone.'

'But if you met them as part of this process?' She angled her head, and a lock of hair fell across one eye. She casually brushed it away.

He wished she'd stop fishing, looking for holes in the logic. His love life wasn't a factor here. 'Everyone we meet during the research and build phase will go into the database.'

'Including you and me?'

'Why not? It's all data.' A smile grew. 'But you're the queen of big data.'

She picked up crumbs with her fingertips. 'Because I've tried and failed with half the county?'

'Well, maybe only a quarter.'

She threw a scrunched-up sugar sachet at him. 'So what do you think? If the company gives us the thumbs down, where next? Pull the plug?' A melancholic expectation lurked in the corner of her eyes.

'You don't want to, do you?'

'It's not my call, Sam. I reckon we'll make a good team, funding or no funding. But I can't *drag* the information out of you. I don't have your brilliant emotional intelligence. And I sure as hell can't code. I can't make you pour hundreds of hours of your *life* into this thing. But let's not get ahead of ourselves. Declan might have an uncharacteristic afternoon of not being a dick, and wave it through.'

'Then let's hope we can successfully turn my... gift... into code. But devil's advocate, what if we put Jon and Rachel and Mark and Anna and everyone in, and *none* match?'

'Then it shows you've not created the happy ever afters you believe.' She frowned. 'None of us want that, but it's possible. More likely, we added their data incorrectly, or need to revisit how we phrase the questions, or do formal interviews, or have a focus group.' She steepled her fingers. 'Or perhaps this thing only works in your head.'

His heart raced. What if this was all a wild goose chase? Yet the "Paul & Lena draft" proved that not only could he codify his skill, but the code matched real life. Of course, this was merely the start. A million things might still go wrong.

'I hope not,' he said. 'Declan will be laughing at you forever.'

She fluttered a hand. 'Sod him. I'm not doing this to prove anything, get one over on him. I can't deny that I really need to back a winner, but this truly feels like one. Besides, it should be fun. Better than flouncing on the sofa, bitching about how Poor Old Beth can't get a break. I'm doing something about it, which is a lot healthier.'

He pointed at the cake crumbs. 'Healthier?'

'We're getting fresh air. And intellectual discourse. And locally-sourced cherry tomatoes. Anyway, we're doing this for Mark and Anna, not us. Are you a picnic person?'

'It feels like a very grown-up thing to do. Or young. We're at that... difficult age.'

'Haha. True. Let's come back to it when we've got kids. Separately, I mean,' she gabbled. 'Do you want kids? I mean, that's Dating Profile page one.'

'It is, and I do. Sounds like you do too.'

'Yeah. One of each. Girl first, ideally, as they don't tend to be as bad at bullying the youngest.'

A cruel thought put a smile on his face. 'Which of your strikeout dates disagreed on the order in which you're planning children? Or was it the precise age interval that was the sticking point?'

She swept up the sugar packet she'd already thrown and lobbed it at his face. 'You're a snake, Sam Carter.'

'Maybe.' He picked up the crumpled paper and squeezed it into an even tighter ball. 'Where do you stand on men throwing missiles at you?' He feigned aiming at her face.

'I did tip a glass of water over Declan, so I need to take my own medicine.'

'In that case...' He lobbed the tiny sphere. It hit her on the cheek.

Her eyes flared, but he caught the micro expression of amusement.

Still, she was out of the seat like a startled hare, face of thunder. 'That's it. We're done. You can forget the app.'

Chapter Fifteen

Beth put on a glower. Inside, she was barely holding it together. Teasing Sam was the new favourite thing in her life. Maybe tickling him would be even more fun. Naked.

He stood abruptly and scuttled round the table. His forehead was knit in worry and pleading. 'What?'

'You could have had my eye out!' She jammed her hands on her hips for the full effect, but the smile gave the game away.

'Hmm. I reckon Declan got off lightly. He should be grateful you two *didn't* end up going out.'

'Or any of the others I ruthlessly cast aside.'

He stroked his chin. 'Should we include a personality trait like "Is completely impossible"?'

She nodded hard. 'Definitely.'

The air crackled with sexual tension, raising goosebumps on her scalp.

With a hiss of air brakes, a bus pulled up to the stop on the road that snaked past the café. A few people disembarked.

Sam pointed. 'Anna's here.'

She tapped his arm. 'Then let's picnic.'

They met Anna, then Mark's car arrived, and the trio wandered over. Beth watched with interest as the two hopefully-future-lovebirds interacted.

She and Sam gathered picnic coolers and blankets from their cars, then all four headed out onto the low hillside, seeking a favourable spot.

Mark and Anna strode ahead, deep in conversation peppered with laughter.

'Looks good,' Beth said. 'Not wanting to jinx things.'

'Fifty quid says they excuse themselves for a walk.'

'A hundred quid says they shag in the rhododendron bushes.'

'Will there be evidence, or should I ask them outright?'

'Don't tell me you can't spot a twisted bra strap or an unzipped fly at a hundred paces.'

'Absolutely. That's the best part of this job, ogling women's underwear.' He said it so deadpan that for a second she thought he was serious.

'And men's crotches.'

'It's always delightful.' His attention darted to her shoulder. 'By the way, your bra strap is twisted.'

Beth turned a gentle shade of crimson. She ran fingers over her shoulder blade.

Sam hustled onwards. 'Made you look!'

'You little...' she murmured. Deep down, she was fluttering. For a guy sworn off any woman outside the Boulevard Périphérique, he flirted with consummate skill.

Yet as she scurried to catch up, she realised that flirting was merely what she *wanted* to happen. Because she'd happily skip lunch and go straight to rolling around the grass.

After a confab, a location was agreed upon. All four had brought their own stuff; easiest as Anna and Mark were veggie. As Beth unpacked her cooler, she noted what Sam had brought. Mini pork pies and cherry tomatoes, as promised. A nutty salad, mini sausage rolls, and a hard-boiled egg.

She surveyed her spread. The same, plus celery sticks.

Sam chuckled. 'Great minds think alike.'

'And it stops me nicking stuff.'

'True.' He grabbed one of her sausage rolls and popped it in his mouth. She returned the favour.

He shoved her playfully. She shoved back.

'Now, children,' Mark said with fake gravitas. 'Play nicely.'

Anna laughed, bright and without side, touching his arm as if to say, "Well done, honey".

Beth tried to recall whether she and Sam had actually made that bet.

For the next delightful hour, conversation danced around the group. She got time to chat with Mark, while Sam and Anna caught up.

In a lull, Mark stood. 'I'm going to stretch my legs. Pop to the loo in the café.'

Anna rose. 'Want company?'

'For the walk, sure. The loo part I can do myself.'

She laughed. 'Anyone want coffee?'

'No, thanks,' Sam and Beth choroused.

'Okay, see you in a bit.'

They ambled off. *Not* towards the café.

Beth crossed her legs and faced Sam. 'Do you want the fifty quid in cash or bank transfer?'

'They didn't technically excuse themselves *together*. I won't take your money.'

'But the company's, right?'

'I believe that's the idea, yes,' he said cheekily.

'So we should start spreadsheeting stuff. Like the people you've put together and why they matched.'

'I already did, with Paul and Lena. I'll add the other couples as well.'

'That's brilliant. I'll list everything I liked and disliked about,' she made speech marks, 'The Thirty-Three.'

'You *liked* some things?' he snipped, a twinkle in his lovely eyes.

'Fuck off.'

'Yeah, see, being told to fuck off is a *big* dislike for me.'

She folded her arms. 'That hardly matters, does it? Firstly, we're business partners, and I'm not *from France,* so no relationship would ever work. Plus my roll call of character shortcomings that The Thirty-Three saw.'

'I'm surprised you don't lose as many clients as you do boyfriends.'

Is that it? Is my sweary gob the big turnoff?

'Oh, I only tell the *special* ones to fuck off.'

He put a hand on his chest. 'I'm flattered.'

She sighed theatrically. 'I'm going to kill Lena for introducing us.'

'Not if I get there first.'

'And make your best mate a widower?'

He shrugged. 'I can always find him someone else, quick sharp.'

Her head dipped. Second time love? Mum and Dad, and her brother, had proven it was possible. That was a large part of why she was seeking Mr Right 2.0.

Yet so far, she was failing dismally.

Chapter Sixteen

S am frowned. What had he said to make her forlorn? Then the penny dropped.

It's second time around for her. Of course it is. Idiot.

'You *will* find someone again, Beth. Unless, and please tell me to fuck off for real if this is inappropriate, the first time around has... changed you.'

Her shoulders slid back. Had he misjudged it?

He held up a hand. 'Never mind. Want me to go for ice cream?'

'Divorce has made me a bitter old sow? Icy exterior over a cold, dead heart? That's the reason I can't find a date?'

'If you're any of those things, you hide it superbly. Or does one G&T over a candlelit dinner trigger the real Beth to come out, claws and all?'

She laughed. 'Then I wouldn't leave the house, would I? One bitten, twice shy.' She fingered the space where her wedding band had been.

'Look, Beth—'

She met his gaze. 'We're working together, come what may, aren't we? If I'm to put my faith in you, that someday I'll be taking *my* Mr Darcy for a walk on the hills, and possibly a roll in the bracken, it's full disclosure.'

'You can stop short of *full* disclosure. I don't need to know that reverse cowgirl is your favourite, for instance.'

'Oh.' A smile played on her lips. 'I hoped that was going to be the *first* profile question.'

'If I was being cruel, I'd say that even matching preferred positions wasn't enough for *Mr* Beth.'

The smile vanished. She sipped from her reusable water bottle. 'Leon and I ran out of steam, that's all. Statistically, that's fifty-fifty. And, much as I believe in you, our app won't dent that figure.'

That was, if not a dagger in his back, a harsh truth. 'I agree. But behind those stats are real people. And it's real people we want to give a happy ever after. Even a few.' He shrugged. 'Every little helps, right?'

'I believe that slogan is already taken.'

'Well, when we hire a marketing genius, they'll come up with ours.'

She stared into space. Had he unwittingly identified the key issue? If they never received funding, the marketing would be sorely lacking. Research, parameters and coding were almost the *easy* part. Without significant customer take-up, the app would die a quick death.

'"The Happy Ever After app".' She scrutinised his face. 'Well?'

'"The *Appy* Ever After app",' he joked, enjoying the pun.

Her eyes widened. 'Appy Ever After! That's it! Sam, you're a genius.' She raised a palm.

He high-fived. 'Joint effort, I think.'

'See what fresh air and M&S munchies can do?'

He surveyed the horizon. 'And being left alone while my latest success story gets down to business.'

'Ha! There's no way Anna is reverse cowgirling Mark in the woods.'

'Yeah. I reckon he's a missionary-or-nothing guy, which would make *her* the one with tree roots chafing the coccyx.'

'And woodlice up her yahoo.'

He shook away the image of Anna sprawled on the ground, legs akimbo. Yes, she was sweet, but rather full-on for his liking. 'Mark would have taken his rug if he had such shallow designs on her. Which he wouldn't.'

'Is that one of the questions?' Beth asked.

'You mean "Do you want or expect sex on the first date?"' Sam waggled his head. 'Maybe. All the profile questions will have to be vetted by my account manager, business consultant, investment whip-cracker, whatever she wants to be known as.'

'I think she'll settle for "Beth".'

'Don't settle, Beth. Never *settle*. Choose.' He winked.

She made a thumb-and-forefinger "gun" gesture. 'One hundred percent.' Then she snorted quietly. 'I didn't *settle*, Sam. Leon and I were good.'

'Sorry.' He patted her hand. 'I didn't mean anything by that.'

'It's fine. But I'm a case study, that's for certain. As well as the dating failures, I'll tell you all the friction points between me and my ex. Or soon-to-be ex.'

His eyes flared, chest thumping. 'You're still *married*?'

She held up her left hand. 'Does it look like I want to be?' She shook her head. 'Leon's not the quickest at stuff. Admin. Letting go, perhaps.' She wiggled her eyebrows. 'But sometimes slow is good. In other ways.'

He swallowed hard. 'Missionary or... whatever.'

'That's not too much disclosure, is it? And hardly a question for the app. "Do you prefer it to be over in less than a minute?"' She laughed at her own joke.

'Too right. I'd never get matched.'

She glanced at his groin, barely a flicker. But she was caught red-handed and looked away.

She coughed. 'I know you're joking, but how do we get over that whole problem of users putting in what they want other people to hear? Everybody will say they are tolerant, easy-going, good sense of humour, are above average in attractiveness, believe in equal division of labour between the sexes, and give great oral. It's only down the line that you find out how much of that was a lie to get to the first date or the first shag.'

He raised a finger. 'But it's the friction that causes the breakups. The mismatches. Things people *don't* like. Or don't value, or are unwilling to give ground on.'

'Like your wierdo wedding girlfriend.'

'Exactly. It's the real-life *examples* we're focusing on. Plus, we phrase the questions in a way that minimises the chances of people gaming the system. We joke about The Thirty-Three, but it's worn you down, hasn't it? The number of times things have fallen at the first hurdle.'

'That's the problem, isn't it? I never get far enough to hit the "real life" issues.' She pinched the bridge of her nose. 'I'm too picky. Reject before I get rejected. That's some skill, being able to hurtle towards something new whilst running away from it at every opportunity.' Her mouth turned downwards.

She shook her head and stood. 'I'm going for a walk.'

Chapter Seventeen

He sprang up, placing a hand on Beth's lower arm. 'Hey,' he said softly. 'Don't be silly.'

That touch, that unrequested care and empathy, turned her heart to mush. She wanted to pull him close, a hug of thanks and friendship. Anything more needed to wait. Possibly forever.

She tutted. 'Yeah. Sorry for spoiling the afternoon. This isn't about *me*.'

'But it can be about your experience. And mine.'

She squeezed his hand. 'Come on then. Tell me your idea.'

They sat, closer now.

'Part of a user's profile is their view on the facets of *another* user, one they hope to match with.'

She frowned. 'Don't get you.'

'Okay, let's take an example. We have a question like, "What should be your partner's position on having children?" Answers, "Want them", "We'd have to talk it over", or "Hard no".'

'And...?'

'Nobody has to state *their* point of view. No chance to lie, or go for the safe "middle" answer. Yes, some people truly are on the fence, but there are usually definite standpoints. For example, your profile says "Want them". But remember, that's not *your* preference, but the opinion or life goal you want your *ideal match* to have. So, I check out Beth Moore's profile, and she's seeking a partner who wants kids. If I do too, then I pass that criterion. Simple.'

'Hmm. It's kind of a giveaway, though. If he has to want kids, by definition, she wants them too.'

He gritted his teeth, sucking in air. 'Okay. Bad example.' He gazed into the distance. 'Try this. "Do you want your partner to have tattoos? Yes, maybe, definitely not." That doesn't imply an equivalence. I might not have any tattoos, but crave a girl who's covered in them.'

She roared with laughter. 'You do not.'

'What, have tattoos myself, or want to settle down with Lydia The Tattooed Lady?'

'Either. If there's a drop of ink on your body, I'll give you that fifty quid right now.'

He held out a palm, eyebrows arched.

She folded her arms. 'Fool me once, shame on you. Fool me twice, shame on me.'

He held the pose for a beat, then winked. 'But you get the logic?'

'I do. Still, there's lots to thrash out.'

'A ton, yeah. If summer keeps going past this weekend, maybe some outdoor working is on the cards.'

'You bring the laptop, I'll bring the Prosecco.'

He raised a finger. 'Nosecco's probably better. Or we'll get bogged down in finessing *your* type of questions. Reverse cowgirl, pretzel dip, seashell or whatever.'

Beth's fingers came to her mouth. 'I can't decide what's worse, the fact you know that stuff, the implication I do, or the suggestion that I'd get bladdered and talk to my client about sex positions.' Her insides knotted at the prospect of trying those three—and more—with him.

'Actually, my software development job is a cover story. I'm actually an adult movie star.'

She squealed with amusement, which set him off. Wiping tears from her cheeks—after the best laugh she'd had in months—she found a reply.

'So if the app goes viral, will you give up the porn? You won't need the extra money.'

'Debatable. I mean, the regular sex is a very attractive bonus.'

'Plus, it doesn't conflict with your dream, because none of these women classify as girlfriends.'

He leant in. 'Exactly. I hope my little secret is safe with you.'

She zipped her mouth, struggling to put away a smile. 'Mum's the word. And I'm sure the secret's not that *little*, or you wouldn't have the job, right?'

'Is this another question we'll get waylaid by when you're pissed? "What *size* does your partner need to be?"'

She pushed at his shoulder. 'It's lucky I know you're kidding. That stuff is *not* the difference between a few fun nights and many wonderful decades.'

'No. I'll bet that most bedroom fights aren't caused by what does or doesn't happen in the *bedroom*, but by what happens in other rooms of the house. Or, worse, the rooms of someone else's house.'

'Hmm.' There had never been any suspicion that Leon had been unfaithful, and she certainly hadn't done much worse than dream about Robert Pattinson when she was in the bath, so they'd escaped that stand-up row, knife in the back, spite and disgust end to the marriage.

Sam was checking his watch.

'Oh, are we on a schedule?' she asked.

'No. But either they've got lost or don't want to be found yet.'

She scoured the area, but couldn't spot Mark and Anna. 'Should we take their stuff back to the car park?'

'And if they come here and find it gone, they'll call the police?'

'Would *you* call the police if your cooler and blanket were nicked? They probably have better things to do.'

'True. We'll have to wait. Chance to get some sun.'

She checked her attire. Only her hands and face were exposed. 'Wow. Great.'

'What? Are you not into tanning? Vitamin D is healthy.'

She nodded sarcastically. 'Ah. That'll be why I'm a car crash on the dating scene. Insufficient vitamins in my diet. But I'm hardly dressed for sunbathing. Want to talk more shop?'

'We already did talk shop.' His lips pursed wickedly. 'Maybe *this* is the thing. The reason. You're always in work mode. Too starchy.'

Her mouth formed an O. She ripped up a handful of grass and lobbed it at him. 'I say again, you're a snake.'

He brushed the greenery from his lightweight jacket, tugged it off and cast it aside. He lay down, folding his toned arms behind his head. The T-shirt bit into his biceps.

Is it hot in here? Out here?

'Chill. Take some clothes off.'

Her eyes became saucers. 'The hell?'

'I meant your jumper. And remember, unless you're wearing a beret and a string of onions, you're safe.' He shot a knowing look.

'Wow. Comes to something when you're mocking your own fantasy.'

'Des-ti-ny. Very different concept. And yes, I'd rather mock it than wait for you to.'

The wind left her sails. 'Sorry. I need to stay in my lane.'

He looked her up and down, pensive.

Time to show him what he's missing.

She pulled off the jumper, making sure to push her chest out. Then she folded the garment to use as a pillow and straightened her short-sleeved white blouse.

'Bra strap's twisted,' he said, rolling over.

'Fuck off.'

He merely smiled, so she lay down. Something dug into her shoulder blade. She reached around with her left hand.

Smart arse.

She untwisted the strap and closed her eyes. Taking deep breaths, the sun warm and invigorating on her face, she stretched her arms out to the side. Her fingers bumped something.

The something moved. 'Sorry.'

She opened her eyes to see him draw his hand in by a few inches. That didn't mean a thing. He'd been teasing her for ages; the first step towards flirting. Why was he doing it if there was no romantic future for them? To keep his banter machine oiled, so that when he met Mademoiselle Right, he wasn't tongue-tied?

No point in sweating the details. She was enjoying the beautiful countryside on a lovely day, with a wonderful bloke. Actually, it was better than virtually every other date she'd had.

Perhaps this was the answer: stop trying too hard.

A few minutes later, she checked whether the water bottle was within reach. It was. Thirty yards across the hillside, a couple were heading their way... holding hands.

Beth waited a moment, sat up, took a drink, then feigned noticing them and waved.

'Lovebirds incoming,' Beth said.

'Anna pregnant yet?' Sam replied, eyes closed.

She quietly tore a handful of grass from the meadow, stealthily leant over and carpet-bombed his face.

He didn't flinch. She tensed, awaiting a lunge, perhaps a tickling, though that would send the wrong signals to Mark and Anna.

Sam spoke softly and evenly. 'You could have had my eye out. That's it. We're done. You can forget the app.'

As the quartet walked back to the car park, Beth pursed her lips against a chuckle, recalling the last hour or so. It would be childish, reckless and naive to believe she'd fallen in *love*, but unarguably she'd fallen in *very strongly like*.

There were hugs all round. Mark drove away, and Anna went to the bus stop.

Beth stowed her picnic gear in the boot and walked over to Sam's car.

'Great idea, great afternoon. Thanks, *partner*. Bring on the next one. Maybe without the missiles, though.' She spied something. 'Hang on.' She carefully plucked a stray piece of grass from his hair.

'Next one's nude tandem skydiving,' he said. 'There's this guy Declan I know—'

She whacked his arm. 'Fuck off.'

He held her gaze. 'Thanks, Beth. Really. This whole thing is much less painful than I expected.'

'Yeah. Amazing, eh? Given how I struggle to spend more than a couple of hours with any bloke before giving them the elbow.'

'I won't dignify that. So text me when the funding is agreed?'

She angled her head. 'And if it isn't?'

'Text me when you want to sit down and go through any detail ideas you've got.'

'Sounds good.' She nodded.

He nodded.

And that pregnant pause. And the tense body language.

Sod it.

She pulled him into a loose embrace. He almost gave as good as he got, but held plenty in reserve. For Mademoiselle Right.

Which made her a little sad, despite the joyous day.

At home, she took Quincunx out of his cage, fussed him, chatted to him, said what a studmuffin Sam was—a silly, private, jokey term she'd used throughout this dating rollercoaster. Quincunx didn't care. His feathers weren't ruffled.

Hers had been.

Chapter Eighteen

On Sunday, George invited Sam along on a shopping trip. The 3-year lease on his car was up, which meant it was time for another, newer, faster one. For an educated guy, the concept of depreciation was strangely alien to George, as was the realisation that revving his engine at traffic lights didn't cause women to queue up at nearby phone boxes, ready to change into bridalwear.

While George talked to the salesman who he wished was a younger, blonder and chestier sales*woman*, Sam toured the showroom, feigning interest in metal he couldn't afford and didn't want. Then, during the test drive, he sat in the customer waiting area, drinking the dealership's passable free coffee, recalling the chats with Beth, and making app development notes on his phone.

'Verdict?' Sam asked when George returned.

'Goes like shit off a shovel. Don't like the satnav though.'

'Never mind. Pub?'

'Pub.'

In the car, Sam made a pantomime of fastening his seatbelt.

George, familiar with his driving being mocked, coughed, 'Arsehole.' Then he trickled the car out of the forecourt, inched onto the main road, and pressed the accelerator to the stop.

'I bumped into Rob the other day,' he announced.

'Going at this speed, I'm not surprised.'

'Fuck off.'

'Rob who?' Sam asked.

'Rob. You know, Rob. The contract. Rob Parsons.'

'Oh. And?'

'His girlfriend was shagging someone else.'

'Ah.'

'He walked in on them.'

'Wow.'

'It was girl-girl, though, so he thought about asking to stay.'

Sam couldn't decide what was worse: discovering something *very* new about your girlfriend, losing her because of it, or trying to sneak a threesome.

'Is this relevant to anything, or gossip?'

'Do you know anyone he might want to date?' George asked, heel-and-toeing a downchange.

'Hmm.'

Rob Parsons was pushing forty—not usually Sam's target market, but with the app, he'd have to broaden his horizons, appealing to those wanting a forever love, whether in their third, fourth or fifth decade. Undeniably, the further on in life you went, the better you knew yourself and what you wanted from a relationship.

Two years ago, Rob's company had requested a quote for a software project. The tender was handled through Sam's team, and he'd done the business spec. Sadly, as Rob was known to have a few quid, VentaTech inflated their quote and duly lost out to a competitor. Rob was disappointed, as he wanted Sam on the project, but the contract decision had been made by his penny-pinching Financial Director.

That encounter had swelled Sam's confidence in his abilities as both a developer and a client liaison. As such, he believed he could make a go of this app, as well as his fledgling consultancy. Still, he had no intention of walking into HR and telling them where to stuff it. For one thing, if the VC people didn't green-light the funding, he'd need his salary to cover the costs. Costs for an app that his employer didn't know, and must never know, he was building.

'What does "Hmm" mean?' George asked. 'Has something happened? Is this project not going ahead? Lena said you and Beth are getting on *famously*. Second date already.'

Sam shot a glare. 'These are research meetings. Planning sessions. Why is it that as soon as I spend more than ten minutes with a woman, suddenly my dreams are out the window? I told you that work is probably sending me to Paris. Why would I risk things now by starting something with Beth? Even if I wanted to? Which I don't.'

She wouldn't have me anyway. She deserves better than someone who can't even sit on a café bench successfully.

'Alright, keep your hair on.' George revved the engine, frustrated by the queue at the temporary traffic lights. 'And what if nothing happens on this trip? How long will you wait? Another month? A year? A decade? Come on, mate, you have to entertain the idea of giving up on this.'

Sam scoffed. 'You mean settling? Settling for something less than perfect, less than what I want?' He shook his head. 'Some friend you are. Beth is my *investor*.'

George moved the car forward six feet. 'She's a suit. It's not her money. And it sounds like she's only interested because the app will help *her*. Not great morals, is it?'

Sam shook his head. 'You have no idea. She's no *suit*. She's incredibly valuable, especially given her extensive dating experience. And, yes, before you say, that's ideal, isn't it, because I don't have that.'

'Look, mate, I know your Paris idea comes from a good place. From what your folks have. If you can somehow recapture that, great. But in the meantime, why not look elsewhere?'

'I don't want the distraction. And I'm fine.'

George appeared sceptical. 'You're happy to be single while twelve other couples have got it working?'

'It's fourteen now. Maybe fifteen. And if the alternative is *my* happiness, that's pretty selfish. Paul and Lena, for starters. Would I turn back the clock, split them up, if it meant I'd walked down the aisle instead? No way.'

George accelerated hard, racing the traffic light, but gave up and braked hard to a stop. They'd be through in the next group. Naturally, no activity was *actually* taking place on the road repair.

'Okay, fair enough. I didn't mean it as a "you or them" thing, but P and L will never split up anyway. Besides, she seems very... clucky recently.'

Sam was open-mouthed. 'Lena's *pregnant*?'

'You do *know* that kind of thing can happen?' George shook his head in feigned ridicule. 'No, she's not, or not that I've heard, but I think she wants to be.'

Scenes from the junkyard golf date spooled through Sam's head. 'Have they fallen out? Oh, God.' He stared at the cupholder stuffed with detritus.

George clicked his fingers. 'Hey. Snap out of it. No, they haven't. Or not that Paul's told me.'

'They better bloody well not. They're the app's guinea pigs. They're my poster couple.'

'Because it's all about *you*.' George tore away from the WHEN RED LIGHT SHOWS WAIT HERE sign.

Sam held back a rejoinder. It *wasn't* about him. It *was* about their marriage. But also his matchmaking skills, and therefore the app.

Change the subject.

'I'll get in touch with Rob. Have a coffee. Does he know I'm the walking anachronism of a dating mastermind?'

'I didn't give him chapter and verse. But stop being so bloody defensive. You've been using your network, your mates, their mates, workmates, aunt's friend's cousin's neighbour, whatever, as your resource pool—'

'You make it sound so underhanded! You're the ones shoving single people under my nose, promising that Cupid Carter will get them married off.'

George brought the car to a halt at the lights on the dual carriageway. Sam clocked the dark blue car in the adjacent lane. George's attention was lasered on the red light. He eased in the accelerator, rode the clutch.

'Er, mate...' Sam warned.

Red and amber. 5000rpm.

'Mate!'

Too late. The car leapt off the line, trouncing the getaway of the car beside them. In four seconds, they were doing 50. In a 40 zone.

'George!'

Streaks of blue light shimmered across the inside of the windscreen. A siren cut the air.

George checked his mirror, then Sam, then the side window. The unmarked police car pulled alongside...

Sam sat in the passenger seat, cringing for five solid minutes, as George was read the riot act. Statistically, it had been coming. He wasn't reckless or angry behind the wheel, merely a bit of a plonker. A show-off.

Sam watched via the door mirror, assessing George's body language, which, after the initial shock and sheepishness, had morphed into something more incredible—playfulness. It was obvious why. Whilst Sam was sworn off dating, he wasn't *blind*. In the same situation, he'd be looking to bail as quickly as possible, his tail between his legs.

Not George. The idiot was flirting. The WPC seemed distinctly unimpressed, but she hadn't yet clapped him in handcuffs. Wise, as that might have played to his fantasies.

Tutting, Sam engrossed himself in his phone.

Two minutes later, the driver's door opened and George plopped into the seat.

'Three points?' Sam asked.

'Yeah. But did you see her? Wow.'

Sam shook his head. 'Unbelievable. Only you could get the hots for a WPC whose sole impression is that you're a bellend.'

'We had a chuckle,' George protested.

'Why? Did you say it was bound to happen eventually, and she was the lucky one?'

'Hey! Live and let live.'

'If you start cruising around at ten miles an hour over the speed limit, trying to get arrested by her, I'll know you've lost the plot.'

George shot a self-satisfied smirk. 'I got her number.'

Sam laughed. 'You did not.'

'I did. 44519.'

'Hilarious. So what's the next step? Ring up the cop shop and ask for the address, phone number, and vital statistics of WPC 44519?'

'WPC *Cole*.'

Sam clapped his hands over his face. 'Oh crap. You're serious.'

'Deadly.'

'Then I can't wait to see what happens first, a date or a driving ban.'

George cocked an eyebrow. 'No contest, mate.'

Chapter Nineteen

For the first three days of the working week, Beth was on tenterhooks. Why was Declan taking an age to sign off a proposal whose ask was a mere fifty grand? She could only presume that such a minnow was pushed to the bottom of his In Tray, or he was deliberately stalling so she'd come begging to be fast-tracked. Begging on her knees...

In the meantime, she'd spent the evenings making notes about her recent experiences, trying—like Sam—to invent the beginnings of a questionnaire which would form the app's user profile. She liked nothing better than a spreadsheet, and, with a glass of wine by her side, painstakingly created a list of over 500 attributes, values and preferences that meeting The Thirty-Three had raised.

It was a sobering experience. Initially, she'd organised dates as an excuse to get out of the house and away from Leon; the atmosphere was too odd. Ten quickfire dates later, she'd realised it was a mistake to select people based on looks—which was how she first chose Leon. This time, she wanted something deeper and more fundamental. True, dating meant discovery, but another twenty-plus strikeouts—and her new spreadsheet—showed that *surely* some things could be discovered before pulling on fancy clothes and then coming home disappointed.

She exchanged messages with Sam. He was hoping to line up another date evening with someone called Rob, but didn't have an obvious match. He'd sent a picture and a few salient facts, asking if she knew someone who fit.

On Thursday, she was halfway through a crayfish and rocket baguette when Declan stood in the doorway of his office and beckoned. She used a compact to check for green leaf shards on her teeth and went to find out what her master/torturer had to say.

He waved her to the seat opposite his desk. Her pulse thudded—which was ridiculous. He'd never make a scene, or an overt preying gesture, not here. She resolved to show no fear; she'd done nothing wrong.

'Good news and bad news, Beth.'

'Okay,' she replied.

'Bad news first. Edgar Hopkirk has absconded.'

Her brow knit. 'Absconded?'

'It means to leave hurriedly.' A supercilious smile appeared.

She didn't rise to that. 'With money.'

'Our money. A million. Dropped off the face of the earth.'

Now, her jugular had a legitimate reason to pulse.

'Oh,' she said, because shouting "Fucking hell!" might have put her on an even slipperier slope to unemployment than she was currently prostrated upon, fingers in a tiny handhold.

'Whether that was his intention all along, we'll never know. I certainly won't, because he is, was, your client, and thankfully, my name's not all over that proposal. A proposal that now looks somewhat crass.' He snapped up a hand before she could protest. 'I'm sure everything was watertight, and maybe some people are godawful sponges, but let's hope it's an oversight and he's not been playing us.'

'Let's hope,' she mustered.

'Yes, plan for the worst but hope for the best. We've alerted the authorities.' He leaned on the desk. 'So your portfolio could use a pep, I think.'

'Definitely.'

Providing there are no conditions attached.

'Your work over the last few years indicates a good judge of investment potential and character.' His nose wrinkled minutely, like the whiff of a bad smell. 'Let's hope you're a better judge of character than *my* experience indicates.'

She took a punt on what the good news was. 'If Sam Carter takes us for fifty grand and runs off to a desert island, I'll hand in my notice.'

Declan Black surveyed her, nodding slightly... whilst probably trying to visualise her naked. 'I've split the funding into three stages. It's gone for approval. I'd be cruel to deny you the chance to back a winner. Even in *that* line of business.'

'Thank you.'

'I also cut the build time down to three months. If your client is such a hotshot at coding and finding hookups for *discerning* people, I'm sure he'll want to launch and start earning as fast as we do. And before the bottom drops out of the dating app market. I read the other day that *office* romances are on the rise.' He looked her a question.

'So are sexual harassment claims.' She stood. 'Thank you, Declan. I'll inform the client that the first stage of funding is on its way.'

She strode out.

At five past six, the first cocktail was inside her.

Danni, as usual, was late. This tardiness had been a sticking point for the suits at work, too. She'd jumped before she was pushed, opting for a career lane-change. She'd retrained as a massage therapist, working from home, which minimised the chances of being late to "the office".

Despite having her hands all over a steady stream of men, this hadn't led to love, merely to a request for "extra" from one guy. Sadly, this wasn't one of the guys Danni wanted to give "extra", and she said she wasn't that type of masseuse, and he should try the place with the blacked-out windows down the road.

At six fifteen, Danni arrived. Apologising profusely, she got Beth a refill and herself a glass of white.

As they hadn't spoken in weeks, Beth caught Danni up on her divorce—still waiting for Leon's lawyer to produce the final paperwork, the dating scene—not unduly successful, and the Declan problem. Best to get the bile out early, before the booze took effect and she began ranting, leading to more booze, higher emotion, more ranting, more booze, etc, until she was woken up at 4 a.m. on a workday, aggrieved because the roadsweeper hadn't had the courtesy to drive around her.

Danni, because she was a darling and familiar with alleviating people's pain, took it like a champ. Then she doled out solid advice: give Leon a nudge, forget The Thirty-Three, and keep playing sweet and nice with Declan.

They ordered four plates of starters to share as mains, devouring them as Danni chatted about her new lifestyle and the inability to find a man... or a man who wouldn't raise his eyebrows suggestively when he discovered what she did for a living.

Beth considered Sam's little black book.

'What are you thinking about?' Danni asked.

'Oh, Sam.'

'Who's Sam? I wondered when the good news was coming.'

Beth scoffed. 'Oh no. Not that. I wish. Just a client.'

Danni tapped the table enthusiastically. 'Spill the tea. Especially the "I wish" part.'

Beth gave her the facts—the intro by Lena, Sam's matchmaking skill, the app, the two enjoyable research dates and, finally, the one sour note.

Danni put a hand to her chest. 'Oh, that's so romantic.'

'It's stupid,' she replied like a sullen teen.

'Maybe. But don't you like romance?'

'Absolutely.'

'So what's wrong with this? Other than you're not the subject of his dream.'

Beth shook her head gently, suppressing petulant, self-interested annoyance. 'He's too... narrow-minded, fixed on it. I could dance naked on a table and he'd give a Gallic shrug and say "Non merci. Do you see the Arc de Triomphe around here? No? Then you're not what I want."'

'Oh, babe.'

She tutted, sipping wine. 'Seems like the only way it'll get into his skull is if our compatibility is proven *scientifically*. So the faster we get the app written, and plug our details in, the sooner he'll realise that destiny is staring at him from across the table, not across the Channel.' Her nose wrinkled. 'Unless I really *am* undateable.'

Danni laughed. 'No way! Maybe his gift isn't perfect. So what?'

'I suppose. Providing it makes a successful app with great reviews, a ton of happy people, and money in the bank for us all, then fine.' She sighed. 'Ironic that he'll be the only person it won't work for. I mean, the Paris thing *is* cute, but it's almost obsessive.'

'Do you want me to point out that time you fantasised about being stranded on a desert island with some hunk?' Danni shot a cautioning look. 'And what about dating a client? Conflict of interest.'

'Okay, okay.' If Beth rushed things and pressured Sam, he might get angry and push back. They'd lose the working relationship, even the fledgling friendship. Worse still, he could abandon the app, which was logically her best route to a man. An available one.

Danni licked her lips. 'Of course, there's no conflict of interest with *me*.'

'Did I not just *tell* you the whole France thing?!'

'Maybe it's not *that* fixed. At least give someone else a chance. He sounds like a catch.'

Either Danni was rubbing salt in the wound, or she had a point. Anyway, didn't she deserve happiness too?

'Okay. I'll tell him about you. Worst case, you can be one of the app guinea pigs. Okay?'

What was there to lose? If Sam fell for Danni, it proved Beth never stood a chance, because they were different propositions. If he even dated Danni once, but it didn't work out, it would show that Sam was open to something other than The Undiscovered Paris Woman.

Also, as the absconding Edgar Hopkirk fiasco had proved, Beth needed to hedge her bets. By fixating on Sam, she might remain blind to other opportunities, which was crazy, because she'd wound up in a position where the chances of finding the right man were higher than they'd been for ages.

Bring on the double dates!

Chapter Twenty

On Wednesday, Sam met a client whose mindfulness app he was working on.

The unfamiliar coffee shop was across town, and the parking nearby was dreadful, so he took two bus rides from the office, arriving in good time.

After a successful hour huddled over the laptop, the client had to run off to another engagement. Sam headed to the Gents: the large Americano was working through his system, and he didn't want to get caught short on the bus.

He emerged from the loo and headed for the door. Two people had collected their takeaway order. The man, forty maybe, pulled the woman into him, and they shared a fulsome kiss.

'Sorry, I have to rush.' He squeezed her arm.

'No problem. See you soon,' she replied.

Every hair on Sam's neck stood to attention.

The man waved casually, pulled open the café door and disappeared into the late morning.

Sam was rooted to the spot.

The woman went to the podium where sugars and stirrers lived, prised off the cup's lid, tipped in one sachet, and stirred.

Blood roared in Sam's ears.

The woman tossed the wooden stick in the cubbyhole, replaced the lid and glanced around, checking that the way was clear. She spied him, and all colour evaporated from her cheeks.

Quivering, Sam could only muster a wide-eyed query. Shock and fear washed her face. Then she spun on her heels and hustled to the door.

Sam's throat constricted.

Fuck. Fucking bollocky fuck.

Sound, which had been shut off for the last half-minute, minute, or aeon, swamped him. The hiss of steam, rattle of cups, chatter of patrons. The aroma of caffeine hit like an invisible mushroom cloud, waking him from what couldn't have been a dream because it was a nightmare.

Cannons went off in his head. He wanted to crouch and scream.

This can't be happening.

The door banged shut.

It *was* happening. And he couldn't be polite and British and shrug it off. He couldn't unsee it. He couldn't erase the happenstance encounter. She would know she'd been spotted. Rumbled. He could barely begin to imagine the implications, the consequences.

He couldn't let this lie, not for someone he cared about.

He hauled open the door and broke into a jog. She was twenty yards away, scurrying, trying to escape from something that would live with them forever.

She glanced over her shoulder. Furtively. He ran.

Shoulders down, defeated, she hustled onwards, but in three seconds the chase was over. He barred her path. She stopped dead, face rent with sorrow.

He took her elbow and eased her into a quiet side street. Thankfully, she didn't resist. He didn't want a stand-up row... although it was still possible.

His mouth moved wordlessly. What to say?

'Sam, I can explain,' she said.

'It better be a *fucking* good explanation.'

'And why is it any of your bloody business?' she spat.

He stepped into her personal space. 'Because Paul is my *best friend*. Remember him? Your *husband*.'

'It's not what it looks like.'

He laughed, hollow. His insides had been scooped out. His world was chaos.

'Ah. Long lost cousin? Old friend? Maybe the first boyfriend, the one you never stopped loving? Or you're in am-dram soon, and were rehearsing with the leading man?'

She shoved him. 'Don't make this any harder than it is.'

He spoke through gritted teeth. 'It can't be that hard if you're prepared to do it.' His head drooped, weighted down by the enormity of the discovery. 'Fuck's sake, Lena.'

She clutched his arm. Tightly, as if he were a lifebuoy. 'You can't tell him. You cannot tell him.'

'Who? Paul, or the guy you're having an affair with?' He sneered, a deliberately patronising glare.

'It's not an affair, Sam,' she hissed, glancing round nervously.

Too late: the horse has bolted.

'Define "not".'

'It was one stupid kiss.' Her eyes were red and full of pleading—not honesty.

'One. What are the odds that I saw the *one* kiss? And, being unexpectedly kissed by this guy you're *not* having an affair with, you kissed him back?' He prised her hand from his arm and squeezed it—lovingly, not hurtfully.

'Okay, I admit it's not the first.'

'Give me a clue. Less than five? Less than ten? Double digits?'

She ripped her hand away. 'Will you stop being such a fucking smart-aleck? It's wrong. Okay? I know it's wrong. But holier-than-thou from *you* of all people?'

'Oh. And what did *I* do?'

'You won't even date *anyone*.'

'Yeah, well, at least when I do it won't be adulterous.'

She slapped him. At that moment, few things could have been more surprising or hurtful than finding out what he'd just found out. But a slap from a valued friend was one of them.

Immediately, she shrank back, bumping into the graffiti-covered wall of a long-closed shop. She looked at her palm as if it were alien. Her lip trembled.

He massaged his stinging face, wishing he'd never seen that kiss. He wanted to erase it from his memory, or go back ten minutes and skip the loo, risk a wet patch on the Number 446, as this would be infinitely less ruinous on himself and those he loved.

Except that wouldn't cure things. It wouldn't mean that Lena wasn't doing *something* with *someone*.

But what?

He was at a fork in the road, his life, their lives. A huge fork, one you buy in B&Q at the start of the barbecue season, use once, then accidentally leave outside until it rusts in the autumn rain. This whole situation was a shitshow. His M.O. was *creating* couples, not splitting them up.

Absent a better plan, he pulled a startled Lena into a bear hug. She clung on, shaking. They stayed like that for a full minute.

'I don't know what to say,' she murmured.

'You'll work it out. You and Paul are strong enough that if you explain simply, he'll understand.'

She broke off sharply, shaking her head. 'I can't tell him!'

'Then I will.'

Her nostrils flared. 'You wouldn't.'

'He's my mate. He needs to know. I want... *wanted* him to be happy.'

'He is,' she snapped. 'And I am. With *him*.'

'Nobody who is *that* happy kisses other men. Not like you were kissing whoever that was.'

'Hamish. His name is Hamish.'

Sam laughed involuntarily. 'You can't fucking date a guy called *Hamish*.'

'I am not dating him! It was one kiss.'

He cocked an eyebrow.

'A few kisses.'

He cocked higher, straining the facial muscle to breaking point.

'I am not sleeping with him!' she spat, shoving Sam's chest.

He fixed her in the most intense, scrutinising gaze, as if trying to suck out the truth by willpower alone.

'I promise,' she said, low and earnest.

He nodded slowly. 'Then maybe, maybe, Paul will forgive you.'

Moisture appeared in her eyes. 'I can't, I can't.'

'One of us has to. Or this is dry rot, and sooner or later, your house will come down. And I thought the seven-year itch was a *guy* thing.'

She shook her head. 'It's nothing. Honestly. Flirting that got out of hand.'

He scanned around. 'Now is not the time or place. I'm not having you get me sacked for being late back to the office. Jesus, Lena. Now I've got to live with knowing.'

She grabbed his hand. 'I'm sorry, Sam.'

'I'm only his friend. Your friend. You're the ones in trouble. I'm certainly not bloody well losing my mate because of it. And I'd rather not lose you either. Especially after... recently.'

A small curiosity, a tiny hope plucked at the corner of her mouth. 'The introduction.'

'In other circumstances, I'd buy you a drink. But I'm not celebrating anything. Given what I just saw, maybe I won't ever celebrate.'

She frowned. 'What does that mean?'

Acid gnawed at his throat. 'It means that you and Paul and... *this*... are absolutely my business. Literally, now. You're the ones who bloody suggested I create an app! So this is *not* being swept under the carpet. Work out what you're going to tell him, and let me know. Soon. The longer I lose sleep over you two, which I will, the sooner I'll come over and blurt it out to him. Which I don't want. Because I care about you both, and my instincts say this is a blip. I certainly fucking hope so.'

'It is, it is, it is,' she beseeched.

He let out a gust of air. 'Of all the couples. Unbelievable.' Then, and he didn't know why, he kissed her on the temple and walked away.

Inside, he was a mess.

His poster couple were on the rocks. If this was a litmus test of his matchmaking skills, of his fledgling database and its compatibility function, Appy Ever After was merely Appy For A While. And who could he talk to? None of his friends. Not his workmates—they'd never understand the implications.

Not even Beth. It would shake her faith in him, his gift, to its foundations. She'd pull the funding. She'd walk away. The app might never happen. And she'd likely lose her best shot at finding someone.

Which hurt, because of all the people he'd met, Beth was one he wanted to see happy. For the right man, she was a real catch.

Chapter Twenty-One

B eth messaged Sam about the funding, but his response was a curiously bland and terse, "Great, thanks".

Had she caught him at a bad time? Or was it a silly expectation of endless sunshine between them, a ridiculous notion that their working relationship would get personal... and *sexy*.

She needed to lighten up. Focus on the positives. He gave her hope. If there was one man like Sam in the world, perhaps there were others. If there had been two good dates, surely there were more.

Keen for research and more time together, she messaged him with Danni's details. Did he know a suitable match? He didn't reply. Had something gone wrong at the office? Perhaps he'd had a change of heart about the app? She hoped not.

When her phone trilled on Friday night, she worried that Sam was calling to bail on the following day's brainstorming session.

It wasn't Sam—but someone who *definitely* loved her. A much-needed smile broke on her face.

She accepted the FaceTime call. 'Hey, bro!'

'Hiya sis.'

'How's things? What time is it there?'

He glanced offscreen. Bright sunlight dappled through the blind behind him. 'Half nine. Fancied a quick catch-up before I get to my desk, and the day is gone. Or the month, more like, knowing how shit I am at calling you.'

'Cuts both ways. How's Alyssa?'

'She's great. Out walking the dog.'

A dog that Beth had never met. A girlfriend she'd never met—but someone who was good for him.

'How's winter? Looks pretty not shit,' she said.

'That's Adelaide for you. Probably warmer than Winchester, right?'

'23 degrees today. Three days of sun. That's summer over for the year.'

He laughed. 'I do miss that. And you.'

She shrugged. 'They have planes. And the spare bed is made up. Just little old me here now.'

He frowned, concerned. 'How's it going? You coping?'

'It's going... slowly, still.'

'But the end is in sight? Soon there'll only be *one* Leon you're related to.'

She chuckled. 'Yeah. I kept the good one.'

'Good? Even after all the duckings I gave you in the sea at Brighton?'

'I did put that seaweed in your shoes. Remember? You screamed like a girl! You thought something was eating your toes.'

He laughed. 'Dropped my ice cream on the beach.'

'On Mum's leg, more like. I was *not* popular.'

'You should come out here, throw some ice cream over Alyssa. Beaches are much nicer. And the ice cream, to be fair.'

'Yeah, I'd be popular, breaking you two up. The Pommie sister from hell.'

'She'd love you. What's not to like?'

Beth snorted gently. 'There's a question.'

He leant towards the webcam. 'Is this about you getting back on the dating wagon? You're not expecting to hit the jackpot straight away, like last time? Come on, sis.'

She sighed heavily. 'Yeah. Sorry.'

'You're trying again, which is good, which is healthy. Logical. There's a lucky guy out there waiting. And it's never too late.'

That both perked and saddened her. Leon's second chance, borne of something infinitely worse than divorce, *had* given her the courage, the belief, to try again.

Like Beth, her brother had found love young. At 23. Georgia was an amazing person. The wedding was picture book. Beth had turned 20, and recently met someone—the person she was currently splitting up with.

Georgia and Leon never split up. Fate had something else in store. After six years, Georgia was diagnosed with late-stage cancer. Beth cried as much as any of them. Leon didn't deserve this. Neither did Georgia.

When she died, Leon needed to get away, put some distance between himself and the heartbreak. He got a job opportunity in Australia and took it with both hands. Mum and Dad were retired, and his sister was happily—at the time—married.

Three years later, he met a woman called Alyssa in an Adelaide coffee shop. She was precisely the tonic, the second chance, he needed.

Compared to this, Beth's current challenges were sour grapes. Her brother had walked through the valley of the shadow of death. Now he'd found the light. Even if it took *another* thirty-three dates, Beth believed, deep down, that someone would come along and rescue her from spinsterhood.

Imagine still being Declan Black's subordinate in five years, and single. How he'd laugh, twisting the knife: "Shouldn't have told me to fuck off, should you? How about we give it another go?"

She shuddered.

Please, Sam—and your funny matchmaking brain—save me from a future like that.

Chapter Twenty-Two

A t ten o'clock on Saturday, Sam headed over to Beth's. He was hoping for a pick-me-up after the gut punch of discovering Lena's infidelity. He told himself not to be a grouch. Every relationship has bumps in the road. Misunderstandings. He needed perspective—moving towards new matchups that he *could* influence.

Beth had an impressive suburban semi with a red BMW soft-top in the drive.

He pressed the Ring doorbell, pulling a cross-eyed, wide-mouthed face into the camera.

She opened the door. She wore navy joggers and a white hoodie, zipped halfway down to reveal a grey tee. Her hair was up in a loose ponytail. She looked fresh, relaxed, and rather cute.

'Police are on their way. Weirdo.'

'Hey,' he said, rather too apathetically.

She angled her head. 'Is... everything okay?'

Clearly, he hadn't successfully hidden the Lena and Paul worries. He pulled a sober grimace. 'Nothing that you or I can fix.'

'You do realise we got the first ten grand?'

'Yeah.' A smile emerged. 'Sorry.'

'Okay. I won't pry.' She waved him in. 'Oh, and morning.'

'Morning.'

As they passed in the doorway, she pressed her cheek to his. 'Coffee or tea?'

'That would be good.' He followed her into the lounge, his face tingling with the intimacy of her soft, fragrant touch.

'What do you want?'

'Honestly, not bothered. Whatever you're making.'

'I'm making either. Which would you rather?'

'Don't mind. Tea. Coffee. Whatever's easiest.'

She stepped in, hands on her hips, eyebrow raised. She could do that *one eyebrow* thing. 'Half tea, topped up with coffee. Alright?'

He pulled a face. 'Nah. Half coffee, topped up with tea.'

'This is going to be a *long* day.'

'Coffee. Please.'

'Good choice. I grind fresh. White, no sugar?'

'Very observant.' He frowned, not recalling how or why she knew.

'Picnic café. Remember? You threw stuff at me.'

'Oh. Yeah. Hang on, you started that. And finished by dumping half the countryside on my face, as I recall.'

'Nyah nyah nyah nyah nyah,' she whined.

He thumped onto the sofa with teenage petulance. 'This is going to be a *long* day.'

She laughed, pulling at her ponytail. 'White, no sugar, just a spoonful of arsenic.' She disappeared into the kitchen.

He gazed around, intrigued by the object in the corner—a cuboid with a cloth draped over it. Nearby, trinkets were dotted around the tall bookcase. Parrots. Many diverse parrots. Glass, ceramic, wood, metal.

He now had an idea what was beneath the drape, but couldn't resist lifting the lower edge by an inch.

'SQUAAWK!'

'Wha!' He nearly shat himself—because the noise *didn't* come from under the cloth.

He spun.

Beth clapped, a grin splitting her face. 'Priceless!'

'Yeah, brilliant,' he grumped deliberately.

She guffawed. 'Oh, man.' She wiped a tear from her cheek. 'Forget the arsenic. Death by a thousand embarrassments is the way I want *you* to go.'

'Thanks. At least wait until I've built the app and earned you a fat pension.'

'Sorry. Wanna meet him?' She pointed at the cage.

'Sure. With any luck, he'll bite my finger off and you can have another great chuckle.'

'Aw, he wouldn't.' She carefully removed the drape. 'Would you, Quincunx?'

The parrot sidestepped along its perch, burbling softly.

'Good name,' Sam said.

'Thanks. You know me, I like numbers.'

'Yeah. Thirty-three is a favourite, as I recall.'

She leant against the bars. 'Kill, Quin! Kill!'

The parrot sprang onto the cage wall. 'Stud-muffin,' it squawked with faintly ridiculous realism.

Beth's hand came to her mouth.

Sam shot her a query. 'I'd have thought if you were teaching it to speak, some world-class swears are more your type of thing.'

'Stuuud*muffin*,' Quincunx announced.

Beth was nonplussed. 'He's never said a single word. Have you, Quin?'

The parrot climbed the bars until it was level with Sam's head. 'Whaaat a studmuuuffin.'

'But it's definitely been listening,' she breathed, screwing up her eyes.

'Ah. Been looking at pictures of Declan, have you?' Sam asked.

She punched his arm. 'Fuck off.'

He tapped the cage. 'Great pet.'

'Yeah,' she said through clenched teeth. 'Can't wait to have him stuffed.'

'Aw. Poor thing.'

'Want me to get him out? Have a play?'

'Maybe in a bit. Let him get used to me. Show I'm not a threat.'

She tutted. 'Spoilsport. A bit of blood would be hilarious.'

'Absolutely. Unexpected win. But I'm not here for the petting zoo.'

A smile played on her lips. 'Oh, yeah. Aren't you the dating app guy? Expecting some meeting or other?'

'That was the general idea. I did ask for coffee, but the staff here are *shocking*.'

'They really are. Probably can't find the arsenic.' She faced the doorway, cupping a hand around her mouth. 'Top shelf, Mavis! Behind the instant mash.' She shook her head in fake despair. 'Take a seat, Mr Carter, while I administer a quick flogging.'

She hustled away.

He couldn't wipe the grin from his face.

Chapter Twenty-Three

Beth leant against the worktop, fanning herself with a hand. It was warm in the room, but something else was hotter. Sam.

Hell did he tick every damn box. If she steered clear of the France topic, anything else was within bounds. Which was good, because this project involved discussing life and love... plus multiple choice vs. true/false, inward and outward-facing questions, database logic, marketing verticals, and a ton of other aspects.

She was blessed to be working on this—and with *him*. For the first time in too long, she felt like perhaps she *wasn't* picky, impossible and cruel. Two non-dates with a person she couldn't date had changed her mind about dating.

Oh, the irony.

As she brewed the coffee, a few atonal notes kissed the air.

Sam apparently had no problem making himself at home. She put the refreshments on a parrot-themed tray bought at a garden centre, and carried it to the coffee table.

He stopped playing what was *almost* Chopsticks.

'I'd have thought "As Time Goes By" was your favourite,' she said.

He rose from the stool. 'How do you know I like Casablanca?'

'Well... the whole "love in Paris" thing. Plus, it's a classic.'

'True on both counts.' He pointed. 'Yours or your ex's? If it's not a personal question.'

She sat beside him on the sofa and sipped from her mug. 'I'm an open book. The piano's mine. I got to Grade 8, but never followed through. So please don't ask me to play. Too embarrassing.'

He bit into a biscuit. 'I thought embarrassment was your middle name. Or am I just lucky to be the target of your vendetta of mirth?'

She nudged him. 'So this is why I keep striking out. Too cutting. Too presumptuous. Too *familiar*.'

'Not the working relationship I expected, for sure.'

'We're creating a dating app, Sam. Part of the job is understanding people's likes and dislikes.'

He raised a finger. '*People's*. Not mine.'

'You're a person. Oh, wait, sorry, I forgot you're not going on the app. No need.'

He wrinkled his nose. 'Ah, the gentle mocking. It's been five minutes.'

'You love it really. It's all in fun. Only trying to understand you. As a colleague. And friend.'

'Not even my *longstanding* friends understand.' He growled. 'Arseholes.'

She angled her body towards him and crossed one leg over her lap. 'If you're that invested in this dream meet-cute, so believing, so confident it's the answer, why are you always defensive?'

He inspected her face. 'Honestly? I think years of piss-taking have got my back up. Why can't people live and let live? I don't judge the people I set up for dates, or mock them because they like... acid jazz or threesomes or Mrs Brown's Boys.'

'"Threesomes"?'

127

'Random example,' he said defensively.

'Hmm.' She shot a pointed look.

'Ah, now *I'm* being judged.'

'Not at all.'

'Why, sore topic?'

She fluttered her eyelashes with deliberate theatre. 'A lady never tells.'

'True. But what about *you*?'

She whacked his arm. 'How dare you imply I'm not a lady.'

'Okay, let's analyse. Do ladies even *have* threesomes?'

She played with her lip almost flirtatiously. 'I think if they do, it's a "two girls, one guy" setup.'

He frowned. 'So a lady is more into ladies than men.'

'I may be the numbers person on this sofa, but if you do the maths, there's one of each available. That's kind of the point of threesomes, isn't it?'

'For a lady. Or at least a *woman*, yes.'

'But for you blokes, it's a wonderful smorgasbord of choice.'

He pursed his lips. 'I'm not sure two is sufficient to be called a smorgasbord.'

'Why, how many would you like? What is sir's minimum pussy quotient for a fun night? Three? Four? A full netball team?'

His lower jaw hit the floor.

She let out a guffaw. 'Oh, shit, that's done it! I said "pussy" in front of my business partner, and now I'm nowhere *near* being a lady. Possibly a tart. Do I qualify?'

'Depends. What is madam's *man* quotient for a fun night? Two? Three? The Coldstream Guards?'

She laughed, shoving him. 'Ladies do not answer questions like that!'

He shoved back. 'No. But tarts do.' He winked.

God, his wink is enough to turn me on.

She cleared her throat. 'We're getting off-topic, aren't we?'

'That's okay. I know you tarts have trouble with decorum and polite conversation.'

'We do. But we *will* have to discuss the,' she lowered her voice for comic effect, '*sex* part of the dating profile.'

'Of course. I'll bet your answers will be enlightening.'

'Definitely, compared to you.'

'You really have me figured out, don't you?' He drained his coffee.

'Dunno. Care to answer the threesome question?'

'Not especially. And, what's more, as I won't *be* on the app, you'll never find out.'

'Ahem.' She raised three fingers in turn. 'First, you *are* going on the app. Secondly, why do you think I care what your answer is? And thirdly, we haven't confirmed the question will be included in the database anyway.'

'True. But will I care? No. We're colleagues. Alright, friends, too. Do I have an unhealthy interest in your sexual preferences? No. Why would I? Even if I do, under duress, put a profile on the app.'

She inspected his face. 'Then why is my stomach churning at the thought of you finding out?'

'No idea. Because your whirlwind weekend with the Coldstream Guards will mark you down in my estimation?'

She laughed, whacking the cushion, then became introspective.

Her chest pattered. 'I *do* care what you think, Sam. Not for the app, but because out of everyone I've met, you're the best at assessing people, understanding them. And if I bare my soul, which *has* to happen if I'm to work out why I'm this undateable, unforgiving person, then when you find out what makes me tick, I'm worried it'll give me an answer I don't want to hear.'

He held her gaze, which did nothing for her roiling tummy. His voice was soft, mollifying. 'But it's not about *me*. What matters is honesty, completeness, accuracy, and then matching you with Mr Right. Who, I firmly believe, is out there.'

She explored his compassionate face. 'I seem to make a rod for my back every day I spend with you. My stomach *is* churning about the whole threesome thing, but *I'm* the one who brought the bloody subject up. It wouldn't be an issue if I'd kept my mouth shut. And who cares anyway? It's just one more question. In what universe is *that* the difference between a match and no match? How shallow would a person have to be to flip the switch of their future life on *that*?'

'You're forgetting tarts. I bet, for them, it's mandatory.'

She jabbed his shoulder blade. 'Very funny.' She threw her hands up. 'Sod it. We're supposed to be having a *meeting*, and I hijacked the agenda. You know what?' She looked at him unwaveringly. 'Sam, I've never had a threesome. There. Would I? Possibly. Can't rule it out. Okay?'

He turned away. Embarrassed, probably. *Again.* 'I didn't mean to—'

'Another girl, almost certainly. Yes, the guy would have more fun than me, but, you know, if I loved him, and I'd have to, because it would never be a... casual thing after a game of junkyard golf or whatever, then maybe it would be a laugh. Maybe it'd make my head spin. Maybe it'd be a total car crash. Naively, I'd hope it was a "have a go, get it out of my system" thing. Before the two-point-four kids and the inevitable decline in bedroom activity. Not later down the marriage road, in desperation to put the spark back. Because hopefully this app future-proofs the bedroom stuff, keeps things healthy for years.'

He was facing her, only displaying modest astonishment at her rambling outpouring.

She shook her head. 'Sorry. I'm delusional, aren't I? Expecting decades of bliss. And making it all about the bedroom. Christ, now I *am* worried what you think.'

It was suddenly hot. She unzipped her hoodie, tugged it off and lobbed it over the back of the sofa.

Chapter Twenty-Four

I t was suddenly hot under his collar. Whilst the French doors were letting in a bounty of June sunshine, and the mercury had hit 25, it wasn't helped by Beth discussing threesomes and then thrusting her delightful chest in his direction. He forced an image of the Arc de Triomphe into his mind's eye.

She put the two empty mugs onto the tray and brushed biscuit crumbs from the cushion.

'Beth. Beth.' He stilled her busy hand. 'Everyone has a dream, their expectation of an ideal forever. Nobody is right or wrong. And I'm the *last* person who should judge you. If everyone followed my path, the dating app industry would be on its knees!' He grinned.

She drew circles on her leg with an index finger. 'True. But I *am* looking for love, not sex, Sam. Don't get me wrong, okay? Maybe because it's... been a while... my priorities are off.'

'I think, finally, that qualifies as too much information.'

'I am a bit in-your-face, aren't I? For a work colleague.'

'And friend,' he added, squeezing her hand.

She frowned. 'Too much for a *friend*?'

'No. I mean, you are a friend, and no, it's not too much.' He swallowed hard. 'And I'm still on the start line when it comes to threesomes too. There. We're even. And now, can we *please* move on? I don't know what you're doing for the next few hours, but there's this app idea I hoped we could discuss.'

She beamed. 'Great. More coffee?'

'Yep. Hold the arsenic.'

They rose.

'*Stud*muffin,' squawked Quincunx.

'Hardly,' she called. 'The loser's not even had a threesome.'

He shook his head. 'I don't know which of you to throttle first.'

They sat at the dining table, side by side, laptops open. Coffee, biscuits and water were on the go. He showed Beth his spreadsheet behemoth, which covered everything from looks, height and age to wedding location, parenthood and expat retirement. Plus, literally, 1000 things in between, mostly gleaned from his twelve success stories.

She'd listed The Thirty-Three, their particulars, her likes and dislikes, and all the dealbreakers that had made her decide "He's not for me".

At one fifteen, she suggested lunch. 'What do you fancy?'

'Whatever you're making.'

'What do you want?'

He smirked. 'Honestly, not bothered. Whatever's available.'

'Arsenic on toast?'

'Sounds perfect,' he replied.

She made chunky cheese and ham sandwiches on granary, with tomatoes and kettle chips on the side.

'We need to have a cooking question,' he said, munching on her fine fare.

'Definitely.'

'How about, "Do you cook?". Answers, "Love it", "Don't mind it", "Can't", "Can't be bothered", and "Not my job".'

She nodded enthusiastically. 'Like it. Especially the last one. If he thinks it's her job to be in the kitchen, he can get fucked.'

'I'd imagine, in that household, those would be her sole responsibilities. Get dinner, and get fucked.'

She pointed a crisp at him. 'Ah. We're back onto sex again. Mr One Track Mind.'

'I won't dignify that, Mrs Coldstream. Remember, each to their own. There will be a matchup between someone who wants to be that version of womanhood and a man with old-fashioned values.'

'Fair enough. Providing I don't get matched with any dinosaurs, I'm good.'

As they finished lunch, her mobile pinged.

She scrolled through. 'Ah, bollocks.'

He wondered whether an app question about swearing was appropriate. 'Everything okay?'

She pulled her hair out of its clasp, floofed it up, then gathered it again and slipped the band on.

She growled. 'This guy called Callum. Number thirty-three. I deleted the app we met on, but he found me on another.'

'Hassling you?' Sam hoovered up the remaining crisp shards.

'No. Chasing, maybe. Perhaps I didn't give him the message clearly enough.'

'Callum tracking you down is a *bit* stalkery.'

'Seems like I'm *too* delightful and desirable for men to stay away from.' She put her hands under her chin like a movie starlet.

'If I'm being pedantic, the problem is that it's not yet *mutual* with anyone.'

'True. But... you *are* still looking? For a match for me?'

'You're never far from my mind, Beth.'

Chapter Twenty-Five

*N*or *you mine. Which is a waste of time. But a girl can dream.*

'Thanks,' she replied.

'But the needs of the many outweigh the needs of the one.' He pointed at the laptop.

'Yeah. Sorry. Not all about me. Let's crack on.'

They forensically analysed the criteria he'd listed, then brainstormed the last two dates, recalling all the snippets of conversation. This was a vital part of his approach: what did people really talk about on dates? Not the details on their profiles, their public likes and dislikes, but the day-to-day stuff, the avenues that conversations went down. Ignoring the hot potatoes like religion and politics, even something as simple as a comment about tipping could open a can of worms.

Number 27 had flatly refused to tip the waitress, believing it was reserved for superior service. Beth had disagreed and got sniffy, pigeonholing him as a cheapskate arsehole. Now she recognised that it was merely a difference in views and values. Number 27 was as deserving of a life partner as she was, but they were at odds on this matter, and was it the thin end of the wedge?

She recounted the story to Sam, asking if she'd been unreasonable or picky. He sat on the fence: it mattered to her, and it was a dealbreaker.

'Besides,' he added, 'I've ruled out everyone this side of the Channel, so I can hardly say that *you* need to be more accommodating.'

'It's good that you can joke about this.'

He offered a sober expression. 'I don't expect you, or anyone, to *understand*. Only accept.'

She touched his arm. 'I'd like to understand.'

'Maybe later.' He checked his watch. 'Wow. Cuppa?'

The wall clock said 4:22. 'Definitely.'

They went into the kitchen, made tea, and returned to the sofa. Hanging with him felt so natural.

'So why the double dates in the first place?'

'The first hookup, I double dated because the newbies were apprehensive. I went with someone. The second time, I was hedging my bets, setting the guy up with two possible girls.' He grinned. 'I wasn't this "expert" back then!'

I adore his cheeky grin.

'Look at you now. App and everything.'

'Yeah. Anyway, that date wound up with Paul choosing Lena. Next time, Lena brought a friend. Lena agreed to be my... fake date, to make up numbers.' He shrugged. 'Then it became a thing. It's fun to people-watch, make friends. Anyway. On date four, Lena was still my wingman—'

'Wing*woman*.'

'Pedant. And the other guy said Lena and I made a great couple. Embarrassing as hell.'

'But you got over it? Lena wasn't *offended*?'

'No. We rolled with it. Had fun, actually. Later, we kind of... said Lena had found someone else. Which was true. She and Paul were very serious by then.'

She nudged his knee. 'There you go then! You're a dab hand at this, mate. You can fake date like the best of them.'

'That was in the past.'

'But I suspect we'll have to do it again, or be ready to. The matchmaking used to be a bit of fun for you. Now we're building a product. To get research, you might have to go out on a limb. I want my clients to be invested in their business idea.'

His nose wrinkled. 'I suppose. And I am *very* invested.'

'Good. I am backing you *and* it. I've accepted that you won't try to find love through the app, but at least *play the part* of endorsing your product. Plus, these double dates are good practice for when you bump into Miss Right in Paris. You said you've not had much experience recently.' She winked.

He sighed. 'Yeah. I am rusty.'

'Besides, the stats say I'm this picky, impossible person, so if I can have a good time with you and the people you bring, maybe I'll stop feeling down about *my* chances. Of course, if you'd rather *not* be romantically associated with me, I understand.'

'You're not too shabby to hang out with.' He nudged her.

'Thanks... I think. And look at the bigger picture. From the outside, it's a pretty good ad for the app if the two people building it are "together".' She raised her eyebrows.

He chewed his cheek. 'Yeah. Okay. If you reckon keeping up the pretence has more pros than cons, fine. On your head be it. *You* can be the one to explain to *everyone* when the ceiling falls in.'

'You started it.'

His jaw dropped. 'I did not.'

She counted on her fingers. 'You did the double date thing ages ago. You came to me about the app. You agreed that research was a good idea. You've never tried to sub me out as your fourth seat. And you did say it means we don't have to come clean about doing these dates partly for spying.'

He stroked his throat. 'You're a persuasive woman, Beth Moore.'

'Good. Now let's crack on.'

They worked on grouping the criteria into categories, and debated which were best as "What do *you*...?" questions, and which as "What should your *true love*...?" They thrashed out a shortlist of answers or options for every point, mostly without getting sidetracked by their opinions or hangups. They did, however, end up down a rabbit hole of discussing favourite spreadsheet functions, leading to a fifteen-minute blind alley about the multiple classifications of the concept of infinity.

On one level, it was a slick, productive, professional—and sometimes nerdy—meeting. On another, it was warm, cooperative, and enlightening. And it filled her soul with hope.

He cracked his knuckles, grabbed his empty water glass, and stood. 'Back in a mo.'

She watched him go. His gait. Those broad shoulders. That backside.

Keep a grip, Beth. Only a few more weeks of this.

Except she was judging him on more than that. Sam was delightful company.

He re-entered the room.

'Studmuffin,' Quincunx announced, like the maître d' at a Regency ballroom dinner.

Sam did a little bow. Beth spluttered a laugh.

He checked his watch. 'I should go. Burned up too much of your day already.'

'Yeah, I've had more than enough. Take your stuff and bugger off.'

He eyed the cage. 'It's alright, Quin, you're safe. I've decided to throttle *her* first.'

'*Finally*. Now you've sucked out all my brilliance and insight, time to kill your co-creator and take all the credit.'

He flapped the laptop closed. 'You should have spiked that last cuppa, shouldn't you?'

'Maybe next time.'

'Well, it was fun while it lasted. I hope you'll give me a great eulogy.'

'You want La Marseillaise playing during that slow, closing-the-curtain bit?' she asked.

'No. Let's go with Je Ne Regrette Rien.'

'Obviously you'll be regretting meeting me, but we'll gloss over that.'

'I'll be dead, so no chance for regrets. Actually, it'll be a blessing. I'm already feeling the pressure to make this thing succeed, and we've barely started.'

She assumed he meant the app, not their relationship. 'Barely started? We've had a brilliant day.'

He smiled, breaking the deadpan he'd commendably held. 'Yeah, we have.'

And there it was again. That awkward pre-departure silence.

Unless...

'You want to get a bite to eat?' she suggested.

'Um... What do you have?'

'I meant *out*. We've earned it, right? Oh, unless... Sorry. Saturday night. You head off.'

He laughed. 'Don't pretend I have a life. Where were you thinking?'

'Dunno. What do you fancy?'

'Wherever's good,' he replied, eyes playful.

'No, but what do you want?'

'Honestly, not fussed. You choose.'

She suppressed a smile. 'What kind of thing do you like?'

'I'm easy. Any thoughts?'

Her tummy was cartwheeling. Banter with Sam was life-affirming. If he made love like he traded comebacks, Mademoiselle Right would never leave the bedroom.

Gently, she took a fistful of his T-shirt. 'At the same time. One... two... three.'

'Italian,' they chorused.

She smoothed the shirt back over his chest, wishing her hands could wander further. 'Right, I'll go and change into something presentable.' She skipped out of the room and clattered upstairs.

I basically asked him out. And he said yes.

She stood in front of the mirror, made a Zen pose with her fingers, and took a deep breath.

And if you treat this like a date, you will ruin everything.

'Working dinner, working dinner, working dinner...' she murmured, stripping.

Chapter Twenty-Six

They took a cab to a place she knew. It felt oddly like a real date—though he doubted she'd ever see him that way.

While he scanned the menu, she was absentmindedly folding a paper napkin into what looked like a rabbit.

'Thought you'd have done a parrot,' he commented.

She handed over the rabbit, grabbed his napkin and folded it into a bird shape. 'Ta-da!'

'A woman of many talents.'

She didn't get a chance to confirm or deny that, as the waiter came. They ordered, then she fell pensive.

'What?' he asked, concerned.

She regarded him empathically. 'You want to tell me why you were on a downer earlier? And during the week?'

His stomach bottomed out. He played with the thing-that-wasn't-quite-a-parrot. He owed Beth an explanation. Yet discussing the Lena situation was fraught with danger. The women were already friends—if he blabbed, would it drive a wedge between them?

This is impossible.

Still, Beth needed to know, because if Paul and Lena were on the rocks, were all the other couples destined for the same fate? If his ability was flawed, shouldn't he come clean and let Beth decide whether to pull the plug on the app? He couldn't lead her up the garden path. He respected her, cared about her, too much.

He took a preparatory sip of 0% lager, then recounted every last detail about Lena kissing someone else.

'What the hell do I do?' he asked plaintively.

She methodically unfolded the rabbit, smoothed the napkin, then created another bird. She stood the two creations together, facing. Kissing, almost—but that was his silly imagination.

'My opinion? You have to get Lena to tell Paul. Or drop enough hypotheticals, information, *something*, so he asks her, or creates the circumstances for her to fess up. I don't think telling Paul, behind Lena's back, is the way to go.'

'*You* could put pressure on her. Woman to woman. Talk about the app, and how grateful you are for the intro to me, and how you *crave* what they have, the perfect marriage without bumps and hitches. A relationship built on huge compatibility and *trust*. Then I reckon she'll come clean.'

Beth drank pensively. 'Did you ever consider that maybe this... pseudo affair is a sign of something? A crack that was always going to develop?'

He shook his head forcefully. 'No. That would mean I have *nothing*. No magic ability to create forevers. It means you've put all your eggs in the wrong basket, Beth.' He pressed a fist into the tabletop.

She clasped his wrist. 'That's bollocks. This off-piste trip of Lena's is a blip. I honestly believe that. And if I'm wrong, then it's definitely not your fault. And it has no impact on the app, if that's what you're worrying about.'

'Of course I am! They're my golden couple, the first people who proved the theory works.'

'Maybe. But, and this may sound cruel, they're also a data point. You've created twelve couples in long-term relationships. Even if they split up, it's still eleven out of twelve. And they had years together! You're not foolproof, Sam, for Christ's sake.' She prised open his fist, interlacing her soft fingers with his.

'But—'

'Shush. Yes, the seed for this idea was a brilliant success rate, a mad, inexplicable knack, but we have to get real. No user is going to sue us if their happy ever after only lasts six months. Come on, mate. Please don't torture yourself. It's *amazing* that you care. That is *such* an admirable, attractive quality.' She contemplated him. 'But if you insist on perfection, burning the midnight oil trying to squeeze all the perceived faults from your logic and the questionnaire and the algorithm, then we'll fall out. And I don't want that.'

He drank, sating his parched throat. What was worse—that he'd built this matchmaking into too high a tower, or that it was leaning? Clearly, Beth cared deeply. Also she had beautiful eyes.

'Me neither,' he mustered.

'You're better than this, Sam. Don't let one failure, and it's not even proven to be a failure, get you down.'

'Like you,' he said. 'You've been amazingly sober about the divorce. Ready for a second chance.'

'Too bloody right. Mum and Dad are second time around. My brother, too. It *works*.'

There. Beth had thrown his dream a lifeline. 'And my folks, and my sister, their happiness is tied to France. That's why I hold onto what *I* do. Isn't everyone allowed a rose-tinted vision of the future?'

Chapter Twenty-Seven

She grinned. 'Well, I always dreamed of marrying George Clooney, so...'

'You and a million others.'

'Except your ideal is much more achievable. And romantic. Laudable.'

He shrugged. 'I am who I am.'

Her finger drew patterns on the tablecloth. 'And you're... great. As a friend, I mean. Client.' She scrutinised his face. 'Sorry for mickey-taking, Sam. We all mock what we don't understand.'

He'd fallen sober. 'Hmm.'

At that moment, the food arrived.

She'd ordered spaghetti carbonara; he dug into spaghetti and meatballs. As they ate, he seemed to be debating something. Concentrating too hard on his eyes, whose brown tones concealed secrets she hoped to discover, she missed her mouth with a forkful, sending a spaghetto, dripping with sauce, onto her shirt.

'Fuck.'

He tittered. It broke the tension, but sprayed flecks of meatball sauce onto *his* T-shirt. 'Fuck.'

Laughing, she dropped her fork into the plate with a clang. He snatched up his parrot, shook it back into a napkin, and pressed it over his mouth, holding in food and mirth.

Shaking their heads, they regained composure, toasting mutual incompetence.

A few minutes later, he pushed the empty plate aside, pulled his chair inward with a screech, and loosely wrung his hands.

He took a breath. 'I broke up with Milly six years ago. For the last few months, my stupid, analytical, forward-looking mind was finding issues. The problem was lust. Or I was shallow. Whenever I saw her, I wanted her. She didn't exactly *milk* that, but she knew she was desirable, and avoided The Commitment Chat.'

'But she obviously wanted to stay together. If she had functional eyes and brain, she'd know she had a winner in you.'

'Very flattering. But she couldn't spot the incompatibility in so many things.'

'So you broke up?'

He nodded, lips pursed. 'I'd seen what Paul and Lena have, the deep love and connection. I realised I was settling and being lazy.'

'Hmm.' She wiped condensation from her glass. 'Holding out for a specific dream is definitely the harder road.'

'Actually, it sounds like jumping into marriage and failing is worse.'

That took a breath from her. 'Mmm. But isn't your dream based on instant decision-making making too? After one date, you'll *know*?'

He smoothed the tablecloth. 'Maybe.'

'But this doesn't answer the "Why Paris?" question. Destiny can hit you anywhere, right?'

'You may have heard that it's quite famous as a romantic hotspot.'

She poked him. 'Snake.'

'I'm only saying that nobody's idol is the local scrap metal merchant. It's George Clooney. Why would I pick a lesser dream? Eyes met over fish and chips on Cleethorpes Pier?'

She chuckled. 'True.'

'And... the city's in my blood, in my soul.' He took a drink. 'Mum and Dad met there. We reckon I was conceived there. And when I was seven, we had a week's holiday there.' He leant in. 'For a wide-eyed kid, that big metal tower is pretty awe-inspiring. We bought a poster. Had it in my bedroom for years, looking down at me. The place... pulls me, that's all.'

The wind left her sails. This dream had a purity, an adorableness. And provenance.

'Okay, sold. So humour me. Do you have a place in mind? A sunny July day, you bump into her underneath the Eiffel Tower—'

'No. It would be some little bistro, in the morning, so we could spend the rest of the day together. We'd have ordered the same thing. She'll apologise in French, even though it's not her fault, I'll probably misunderstand because I'm really slack on my Duolingo, and it'll turn out we're visiting the same building, probably the Musée D'Orsay, and she'll say that one of the Metros is messed up, and point me to a different line, and I won't understand, and we'll laugh, then she'll walk me to the station, and we'll end up touring the museum together, and then she'll ask if I've tried this great local *moules frites* place down a side street, and I'll say "No, I'm not local", but I'll buy her dinner as thanks for avoiding a crush on the underground, and over dinner it'll turn out she's actually British by birth and from a town near where my folks live and—' Breathless, he took a gulp of air, then of beer.

'Okay, okay. You expect the *perfect* date. Where you find out *everything* about the person and then sleep together.' She frowned. 'You don't seem like the sort of guy to expect sex on the first date.'

'Hell, no.'

'So how many dates?'

'Dunno. Three?'

'Three before sex? Then make your life decision after the first night together?' She raised a palm, wickedness and logic playing on her mind. 'Obviously, you can't decide *before* that! What if you think she's perfect, and then she says, "No sex before marriage"? Or you get into the bedroom and she has swastikas on the walls, or a tattoo on her panty line saying "Slippery When Wet"?'

A grin split his face. 'You mock well, Beth Moore. And make good points.'

'So? What *type* of girl do you want?'

He frowned deeply. 'Never really thought.'

I mean, this is getting silly. It's like trying to hit the North Pole without a compass and a map.

'Come on. Tall, short, size zero, Rubenesque, blonde, redhead? You must have *criteria*, Mr... King Of Criteria.'

He cracked a knuckle. 'Alright. Decent job, early thirties, probably a brunette—'

'Now we're getting somewhere—'

'But this is not a... love at first sight thing, okay! Maybe *fancy* at first sight, but it needs romance and conversation and shared experiences, and through *that* comes the peeling back of layers. She has to tick the other boxes. The compatibility stuff.'

'Which means *you* need to tick those boxes for *her*.'

'Obviously.'

'Obviously.'

With their eyes, they circled each other. Her skin danced with electricity.

'Beth?'

'Yeah?' she asked, filled with a crazy hope.

Decent job. Early thirties. Brunette...

'Can we take a timeout on all this?'

'Sorry. I've made it an interrogation. Character assassination.'

'No. Not assassination. But maybe... take your finger off the trigger.'

She held up two fingers and thumb in a gun pose, then feigned holstering it.

'Thanks,' he said. 'Pudding?'

'Definitely. Sharesies?'

'Do they have cheesecake?'

'It's the *best*,' she said.

'Then sharesies.'

Five minutes later, the waiter delivered a plate and two forks. They dug in, clipping off pieces of dessert—him, her, him, her, like a tennis match.

Then one piece remained. He pointed his fork at her. She waggled hers at him. He inched the plate across. She inched it back. He fluttered his fork. She arrowed hers. He cocked his nose at the last piece, as if ushering it towards her. With a sigh of resignation, she speared the tines towards the tasty morsel.

He jabbed in with lightning speed, piercing the titbit and shoving it gleefully into his mouth.

She rapped her fork onto the plate. 'You're a snake, Sam Carter.'

'I'll be sure to put that on my profile. "Buyer beware".'

While they awaited the bill, she lifted a spare napkin off the adjacent table, fashioned a replacement bird, and laid it in front of him.

'Bird eats snake, or snake eats bird?' he asked.

She raised a single eyebrow. 'Do you prefer eating, or being eaten?'

He flushed red and looked away. The waiter arrived, so she buttoned her laugh.

They split the bill, ordered a cab, and headed back to hers.

'So you'll think about the Lena thing?' Beth asked. She was happy to get involved, but nervous that Lena might take offence that Sam had broken silence.

He turned away from the car window, where the reflections of streetlamps flickered across his face. 'Yeah. I'll... find a way to navigate it. And thanks for listening.'

'No problem. Even snakes need friends.'

Back in the living room, he collected his belongings and then said goodbye to Quincunx. 'Nice to meet you, mate. And congratulations on putting up with her.'

'Fuck aaawwff,' the cockatoo replied.

Beth corpsed.

'I was about to,' he said. 'But thanks for the prompt.'

She followed him to the front door.

He stopped in the hall. 'Oh, a few of us are going to a comedy night next weekend. If that's your thing?'

'Sounds like a laugh.'

'Hope so, or I'll get the Trades Descriptions people onto them.'

She pulled a straight face. 'Yeah. Hilarious. Don't give up the day job.'

'Certainly not now, right?'

'Definitely. So yeah, if there's room for one more. Not a double date, though?'

'Not this time. I'll text you deets.'

He pulled the door open.

Her heart pattered. It had been a *great* day, like a 12-hour date. Now came the tricky goodbye. On a *real* date, she'd be apprehensive about the parting gesture. A fizz of excitement that he might kiss her, a delightful awkwardness, or nerves that New Date Man would make a move she *didn't* want, or how he'd respond to "No, I don't want to see you again".

Yet it was all imagined. Clichéd. She'd only kissed two men since Leon, one on the first date. This was a *hateful* calm. She ached to kiss Sam. The issue was the same sticking point as with The Thirty-Three: it wasn't mutual. Sam *didn't* want to kiss her. Whatever else was true, she failed his single biggest criterion. He'd never said the first *kiss* or first *night together* had to be in France. It had to be the first *meeting...* and Beth had met him in Winchester. Which *did* have a cathedral, but not Notre Dame.

So the future was set. Still, she pulled out the napkin she'd snaffled, smoothed its lame avian origami, and tucked it into the pocket of his overshirt.

'Thanks,' he said.

'No problem. A lot less annoying than Quin.'

'And you, in fact.'

'Thanks for that.'

He did a little bow. 'My pleasure.'

She clasped his shoulder. 'Louis, I think this is the beginning of a beautiful friendship.'

'Hmm. That's a rather downbeat ending. For the love story, anyway. How about... "I've had a nice day. And thanks for being part of the app, the thing that keeps me going".'

A grin broke. She patted his pocket. 'We'll always have parrots.'

He pulled a straight face. 'Yeah. Hilarious. Don't give up the day job.'

'Certainly not now, right?'

'Definitely.' He drew her into a hug. Almost a proper one. 'Have a good week.'

'You too.'

She considered a kiss on the cheek, but played it cool. Acted like she didn't fancy him. Didn't want him to stay the night. The week. Forever.

He sidled off. She closed the door, then stood there, listening hard, hoping against hope that he'd come to his senses. That he'd knock on the door, burst in, and carry her straight upstairs.

Nope.

Chapter Twenty-Eight

After the feel-good high of Saturday—making tremendous progress with the app and enjoying the good-natured sparring with Beth—Sam woke on Sunday with a heavy heart... but also determination.

He had to confront Lena, discover what was going on and what had caused it. Could he help, or solve anything? Probably not. Would it lessen his fears about the validity of his matchmaking skill? Probably not. Might it, in some small way, help him prevent other people from going through rough patches or breakups? Again, probably not. But he had to give it a shot.

Halfway to Paul and Lena's house, he noted a flashing blue light beside the road ahead and slowed, despite already being under the speed limit.

In the lay-by sat a dark blue saloon, its tail lights winking, and, in front, a familiar hot hatch with the *almost* cool plate G130 RGE.

Sam pulled in, leaving a big gap to the unfolding incident. 'Stupid idiot,' he murmured.

Two minutes later, the uniforms climbed back into their car, WPC Cole removing her hat as she did so. The car rejoined the road.

George opened his driver's door, then spotted the unexpected visitor. He wandered over with brazen good humour and leant on Sam's roof.

'I wasn't cruising for a ticket. Honest.'

'But you got another three points?' Sam asked.

'Yep.'

'And her number?'

'I'm not an idiot. I'm not asking her straight out!' He glanced up the road. 'Not with her buddy there.'

'If she ever gives you her number, it will prove the police have *really* dropped their minimum IQ requirement.'

'Thanks for the vote of confidence. I'm going to look her up on Facebook.'

'Why not hang around the cop shop until she goes off duty?'

George's eyes lit up. 'Now *there's* an idea.'

'I'm kidding, dickhead. If you want another girl in uniform, set your house on fire and hope one of Amy's mates saves you.'

Much as Sam hated the ribbing he got about his Paris motif, he gave as good as he got with George—a guy who, if not *technically* attempting to bed every uniform conceivable, did have this as his 'theme'. Was it a sex thing? An authority fixation? Certainly, it was good-natured rather than worrying. George had even joked that dating a barrister didn't really qualify as another uniform, though a nurse, cabin attendant, paramedic and chef still formed an impressive roster.

Undoubtedly, Sam and his mate had one key thing in common: neither had a girlfriend. As such, there were no bragging rights to be had. A person could date as frequently as Beth, as little as Sam, or somewhere in between—like George—and still not find The One.

153

No approach was foolproof... or foolhardy. Though George's did feel idiotic at times.

George rubbed his chin. 'A woman firefighter. That's an even better idea.'

Sam shook his head in disbelief. 'Well, you're coming to the comedy gig. Amy will be there with Rhianna. See if you can get an intro. Or, try to find a girl there on the night. It's dark and you won't be speeding.'

'Bugger off.'

Sam fired a fake salute. 'Gladly.'

He sat in the car, outside Paul and Lena's house, for ten minutes, gathering his thoughts.

When Lena let him in, her embrace was guarded, self-conscious. Guilt-ridden. He tried not to think less of her. People change. Relationships evolve.

She led him into the kitchen, whose wide window overlooked the expansive rear garden. They'd moved here a year ago, a pre-emptive upsizing for a little Lena or a pint-sized Paul. Was that future still possible?

Paul was mowing the lawn. That was a lucky break: Sam could talk to Lena without being overheard.

'How's things with Beth?' she asked.

An odd opener. Probably deflecting, putting off the inevitable. She knew I was coming round, and she's smart. She'll know I have an agenda. Did she tactically ask Paul to cut the grass?

'Things are good.'

Lena ladled coffee into a cafetière. 'Beth gave me a bell this morning. Said you had a great day yesterday. I think she likes you.' She shot a knowing look.

He ignored the subtext. 'Yeah, we had a productive session. Was... that why she called?'

'Yeah. Thanking me for the intro, said what good company you are. Loves your intuition, your logical mind. Your dedication.' Lena stood on one hip. 'And she's hoping you'll find her a man.'

'Beth finding men isn't the issue. Keeping them is the biggie.'

She whacked his arm playfully. 'You're a one.'

'Snake, she calls me.'

'Fair.'

He zeroed a glare. 'Pot kettle black, don't you think?'

Lena leant heavily on the worktop. 'I do know why you're here. I'm not an idiot.'

'Hmm. Could have fooled me.'

'Fuck off,' she breathed.

'Not until you explain yourself. Either you tell him or I will.'

'I'm not ready.'

'Why, you need to break it off with your lover first? Does he get priority?'

'You're blowing this up into something it's not,' she hissed, pouring boiling water into the cafetière.

'Good. Then I'll casually mention to Paul that I bumped into you the other day, kissing a mate of yours. On the lips.'

She spun, grabbing his arm. 'But he'll get the wrong idea!'

'Then *you* tell him. Warts and all.'

She screwed her eyes up, chest heaving. His reservoir of empathy quickly overcame a contempt for her out-of-character actions. He pulled her into a hug.

She squeezed tight. 'Oh God, Sam.'

He looked into the garden. Paul was tipping grass cuttings onto the compost pile, oblivious to the embrace—an innocent one this time—his wife was engaged in. Then Paul noticed Sam, waved a gloved hand, and resumed his toil.

Sam let Lena go. 'So what's the story?'

She served the coffee. 'I'm ready for kids, and he's not.'

He assumed she meant Paul. Hoped she meant Paul. 'But you two always wanted them—'

'We do. He wants to wait. Says it's still safe at 38, 40.'

'Isn't it?'

She handed him a mug. 'Yeah. But the risks go up. And I'm the one with the burden. I'm the beached whale for months. I'm the one with the career break, or end of career.'

'Surely Paul *gets* that?'

'I mean, he's not stupid. But he's still avoiding the topic. Avoiding... sex.' She sighed heavily. 'Some women would *accidentally* stop the pill and get pregnant by stealth. I'm trying to make this a joint decision. But how can it be joint when we're wildly different in our opinions of when to start a family? Huh? And now he's playing the young buck, out with his mates at every chance. The subtext is written in bloody capitals. "I'm living my life before a baby removes all my free time".'

Sam prised open the biscuit barrel and helped himself to a bourbon. She playfully rapped a teaspoon against his hand, yet her expression remained vexed.

'And you fought about it,' he inferred.

'No slanging matches, no. But...' She pressed the heel of her hands into her eyes.

'Frost in the air.'

She nodded. 'So... there was a guy at work. We got talking. He thinks Paul is being selfish. Which is obvious, especially if you're me.'

'The guy is... *that* guy.'

'Hamish.'

His lip curled. 'Oh, sure, have a *dog* and call it Hamish by all means, but not—'

'Unhelpful. The point is he's been supportive, and he listens, and he's independent, and, fundamentally, not the person who's refusing to impregnate me.'

'Thanks for the image.'

'You know where the front door is,' she snipped.

'I'm not leaving until—'

She raised a hand. 'You want the full story? Then, much as I love you, Sam, shut the fuck up.'

He nodded tersely, then sipped his coffee politely, like a truanting child who's trying to avoid detention.

'We went for a drink. Hamish and I. Had a couple. I was grateful for his... arm around my shoulder.'

'He single?'

'Yeah. Anyway, goodbye hug, we both went for a peck on the cheek, turned the same way, became a peck on the lips, he's not too shabby looking, he's on my side about the baby thing, I'd had a couple—'

'You said.'

'—and it was a kiss. Less platonic than it should have been.'

'It shouldn't have been one at all.'

'I know that!' she barked. She glanced into the garden, worried, then pressed her shoulder against Sam's. 'I know that. But with Paul being... romantically cold, and Hamish walking me to the bus...' She shrugged.

'Another kiss. And he thinks he has a chance, that this wedge between you and Paul will deepen.'

'Dammit, Sam, I am *not* having an affair. Three sets of kisses. That's it. He doesn't know what he's doing. Me neither. I wish I'd never spoken to him, certainly never kissed him, but... how can I tell Paul that? What if he comes to the wrong conclusions?'

Sam lasered a gaze. 'No hotel rooms? No after-work rendezvouses concealed by lies?'

She shook her head vehemently. 'I don't *want* this, Sam. Hamish is... getting the wrong idea.'

'So he *does* want the hotel room?'

'Well, he's a tactile person and a good listener and—'

'No more drinks, Lena,' he insisted. 'No more goodbye kisses at the bus stop. If you want to lean on someone, lean on me. Okay? Because I'm a relationship *creator*. Fixer. Not breaker-upper. But even if you move ahead, if you agree on a timetable for kids, this Hamish thing will still have *happened*. And that's a secret. And secrets can kill marriages. So you *have* to tell Paul. Or I'm not sure I can look you in the eye again.'

She scrutinised him for an age, lip wobbling. 'Yeah. You're right. I'll find the time, and the way, to do it. *Soon.*'

Her face spoke the truth, so he nodded. 'Okay.'

The buzz of the lawnmower stopped. Paul made a drinking motion.

'Is he wanting his eleven o'clock whisky?' Sam joked.

Lena snorted sadly. 'He'll bloody need one when I tell him.'

'I suggest coffee. Don't want him mowing his foot off. Otherwise, he'll be laid up in hospital and that'll put an even bigger crimp in your sex life.'

'You're a prick sometimes, Sam.'

'Yeah. But at least I'm not snogging Big Jock McSporran on the side.'

She thumped him. 'It's a good job I love you.'

'Just love *Paul* more, okay?'

Lena pressed a fresh mug of coffee into his hand. 'Here. He can have this... until I perfect a recipe for an aphrodisiac.'

Sam kissed her forehead, snaffled two biscuits from the barrel, and hustled out the back door.

Paul was leaning against the shed. 'Alright?'

'Yep.' Sam handed over the mug and one biscuit, scoffing the other.

'App coming along okay?'

'Yep.'

'You and Beth seem to be going well.'

Sam shrugged nonchalantly. 'You know me, the old master.'

Paul slurped. 'The original. Seven years for me and Lena in a few days.'

'You should take her away. Surprise weekend.'

Paul frowned. 'Why?'

'Romantic.'

'Romance? We're *married*.'

'Take her away. At least for a night.'

'Again, why?'

He gripped Paul's shoulder. 'Trust me. Like when I introduced you two.'

'Er... okay. Any suggestions?'

Sam's mind whirred. 'Well, there is *one* place.'

Chapter Twenty-Nine

After a full-on week at work, Beth was yearning for a fun night out.

Each lunchtime, she and Sam had exchanged texts about the project. He'd also updated her on his chat with Lena and Paul. She worried for her friend, and Sam—not to mention potential implications for the app—but it was out of her hands.

However, that was put aside as she took a bus into the city for the comedy night. She'd worn something slightly more daring—higher heels, plunging neckline, her best-fitting trousers. This was a club, a place for mingling, and she needed to be ready in case Mr Right walked into the room. She hoped there would be great jokes, no annoying hecklers, and that Sam's friends would be good company.

It was nice not to be in "work mode", doing subtle research. As this wasn't a date night, she and Sam wouldn't have to pretend to be a couple—something he seemed uneasy with.

She arrived at six thirty, ready for a seven o'clock kick-off. The auditorium was set up in cabaret style, making the place appear more classy whilst also setting an expectation that the audience wasn't big enough for rows of closely packed seats. A small, raised stage was lit by a single spotlight focused on a mic stand.

Sam was at the bar with two women—one tall and dark, one shorter and blonde—and a guy who, from Sam's description, must be George.

Sam spotted her, his face brightened, and he briefly surveyed her attire. He introduced her to Amy, Rhianna, and then George, whose attention lingered momentarily on her cleavage. Still, she let him buy her a drink while Sam did the "polite explanation of who's who".

George knew about the app project and how Beth fitted into Sam's life. Sadly, he'd also given Amy and her girlfriend one too many facts. A false one.

Rhianna was glancing back and forth between her and Sam. 'So I hear you two are going great guns.'

Amy tapped Beth's arm and, in her Welsh Valleys twang, added, 'You look adorable together.'

Beth's chest tightened.

Oh shit. Sam's going to tear someone a new arsehole. Probably George, for stirring.

Sam took a half-step away from Beth. 'No, it's—'

'It's early days, Amy, that's all,' she blustered. 'Sam isn't one to rush into things, so we're taking it slow.'

George arrowed the neck of his beer bottle. 'Still, like I said before, they go on lots of dates.'

Amy cocked her head. 'Aw, how romantic.'

'Isn't it?' Rhianna craned up to kiss her.

George put his arm around Sam's hunched shoulders. 'I'm proud of my mate. It's taken a while, eh?'

Sam laughed with transparently crippling nervousness. 'Haha, yeah.'

Beth took a calming slurp of G&T.

Oh crap. The poor sod. Please roll with it, mate. We discussed this. You were okay with a white lie. Neither of us expected this tonight, but think of the bigger picture.

She squeezed Sam's arm affectionately. 'Better late than never.'

The rabbit in the headlights patted her hand. 'Yeah. Funny old world. Anyhow, we want to keep it quiet.'

Rhianna frowned. 'Why?'

'Well, we met because of the app.' Beth chimed in. 'We were doing some testing, and… it turns out we're a match. Crazy, huh?' She faked a nervous, embarrassed titter.

Sell. Sell the idea that we're dating. But make sure Sam knows I wish this conversation wasn't happening.

'Wow,' Rhianna said.

'But that *can't* be public, okay? It's part of the marketing spiel for when we launch. You know, "Founders of love app find love themselves".'

That works. As a cute story. Real life hasn't got a hope.

'That's it,' Sam said swiftly. 'But the app's nowhere near live yet, so if you can, like, keep all this under your hat. I'm… *we're…* playing it cool. Besides, this app is not about me, about *us*. It's about other people.'

Amy clutched Beth's wrist, a firefighter's grip. 'Hey, I've had a brilliant idea. Why not ask venues like this to advertise on the app? Y'know, places for great dates. It can help pay your costs, or make more money, or whatever.'

Rhianna beamed. 'See, she's not only a smoking hot gal and a fearless public servant, she's also smart as a whip.'

Beth rubbed Sam's shoulder. Softly. Affectionately. 'What do you reckon, babe?'

His Adam's apple bobbed. 'I... think it's a great idea. Babe.' The last word came out as if he'd never uttered it before—and was having to act like he said it every day.

George circled his finger around the group. 'More drinks? Only got five minutes before it starts.'

They placed orders, George stayed at the bar awaiting service, and Amy and Rhianna went to find a table.

Sam, his smile painted on, took Beth aside. Well, not took. Yanked. 'What are you *saying*?' he hissed.

She glanced around. 'I'm telling the *truth*. The project *did* bring us together. As workmates. We *are* going slow... on the app. And we *have* been on dates. We talked about this. About living the part of "happy matchmakers". Arousing less suspicion. Plus, see how *delighted* they are for you.' Her expression was gently pleading. 'You're *lucky* to have great friends.'

His lips pressed together. 'It just... feels weird.'

She sighed. 'Okay, I promise that when the app is done, we'll have a flaming row in front of everyone and break up. Problem solved.'

'I'm not a flaming row person.'

Please get with the program. I'm trying to make this easier on you.

She rolled her eyes. 'Either that, or be stuck pretending with me *forever*. Besides, it'll be a *legitimate* fake breakup because you'll have met the future Madame Carter by then. We can say you were shagging her on the side, and I found out.' She grinned at her brilliance.

He looked unamused. 'Am I *that* kind of person, either?'

She smirked. 'Of course you'd never cheat on *me,* but—'

'Moot, as this is all a fabrication.'

'Alright. You're *not* a two-timer. Satisfied?'

'Blissfully.'

Amy was waving from a table near the front. Beth gave a thumbs-up.

'Come on. And don't worry. You don't have to put your arm around me or hold my hand.'

Sam's nose wrinkled. 'Am I really this... awful, inattentive person?'

'Hey, I *tried* to tell your mates to keep quiet about us, not expect that I'll be sitting on your lap and whispering sweet nothings in your ear.'

'I'd bloody well hope not.' A wry smile appeared. 'It'd be rude to the performers, if nothing else.'

She leant in. 'Why, *is* there something else?'

'Yes. The whole room will see you snuggling up to another guy. Admittedly, the best looking and most eligible one here—'

'Definitely.'

He growled. 'I *mean* that if you're keeping your eyes peeled for a date, you'll put other suitors off. See?'

'All those other suitors might simply assume I'm flirting. Unless I've got my tongue down your throat, it's possible I'm just trying it on.'

'Too bloody right you're trying it on.'

She grasped his hand. 'Firstly, I am *not*. Secondly, it's for appearances and to stop people asking questions.'

He scoffed. 'They'll be asking questions soon enough. Ones like "What's she like in bed?"'

'I'm sure your mates aren't like that.'

He pointed at George.

'Okay, well, tell him I'm a dynamo in the sack.' She winked.

'So now *I'm* lying too.'

She nudged him. 'It's not a lie.'

'Grrr. I *meant* it's a lie to say we've slept together.'

'Fuck's sake, Sam. Dodge the question. Bland answers. Lean into it a bit. Which is worse, a few white lies that'll pass quickly, or more months of your mates saying "Forget France, it's a silly dream"?

Which I *know* rubs you up the wrong way.' She grinned. 'Certainly does when *I* say it.'

He eye-rolled. 'You're impossible, Beth.'

'Thirty-three failed dates would certainly support your analysis. Now *please*, roll with this façade, or I really *will* sit on your lap.'

'And I'll be the one whispering in *your* ear. "Lose some weight. I can't feel my legs".'

She poked him in the chest. 'You know what? You're as impossible as I am.'

He beamed. 'Then we make a great couple, don't we? *Babe.*'

She playfully bopped his nose. 'Certainly do. Babe.'

The lights dimmed. George hustled over, juggling five drinks. Beth grabbed her cocktail, passed Sam his beer, then led him to their table.

The first two acts were nothing special. Actually, she'd laughed more during her time with Sam.

Then Hannah came on stage. A petite girl, she seemed nervous, approaching the microphone cautiously. Wincing against the spotlight, she peered into the audience. Away to Beth's right, in the front row, a dimly lit figure eased forward in his chair.

Immediately, the comic's shoulders went back, and she came alive. 'So... my boyfriend once joked that he couldn't even find my G-spot if he had a scale map and a torch.' A pause for effect, and nervous audience chuckles at the mention of "G-spot" in the opening sentence. 'So guess what I bought him for his birthday?'

A healthy ripple of laugher washed the room. Beth glanced at Sam, who met her gaze oh-so-briefly, then looked away, probably embarrassed that she'd used a sex joke to make eye contact. Which she had.

Don't worry, mate. I'll buy those things if you need them.

Hannah extended her hand. 'My boyfriend, Drew, ladies and gentlemen. Stand up, baby! God, he loves it when I embarrass him in public.'

The boyfriend, a pretty hot, fair-haired guy, stood, sheepishly waved, then retreated into half-shadow.

However, Hannah's gentle ribbing wasn't over.

Beth watched Drew gently squirm, but the love, the bond between him and the stand-up was obvious. She saw a hint of Sam in Drew, and vice versa. Certainly, she loved teasing Sam and reckoned he secretly liked it. Sometimes, he even gave as good as he got.

When they were on a roll, she believed they could—theoretically—do this dating thing for real.

Chapter Thirty

S am watched Drew laugh nervously at his girlfriend's jokes and felt a kinship with the guy. At least Beth's jibes weren't done publicly, and besides, he'd ridiculed her, too. It was time to stop fighting the chance to have fun. He'd play along with Beth's mischievous side. Fakery was beneficial for the app and for maintaining a smooth working relationship. It was like a marriage of convenience... without the cost of the wedding, having to make a speech, or the drunken uncle.

He tuned back in to Hannah's set. She was hilarious, though George's expression suggested he hoped she'd round off her set with a striptease, which was idiotic because this Drew guy had got the girl first.

Too soon, she walked off to huge applause, and the emcee wrapped up. The lights came on, and soft music wafted through the venue. Punters either headed for the exit or thronged at the bar. Amy and Rhianna made a beeline for Drew, who had Hannah in a bear hug.

Beth leant in. 'Drink?'

'Definitely,' Sam replied

'George?'

George was miles away, focused on something across the room. Or someone.

'Get him a beer. Or smelling salts,' Sam said.

She tapped his arm. 'Will do.'

He stood at George's shoulder. 'Now what?'

'Over there,' George hissed, like he'd spotted Lady Gaga. 'WPC Cole.'

Sam peered intently. 'Oh. Yeah.'

It wasn't easy to make an informed judgment from thirty feet away, but he had to concede that George was chasing quite an attractive woman.

The WPC, who appeared to be with a female friend, noticed them. 'Shit,' George said.

'Why "Shit"? You want to... *take down her particulars*, don't you?'

George wore a pained expression. 'The thing is...'

'Don't tell me? Stage fright.'

'Don't be a dick. It's...' George glanced around, then manhandled Sam towards the exit. Their progress was duly tracked by an officer of the law.

They burst into the balmy June evening.

'What?' Sam demanded, fed up with his mate's odd behaviour.

George picked at his strong chin. 'You remember that trouble I got into? So... she'll know. Bet she's looked me up. Realises I'm a waste of space. A prick. A criminal.' He shook his head, leaning heavily against the wall. 'So fancying her is stupid. Fucking idiotic.'

Sam laughed. 'You're not a *criminal*, mate. It was shoplifting. A decade ago. And if you were so bloody worried, chasing a copper is exactly the wrong thing to do.'

'Can I help it? We all have something. You of all people know that. Takes all sorts, doesn't it?'

'I suppose.'

'So what do I do?'

'Look, she's spotted you. But not followed you. Or put the bracelets on you.' He snapped a hand up. 'And please, no jokes about wanting to get handcuffed to the bed.'

George ruffled his hair. 'But she's collared me twice! So perhaps I'm not *that* good.'

'It was speeding tickets, mate, not GBH. And she's off-duty, it's a Friday night, and she might *not* have recognised you, as you weren't travelling at one hundred miles an hour in a built-up area.'

George socked him. 'Fuck off.'

Sam sighed. 'I'll vouch for you, okay?'

'What? "My mate is a nice guy, really. Please sleep with him"?'

'Hell no. You're on your own with getting her in the sack. But maybe come clean about your past, don't try for a one-night stand, or say you have a thing for uniforms.'

George grimaced. 'I dunno.'

'Maybe she won't care because your minor slip-up was ages ago, and she's a forgiving person. Alternatively, she's already head over heels, and is one of those people who'd date a serial killer provided he could do amazing things with his tongue.'

'Well—'

'Not interested.'

The venue door opened. George went ashen.

'Small world, eh, gentlemen?' said WPC Cole.

Sam slapped George on the back. 'Don't worry, mate. Remember, you are allowed one phone call.'

The woman's eyes creased into a smile, so Sam winked, then headed inside.

The crowd had thinned, but Beth wasn't visible. Then musical notes filled the room. He got an inkling and wandered over. On top of the piano were two drinks, hers and his. He took a long draw on the bottle. She looked up, hands dancing over the keyboard. Clair de Lune.

'Very funny,' he said.

'It was this or The Entertainer.'

'Good choice. You don't strike me as an entertainer.'

'Fuck off,' she mouthed.

Amy sidled over, with Hannah and Drew in tow. Beth stopped playing, and introductions were made. Mercifully, Amy didn't intimate that Sam and Beth were a couple.

Although a fake girlfriend who can play the piano—and looks pretty fine tonight—isn't too embarrassing. In fact, they probably think I'm batting way out of my league by dating Beth.

Amy pulled Hannah into a sisterly clench. 'Did you hear how these two met?'

'Nope,' Beth replied. 'Not an app?'

'No. And no burning buildings involved.'

'Thankfully,' Drew said. 'But I'd run into burning buildings for her now.'

Hannah switched her hug partner, biting her lip nervously.

'Go on then,' Beth prompted.

'You wouldn't believe me if I told you,' Drew replied.

'Should I put it in my set?' Hannah looked up at him with wide eyes.

'Hell yes, baby. The comedy value at my expense is *huge*.'

She poked him in the ribs. He replied by giving chapter and verse on how she'd pretended to be a talking lift, they'd ended up chatting, and a date had finally ensued. Sam was gobsmacked. You really couldn't write this stuff.

Soon, Drew and Hannah said their goodbyes and headed away, fingers entwined.

'Well?' Amy asked.

'Adorable,' Beth said.

Sam's people-watching radar had been going full pelt. 'Is Hannah...?'

Amy nodded. 'Yeah. She's on the spectrum.'

'Wow,' Beth replied. 'How she stands up and does comedy is amazing. She is *gold*. Drew's a lucky guy.'

'Yeah,' Rhianna said. 'And if she was gay...'

Amy pinched Rhianna's backside. 'Oh no. You don't get rid of me that easy.'

Beth eyed Sam mischievously. 'And if Drew was single...'

'I'm in the "getting together" business, not "breaking apart",' he said.

Beth bopped his nose. 'And you're great at it.'

Sam held his breath, but she didn't add "babe" or "honey". Someone moved into his peripheral vision. No... two figures.

'Hey, people,' George said.

'Evening all.' WPC Cole flexed at the knees.

Oh, I like her. And George really likes her. And it seems to be mutual.

George introduced her as Maya, a servant of His Majesty's Police Force, whom he'd allegedly met at the bar. Maya and Amy hit it off immediately, both being emergency responders.

After a few minutes of general camaraderie, Rhianna and Amy exchanged a glance.

'Right, you lot. We're off. Amy has an early shift. Just wanted to be here to support Hannah. Lovely to meet you all.'

There were hugs all round, then Amy and Rhianna left.

George took Maya's hand. 'We'll make a move too. Maya knows a late bar down the road. Fancy joining us?'

Beth looked at Sam. 'What d'you think?'

He wasn't keen on watching George try to get the long arm of the law to touch him below the waist.

'Not sure, babe. We've had a long work week. And I need to do some app stuff over the weekend. Busman's holiday.'

'True,' Beth replied. 'So thanks, George, but we'll pass. Have a good night.'

'I intend to.'

Sam pointed at his mate. 'Sorry about him,' he said to Maya.

'Don't worry. I intend to have a good night too,' she replied.

Sam watched them go. A new couple. One he *hadn't* created.

Beth leant in, lips pursed in amusement. '"Babe"?'

'Someone told me I should lighten up about this pretend relationship. Relax, it's not like I sat on your lap or stuck my tongue down your throat.'

'Chance'd be a fine thing.'

His pulse thudded. 'I'll pretend I didn't hear that.'

'I know, I'm impossible. Change the record.'

'You're not impossible. Just...' He sought a word.

'A tart?'

'An *outrageous* flirt. Luckily, because we're mates, and I desperately need your help with this app, I'll have to put up with your shenanigans.'

'Well, I *would* ask if you wanted to meet up over the weekend for more brainstorming, but I'll let you crack on with the coding. The faster we get this thing live, the sooner we can have that breakup scene and head off on our *own* happy ever afters.'

That shook him a little. Saddened him. 'Still as friends, though?'

'Of course. Friends would be lovely...' She pulled him into a hug and whispered '...babe.'

Chapter Thirty-One

The following day, Saturday, Beth did chores around the house. Her spirits were low, which was silly considering the good time she'd had at the comedy night. Everything was in her favour, yet the frustration continued. Things were worse because of the problem between Lena and Paul. Was Sam's gift nothing more than a lucky string of successful hookups? If so, the app would flop.

Focus on the positives. There's a great rapport with a fantastic guy. I'm getting dating practice. I'm having fun, not wallowing in thirty-three failures. Who saw that coming?

All the same, it didn't say much for Sam's sixth sense if he didn't grasp the bleeding obvious bond they had.

She walked to the Sainsbury's Local, bought a lemon drizzle cake that was marked down for Clearance, went home, made a pot of tea, and ate half the cake.

Then, feeling the need to do something constructive, relationship-wise, she texted Lena about a Sunday brunch date.

They met in the café at eleven o'clock: prime smashed avocado and latte time.

Lena—slim, beautifully attired, and with perfect cheekbones—had come directly from the nail bar. The first five minutes of the chat were about how the new and inexperienced nail tech had misunderstood Lena's booking. Having got that out of her system, she asked about the comedy club.

Beth gave her the rundown, skipping over the fake dating. Still, Lena asked how she and Sam were getting on. Beth said that on a professional level, the meeting of minds was brilliant.

'And on a non-professional level?' Lena sipped her flat white.

'Honestly?'

'No, lie. Yes, honestly! You're my friends, and I want things to work out.'

Beth narrowed her eyes. 'Work out how? This *was* a business introduction, wasn't it?'

'Of course.' A light went on in Lena's face. 'Ah. You've run headlong into the "destiny" problem.'

Beth leant in. The café was buzzing, and she didn't want secrets to leak out. The Winchester network had tendrils everywhere, which was helpful for Sam's big matchmaking Contacts list, but bad for rumours.

'You warned me he had this fixation.' She picked up toast crumbs with her fingertip. 'I didn't mean to fall for him.'

'Ah. Shit.'

'Yeah, "shit" is right. Everything is wonderful. He's what I want. But he has another agenda.'

Lena sighed. 'Seems like we both have men who won't play ball.'

'If you want to bring Paul round to your way of thinking about starting a family, why is it wrong for me to hope for something with Sam?'

'Because it's a hiding to nothing. Sometimes you have to let a person carve their own path or make their own mistakes.' She drained her cup. 'And you can't damage your working relationship. Sam needs the investment capital. And he needs someone who believes in the product.'

Beth stroked the tabletop. 'Yeah.'

Her mobile pinged. She read the message. Her shoulders fell.

'What?' Lena asked.

'Leon. Still stalling. He says, "This all feels very real now. Are you sure you want to go ahead?"'

'Well, duh!'

Beth bit her lip. 'He... asked to meet. Like a final... summit. Last chance for peace.'

'But you *are* at peace. There was never much friction.' Lena inched closer. 'Or is there something I don't know?'

Beth's spirits rose. This was a gilt-edged chance. 'There's never been one particular thing. Every couple has ups and downs. Scrapes. Misunderstandings. At least the guy was faithful.' She pulled a face. 'Or I hope so. God, that would have been awful.'

Fear sprang into Lena's eyes. She fussed with the cutlery, her fingers jittery. 'Look, can we go? I'll pay. I need some... air.'

Ten minutes later, sitting on warped wooden playground swings in the park, Lena opened her heart.

Beth listened intently and had sympathy for her friend's situation—but not for how she'd reacted. She took Lena in a hug and softly read her the riot act.

Did it make Beth feel any better? Not particularly. But she sensed movement towards understanding, and thence happiness. Which was all she wanted for her friend. For all her friends.

Chapter Thirty-Two

S am spent the weekend working on the app. He was more invested, more passionate about this project than he'd ever been at work.

But was the universe telling him to rein in his expectations and dedication?

Besides the Paul and Lena issue, Jon had messaged. He and Rachel had really hit it off, but now he'd taken a job opportunity in Dubai. He'd be gone for three years. Long distance wasn't what either wanted, so they'd agreed to call it a day.

Whilst it wasn't Sam's fault, merely circumstantial and unforeseeable, disappointment was inevitable. He needed another win to boost his spirits. Beth had emailed about a friend called Danni, giving some of the woman's key attributes and preferences.

Whilst the app's Profiles spec wasn't finalised, the algorithm was a draft, and the front end was non-existent, he set up dummy users for Danni, Rob, and Beth. How would they fare?

Rob and Danni had an 88% match. Rob and *Beth* were 72% compatible.

He brewed his habitual Sunday afternoon cuppa and stared at the laptop.

These figures were ballpark at best. The only half-accurate profile was Beth's. He'd extrapolated certain answers, guesstimated, because he believed he truly knew her.

Then it hit him. It wasn't a penny dropping. It was the vaults of the Bank of England falling down a mineshaft.

He'd met many people, got a sense of who they were, what they liked, what they wanted—not to mention how they looked. And, notwithstanding his single-minded pursuit of a specific destiny, he'd dismissed all the women as not being his *type*. Yet he'd never considered whether he *had* a type—as Beth had pointed out.

Matchmaking other people hadn't revealed the type of woman *he* wanted to spend his life with, but it had revealed dozens he *didn't* want. He'd been *subconsciously* ruling girls out. And that was odd, and crazy, and an unexpected bonus. Unlike Beth, he'd never used a dating app. He'd never hemmed and hawed over tick boxes and TRUE/FALSE.

Now? If he wanted to fill out a profile, it would be pretty straightforward. But this app wasn't about *him*. It was about other people. And her.

He checked the analysis.

Rob + Beth = 72%.

Was that enough?

'Hang on,' he murmured, quickly opening Ideas.docx.

Surely a user should be able to select their minimum compatibility level before considering a date? And surely they would pay more for a better match? And an ability to prioritise criteria?

There was plenty more to chat through with his investor. Consultant. Friend. Fake date.

On Monday, Sam attended a meeting about the upcoming trip to Paris. He'd be liaising with a couple of employees in the small French firm that VentaTech were acquiring. Sam was responsible for migrating the projects that wouldn't be complete before the merger closed.

Leaving the breakout room, he was fizzing. However tedious the day-to-day was, the chance to visit the City of Love trumped everything.

This is it. It's going to happen.

His dating muscles had been warmed in recent weeks, thanks to Beth, so he needed to embrace their fakery. Whilst there was nothing wrong with her as a person—physically, emotionally, intellectually, socially, politically, ethically—pretending to date was purely a means to an end.

Soon, in maybe only a fortnight, she'd be spared the embarrassment and inconvenience of having to hang on his arm.

The office was quiet on Tuesday, as several people were away on training, so over a *slightly* extended lunch break, Sam set aside the project he'd been working on and opened a private folder.

As he was munching on his Pret BLT, staring at lines of code, someone stood at his shoulder.

'What are you working on?' asked teammate David.

'Oh, nothing, only an idea.'

'Which client?'

'Umm... a new one. You wouldn't know it.'

David glanced around, then borrowed a chair from a neighbouring desk. 'Are you sure that's... wise?' Wisdom was David's stock in trade. Strait-laced, a couple of years Sam's senior, and a stickler for cyber security.

'It's just a quick thing,' Sam bluffed.

The game was up. Using company resources for personal time was fraught with danger. He'd never even looked at Facebook on the work PC, but had now fallen into abusing a license agreement. Things had got out of hand. A crime of passion—passion for a love app.

'Hmm,' David said.

Sam closed the laptop lid, which was a huge admission of guilt, but he was pretty sure David wouldn't squeal.

'Shame you're not coming on the trip,' he said, changing the subject.

'I'm not bothered. It's not my thing, all that cigarette smoke and pissing in the streets.' Sometimes, David wasn't entirely strait-laced.

'I hear they use toilets quite a bit these days. Besides, the whole public urination lark has got pretty dangerous. Likely to have your cock sliced off by a passing e-scooter.'

David chuckled. 'You're awfully pragmatic about the dangers of life in your dream city.'

'I never said anything about *living* there. But it's a place where love can blossom, you know?'

'Then I wish you luck, mate. You're sharp as a tack with this stuff,' he tapped the laptop. 'So I hope your skill with *les français* is as good.'

'Let's say I expect this trip to be business *and* pleasure.'

Chapter Thirty-Three

By Saturday night, Beth was beginning to envy Sam's fledgling solo career. Never had working for herself looked so appealing.

Declan, who'd recently been pretty distant and non-combative, had resumed being snide. He'd probably overheard her and Eve discussing recent antics and felt jealous. Clearly, the existing app ecosystem hadn't delivered him a suitable date. Might Sam's creation unlock a future for Declan? Surely even creeps like him deserved someone.

Or perhaps not. Anyway, it wasn't her concern, provided he didn't gatecrash one of Sam's double dates. Like tonight's, which was introducing Danni to a guy called Rob, a work acquaintance of Sam.

Both Rob and Danni were interested in the financial world, were dog people, intelligent, tactile, conservative, entrepreneurial, and not fussed about parenthood. Still, based on Rob's LinkedIn picture, Beth was ready to step in if Danni didn't get lucky. She wore a skirt with a thigh-high split, her most expensive shoes, and a strappy top which suggested more than it revealed. Yes, she *did* want kids, but if Rob's "not fussed" meant "open to negotiation", then perhaps he was a contender.

As she arrived at the shuffleboard bar, Danni was getting out of a cab. They hugged, then walked in together. The place was buzzing. There was no sign of Sam or Rob, so they went to the bar.

Danni's phone rang. Wincing in apology, she took the call, pressed a finger to her other ear, then jerked her head towards the exit. Beth hopped onto the bar stool, sipped her cocktail and absorbed the ambience.

A minute later, Sam walked up. She told him Danni had stepped out, and he said Rob was running a few minutes late.

Sam ordered a beer and sat on the adjacent stool. 'Good week? Excited about tonight?'

'I'm going to be rubbish at this game.'

He leaned in. 'We're not here for the game. Unless you count the game of love. Anyway, this is a cool place. Never been here before. George recommended it.'

'It's very *him*. Or am I being judgmental about the public schoolboy type?'

'Maybe. But he *always* has to be blue at shuffleboard. To match his eyes.' Sam tutted, amused. 'What does that say?'

'We all have quirks. Like chasing uniforms, or hoarding parrots, or thinking the perfect first date meal has to be local French cuisine.' She winked.

He growled, poking her arm. 'Or being certifiably impossible.'

She was about to reply when she noted someone walking up.

They dismounted from their stools and greeted Rob. A few seconds later, Danni walked up. Rob was even better than his photo, and his voice was damn sexy. Danni was enjoying the view too.

But it's not all about the looks. It's about compatibility.

Sam pointed across the room. 'We should head to our game table.'

As predicted, Beth came last in both games of shuffleboard. Still, it wasn't about the winning; it was about taking part. Not even that. It was about Rob and Danni taking part. Not even that. It was about Rob and Danni spending time together. Whenever they weren't at the table, they were deep in conversation, peppered by light nudges, touches on the arm.

The group moved to the bar area. Beth felt nicely relaxed. Not pissed but not stressed. She'd laughed and joked with Sam. He seemed loose, shaking off the Lena and Paul issue.

'So how's the app coming along?' Danni asked. 'Looks like *I've* struck gold anyhow.'

Beth shot her the devils.

'App?' Rob said. 'What's this?'

Sam swallowed. 'Oh, nothing really.'

'Don't be modest, Mr Romance,' Danni said. 'Beth told me you're the king of the double date.'

'Oh yes?' Rob appeared intrigued, maybe a little thrown. 'Do tell.'

Beth glanced at Sam, who was gripping his bottle tightly.

The game is up.

She laid a mollifying hand on Rob's broad shoulder, then confessed to the research element of this date night. Yes, the matchmaking was intentioned, but there was curiosity too. A bigger picture.

Rob pursed his lips. 'Interesting. That sounds like a noble pursuit.'

'You... you're not offended?' Sam asked.

Rob laughed, easing Danni's waist closer. 'Of course not. I'm happy to help. To tell the truth, I've never been on a double date before. And, more importantly, I got to meet this lovely lady.' He kissed her forehead.

Danni rubbed his back. 'And I got to meet you.'

Every muscle in Beth's upper body relaxed.

Rob arrowed his bottle at Sam. 'You seem to have the knack for this. In fact, if your lovely Beth hadn't got there first with the investment, I'd bite your hand off for a share in this.'

'Thanks, Rob, that means a lot.'

'No problem. I wish you huge luck. You two clearly have a great connection.'

Beth stroked Sam's arm, playing up to the implication. 'We do.'

'Yeah.' He flashed that irresistible smile.

Rob glanced between them. 'It must be a great bonus to have that understanding at a personal level, as well as collaborative on the business side. It's rather appropriate. You two obviously know love.'

Oh crap.

She met Sam's eye.

Come on, mate. We can do this. Rob is a mover and shaker. And a dating success story for you.

'Well, I can't say it's perfect, but we're lucky to go on all these dates with such wonderful people, right?' he said.

'Definitely,' she replied.

And whether it was the two cocktails, relief that they'd turned Rob's objections into some kind of endorsement, the convivial atmosphere, a need to put a full stop to this conversation, or—perhaps—because Sam looked relaxed and gorgeous...

...she leant in and pecked him on the lips.

Well, more than a peck. But not a *real* kiss. A stage kiss, perhaps.

Yes, a stage kiss, because this is a performance: See, Rob, we're the dream team, and when I ask you in a minute to keep your mouth shut about the app, I want you to like us, be happy for us, and grateful we found you Danni... and then never repeat what went on tonight.

Then she looked away, took a slug of pornstar Martini and hoped Sam understood.

Inside, she was aflame.

Chapter Thirty-Four

S am's lips tingled with the touch. His neck hairs sprang to attention.

What the hell just happened?

He tapped Rob's arm, businesslike, nodding at Danni and Beth. 'Excuse me. Ladies.'

And he hustled towards the door, trying not to appear annoyed. Because he wasn't. Sideswiped, maybe. Disbelieving.

In moments, he had to dodge a couple heading towards him.

'Alright,' George called, pulling Maya out of the way.

Sam didn't respond. He needed oxygen. He needed to calm down.

Outside, he sucked in lungfuls of Winchester's finest summer city air. His mind whorled at the sudden escalation in the fakery.

Someone arrived beside him. Beth's expression was half amused, half fed-up-of-this-shit.

'What was that for?' he asked.

'Unless you missed the news, we're dating.' She eye-rolled extravagantly. 'Yes, I know, not for real. What happened to rolling with the punches?'

'I *am* rolling with the punches, but...' he glanced around. 'Did we discuss kissing? Not *sure* we did.'

'It's part of dating. Or is that news to you, Mr I Don't Date?' A smirk appeared.

'But *fake* dating?'

She pressed a finger into his chest. 'You should feel lucky to have such an experienced partner. A brilliant actress. One who knows the ropes.' She explored his face.

'Thirty-three ropes, in fact.'

She fluttered a hand. 'Oh yeah. I'll kiss anyone. *Tarts* do.'

That pulled the wind from his sails. Arguing was ridiculous. Dangerous, both for the business relationship and the friendship. Better to let things be. The kiss didn't *mean* anything.

He heaved a breath. 'Okay. So, absent of a discussion, kissing is allowed.'

She wagged a finger. 'Not "allowed". That isn't what I meant. "Necessary for the right circumstances". Okay? Does that sit okay with you?'

She'd nailed it. Again.

'Yeah. But no further, okay?'

'Well, if we get as far as orgasms, that's *probably* overdoing it.' Her eyebrows fluttered.

'Obviously they'd be faked too.'

'Good luck with that.'

A million thoughts crossed his mind. Like whether she'd ever faked it with Leon. Or anyone else. Whether Leon had faked it with her. Was that possible? Any man, with Beth Moore moving beneath him, wouldn't need to fake it. He'd need to think about football or dead kittens.

But how far would he and Beth have to go on this fake dating journey? What trials lay ahead? What front would be needed to convince friends, double daters, whoever, that they were an item? What was the minimum requirement for passing muster as a couple? Hopefully, only occasional kisses. And anyway, it would all be over in a few weeks. Soon, the app would be live, or he'd meet Mademoiselle Right, or both.

He jolted back to reality. Beth was scrutinising his face. 'We okay?'

'Yeah. We're good. Sorry for running off.'

She stroked his arm. 'It's fine. I'm on a learning curve too. But we're keeping the kisses to... "needs must". Agreed?'

'Agreed.'

'Good.' Then she spied something and pointed.

George and Maya had come outside, probably wondering why he'd barged past like a rhino without giving them the time of day.

'You okay, mate?' George asked, frowning.

'Yeah. Just... needed some air,' Sam replied.

'And I came out for company.' Beth clasped his hand. He squeezed back.

'Are you having a game?' He pointed at the door.

'No, we popped in for a drink, show Maya the place,' George replied.

'It's great, isn't it?' Beth loosened her grip so it was more like a big sister's companionship.

'Definitely,' Maya said.

'So... we should double date,' George suggested. 'Properly, not for research. Hang out. The four of us.'

'Research?' Maya asked.

Oh God. Cat out of the bag yet a-bloody-gain.

'Oh yeah,' George said helpfully. 'They're writing a dating app for guaranteed happy ever afters.'

Maya beamed. 'That's *so* cool. Tell me when it's live, okay? I'll definitely join.'

'Hmm?' George pulled her close. 'Should I be worried? How long do I have before you dump me?'

She kissed him. 'I *meant* I'll join up to help your friends. And I'll tell *all* my workmates. You'll need as many users as possible, won't you, Sam?'

Sam's shoulders relaxed. He gave Beth's hand another clasp—one which said, "They believe in this too. We're getting people onside. We can do this. Together."

'Great. Thanks,' he replied.

'And it's adorable that a real-life couple created the app,' Maya said. 'You must know all about true love.'

And it was going so well...

Beth ran fingers through his hair, sending a jolt of electricity down his spine and into his groin.

'True love?' she said, snickering. 'Early days, but we're trying.'

Sam fake chuckled. 'Yeah, she is *very* trying.' Which was only slightly true. She was the best kind of impossible.

Maya patted George's chest. 'Hilarious!'

Beth eyed Sam with hope and encouragement—almost as if she wanted him to read her mind. 'No, but I really am a pain sometimes, eh, darling?'

He put a hand in the small of her back.

Act. Act.

'In a *delightful* way. Besides, the app is the real story. We're helping people find a love that's... truer, deeper and more everlasting than our relationship. Isn't that right, Beth?'

'Indeed. Eloquent as ever.'

Maya frowned. 'What do you mean it's not true and deep?'

Oh crap. The way out of this is not for me to dig, clearly.

Beth wetted her lips. 'Sam... er... means "Not yet, but give it time".'

'Yes, absolutely,' he affirmed.

'Like George and I,' Maya said.

'I'm sure you two have what it takes.'

Was that digging deeper? Or too saccharine?

'Yeah. Keep going,' Beth added, putting her arm around him.

He felt obliged to pull her close and kiss the top of her head. She used nice-smelling shampoo.

'Aww,' Maya said.

The WPC seemed a sucker for tenderness and romance... which didn't feel like a good match with George... but why should Sam care? He hadn't set them up. Still, the app was there as a fallback... assuming the project wasn't kiboshed by getting prickly with the woman he had his arm around. And who, actually, he didn't mind having his arm around. It was all in fun, and appeared to be convincing the audience.

We can do this.

He and Beth exchanged a look. Something passed between them. On one level, an understanding. On another, a calming of the waters. Plus something that made her pop another kiss on his lips.

As it would be ridiculous to run back *into* the venue—and likely to generate questions, ruffle feathers, and bring a storm surge to the waters—he took it like a man.

George gripped his shoulder, as if to say, "Good work, mate".

Maya angled her head. 'Come on, Mister Temporary-til-I-find-someone-better.'

'Ah,' he replied caddishly. 'Time to take down your particulars again.'

She tugged his ear. 'That was funny the first seven times, Mister Six-points-on-my-license.'

He laughed self-consciously, then wished Sam and Beth goodnight and was led away.

Sam watched, his mind blazing, until they disappeared.

Beth took a step away. 'I'm sorry, Sam. I crossed a line.'

He frowned. 'How?'

'The second kiss. That wasn't "needs must". George and Maya had already got the message.' She took a deep breath, shaking her head. 'I overstepped. You and I, in business and as friends, relies on trust. This double date fakery is causing friction. My judgment is off. Which seems to be my lot with men. We've got the app to a good place. You don't need me anymore. I'll... I'll speak to Declan and get your account transferred to another member of the team.' She gave a forlorn expression and turned for the door.

His soul creased. He didn't want anyone else on this project. He wanted *her*. 'Beth?'

She stopped.

He clutched her shoulder. 'It's fine. I get that you're only playing to the gallery. I just... wish it wasn't so convincing. If I didn't know better, I'd think you really do believe we're going out.'

She looked up, brow knit, yet with a perplexed smile. 'I'm not delusional, if that's what you mean.'

'I go to Paris this week.'

'I'm pleased. Honestly. You've waited long enough for destiny. And she'll be a lucky woman. I hope she'll appreciate that you've held on for her. Sacrificed years of happiness. Put up with me getting on your case, trying to push you off course, throwing myself at you like a desperate woman.' She took his hand. 'Sorry, Sam. I don't want to lose your friendship.'

'Or my business and your bonus!'

She grinned. 'That too! But seriously... No more unnecessary kissing. Promise.'

He pulled her closer, so their arms weren't stretched out like a suspension bridge. 'We *could* stop double dating. You're right, I *can* take it from here. I don't want to lose your friendship either. You're a hell of a person, a hell of a catch for some guy.'

She beamed. 'Yeah, I am. And as a fake boyfriend, you're better than any of the *real* ones I had a crack at.'

He laughed. 'Christ, if I'm the best guy you've had on your arm, you've *really* wasted those thirty-three dates. I hope I'm not cramping your style.'

She brushed something off his shirt. 'Tell you what, if I spot someone I want to get with, I'll give you a secret signal to keep your hands off me.'

'Err... why would I have my hands on you anyway?'

'True. On past experience, you'll run a mile if I *breathe* too close.' She winked.

That hurt a little. 'You make me sound cold and spiky. Doesn't say much for my chances at love if I treat friends like that, women like that.'

'Sorry. You aren't cold. Just... you know what you want. That's *good*. This by-the-banks-of-the-Seine woman will strike lucky because she's the product of a focussed search. The man wants *commitment*. Hell, he's building a "forever love" app. Pretty damn attractive, if you ask me.'

His insides softened. 'I don't deserve you, Beth. What a pain in the arse client I am.'

'You want to carry on being a client?'

'If you'll have me.'

'Why not? *Clearly,* I'm only sticking with you for the kisses. The VC world is *crawling* with tarts.'

He coughed. 'Looks like we're back to you being impossible again.'

'I *like* being impossible. We do our best work when I'm being impossible. And brilliant. And perceptive. And a *superb* date partner.'

'As fake girlfriends go, you're a quality item, Ms Moore.' He nudged her.

'Aw, cheers, mate. Gizza kiss then.' She puckered up theatrically, laughter in her eyes, and made slurping sounds.

'Oh, crap,' he breathed haughtily.

Then, to show he wasn't going to be a dick about this anymore, he kissed her on the lips.

'Lothario,' she said.

He took her hand and led her into the venue to see whether Rob and Danni had been getting more or less action than he had.

'Now, behave. Or I'll tell everyone about your adventures with the Coldstream Guards.'

Chapter Thirty-Five

B eth sat at her desk, daydreaming. On one hand, she was happy. Danni had met Rob for Sunday lunch, taken a strategic break to go to the supermarket, and then had dinner with him that night. As this was technically the third date, she'd slept with him. And it had been "everything".

On the other hand, Saturday had been a test, and she was lucky to have come out of it with Sam's friendship intact. He was prepared to up his game, to put on a mask, and then go back to normal: colleagues and mates. That was all she could expect. She might *hope* he'd fall in love with her, but that looked unlikely. If they could pretend, keep friends onside, and nurture the potential PR story, that would be a great fallback.

Mid-afternoon, she was heading to the kitchen area when Adrian trudged out of Declan's corner office and headed for his desk. He eye-rolled, baring his teeth.

Beth shot him a sympathetic grimace. Immediately, he cheered. Adrian was much nicer when he was on song. Early forties, a fellow divorcee, his receding hairline was one of the few demerits in his appearance and character. He'd been at the company for years, but it was only in the last few months that her "available man" radar had beeped. A workplace romance wasn't ideal, but neither was looking gift horses in the mouth...

In the kitchen, she boiled the kettle. Someone entered.

'Well, whatever they hired Declan for, it wasn't his touch-feely interpersonal skills,' Adrian said.

She laughed, glancing around to ensure their nemesis wasn't eavesdropping. 'Too right.'

'Management by being an arsehole doesn't win many friends. Wonder if he was like this at his last place? Or are we the problem?' He spooned instant coffee into a mug.

'Yeah. That... might be me.'

Adrian frowned, bushy eyebrows above grey-green eyes. 'Because of the Edgar Hopkirk shitshow? Not your fault... surely?'

She poured boiling water over her teabag, then filled his mug. 'No. I... er... Declan and I went on a date. And it didn't work out. My decision. I'm not in his good books.'

'Ah. Mr Jealous.'

'Christ knows. He's nothing to be jealous of. Just a sore loser.'

'Tangling with the wrong woman,' Adrian suggested.

'You bet.'

'You'll tell me if he makes a thing about it? In work, I mean.'

She glanced at the door. 'Looks like he's taking it out on you, too.'

He touched her shoulder. 'Maybe. But don't blame yourself. We both know that it's hard to make a relationship stick.'

That kicked her spirits. 'Yeah.'

'At least you're trying again.'

She chuckled involuntarily. *Best not to mention The Thirty-Three.* 'You could say that.'

'Ah. War stories.'

'War *volumes*.'

He laughed. 'We should trade notes.'

'Buy me a jug of margaritas and pin your ears back!'

'You're on.' He raised a hand. 'Sorry, jumping in.'

'No. Not at all. Nice bitching session about you-know-who could be what we need.'

'Hmm. So... you fancy a drink?'

She wetted her lips. He was looking at them.

Sod it. Sam's a non-starter. What's the worst that can happen? A failure, Number 34, and research.

They stirred their mugs. Clink clink, in unison.

A date with Adrian might work out. Besides, all input helps the app, and she'd staked her love life on Sam's—and her—ability to make the app work. But she wouldn't invite Sam to this date.

No. It's not like I'm sneaking around. Why should I pass up a chance to find love without the app? We're separate people, and he can't be jealous as he's clearly not interested in me. He's off to France anyway, which will definitely seal our fate.

'Okay, sure,' she replied.

Back at her desk, the daydreaming resumed. It was a fizz of excitement, of possibilities.

Then her phone pinged with a message. Sam was proposing a meeting on Saturday, a drink and a chat about the app. She suggested they get coffee tomorrow, as the weekend looked tricky, especially if things developed with Adrian...

On Tuesday, she headed to the café near Sam's office building. As she was arriving, Drew and Hannah from the comedy club were leaving with takeaway cups. She gave them a wave.

Sam was inside, with a drink on the go. She grabbed a coffee and went to the table.

He rose. 'Hey.'

She gave him a loose clench, then sat. 'Hey.'

'So why the urgent summit?'

She picked at a fingernail. 'Look, I need to tell you that a guy at work has asked me out.'

His face fell. 'Oh.'

'Is that... okay?'

He glanced away, offering the tiniest shrug, apparent nonchalance. 'I suppose so.'

'What does that mean?'

'It means "fine". Why would it not be fine?'

'Cos you said, "Oh", like it was a shock.'

He chuckled. Clearly forced. 'It's not a *shock* that someone asked you out.'

Pedant, she thought. 'No, okay, not shock. More like... disappointment.'

He frowned. 'Me? No.'

'Okay. Good.' She stirred one sachet of sugar into her latte.

He minutely adjusted the position of the menu card. She sipped her drink.

'Can I tag along?' he asked absentmindedly.

'What? You want to come too?'

'Well... yes. For research.'

'It's not a double date this time. Just me and him.'

'Oh.'

'"Oh" again.'

He smiled, but it was thin. 'Sorry. Not "oh". I see. It's an actual *date*.'

'Yeah. Like I said. Not pretend, like you and me. Not making up numbers. You know, boy fancies girl, that old thing.' She shot a playful look, hoping to diffuse a situation that had rapidly gone from courtesy to awkward.

'I do know that old thing, Beth. It's the whole reason we're together.'

'We're not *together*, Sam. Hence why this date is not an "Oh".'

'Yeah. I meant... never mind. Sorry.' He stirred his coffee redundantly.

'The guy at work, Adrian, is perfect.'

'I'm so happy.' Sam sounded pretty sincere.

Then the penny dropped. 'No, perfect because he *doesn't* know that you and I are dating. I mean, not dating. You know?'

'Yes. And I'm *still* happy. It's great that our pretence hasn't had a casualty.'

'Absolutely. But if it works out with Adrian, we'll have to tell people who know about you and me... I mean, *assume* about you and me, that we've split up.'

'Of course. Makes sense.' He grimaced. 'Won't say much for the app, though. And your relationship fidelity.'

There's always something, isn't there, mate? Bigger picture, please.

'Then, um... I'll say I'm only human, plus the app isn't perfect yet. And we didn't *technically* meet through that in any case.'

He waggled his head. 'True. Besides, we're early days, so it wouldn't *really* count as a failure. Like Jon and Rachel's non-starter didn't.'

'Do I have to go to Dubai for this lie to work?' she joked.

'Haha. No, stay here.'

'I'll say I cheated.'

'But I forgave you so we could keep working together,' he suggested, nodding at his unfolding logic.

'Say it was a mistake for us to go out in the first place. Shows you should have waited for the France thing.'

He beamed. 'Which may still happen. This week, in fact.'

'Win-win!' They high-fived.

He moved the menu card again. 'But if I *could* find a fourth...?'

'Not this time, okay? A night off. Adrian asked me for a drink. I think he's nice. And I don't need your permission as a friend, or colleague, and certainly not as a boyfriend, because you and I are not together.'

'Of course not. So long as nobody spots you and thinks you're two-timing.'

'Adrian and I will go to a pub out of town.'

He patted her hand. 'Good. Glad that's cleared up.'

'Yeah.'

'But... will you give me some feedback? Useful information for the app.'

She mock bared her teeth. '*Please*. I let you know as a *courtesy*. End of discussion.' She folded her arms.

'Okay. Sorry.'

She checked her watch. 'I need to go. Enjoy your trip.' She stood and kissed the top of his head. 'Good luck. I mean that.'

He met her eye. 'You too, Beth. The race is on, right?'

'To the church? You bet.'

Chapter Thirty-Six

S am sat on the Eurostar feeling like a kid heading off to the first day at a new school. Excited and apprehensive. Many things played on his mind.

He was happy that Beth had found a date and that their fakery hadn't kiboshed her chances. A few kisses in fun were harmless, and he felt lucky not to have had to pretend to like someone cold and unattractive. Yet why did he feel a little envious of Adrian? It couldn't be jealousy, could it? That implied he wanted to date Beth, which he didn't, not least because they'd already been on dates. Fakes, yes, but brilliant, nonetheless.

Leave it alone. Adrian gets the real chance, the actual hookup. I hope he treats her properly.

Rob texted with an update about himself and Danni, which partially allayed Sam's fears about his matchmaking gift. Still, he worried for Lena and Paul. He'd heard nothing, although perhaps no news was good news. Any rumblings of a spat or a split would have reached him by now. He didn't dare consider the possibility of a breakdown—what would that say about all his and Beth's development work? He'd run a new compatibility check, using the latest version of the app logic: Lena + Paul = 95%.

Surely an affair constitutes much more than a 5% mismatch!

George was taking Maya away for a surprise weekend and was considering asking her to sleep with him. Sam had read the message three times, searching for the lie or subtext, but when he'd replied with disbelief, George had said, "When you know it's meant to be, there's no rush. Better to savour that moment".

George has been kidnapped by aliens.

Sam was travelling out to Paris on Wednesday—by train, luckily, as he hated flying. Bob, his colleague from the London office, was coming on Thursday morning. Sam didn't fancy a 05:00 start, and the risk of missing the connection at St Pancras. This way, he'd get time to nose around the city. Likewise, while Bob was heading home to Mrs Bob on Friday night, Sam was staying an extra night at his own expense. No point in cutting short a potentially life-changing trip.

In the suitcase above his seat were three days' worth of his best clothes, sundry chargers and adapters, and his work laptop. He'd also brought his personal tablet to make notes on, but couldn't do any app development work. Over the weekend, he'd purchased a new laptop, CarterSoft's first asset. It was risky to keep using VentaTech's licenses. Sooner or later, he'd get rumbled. This new PC was much better suited to the task than his old device, and the investment capital had barely been touched. He'd only had to shell out for company registration fees, website, software, and some graphic design work. The real costs lay further ahead.

The train pulled into Gare du Nord at 15:33. The weather was glorious. He emerged from the station into less-than-fresh air, but didn't care.

I'm here. Twenty-five years on, and I'm back.

He absorbed the city atmosphere for a couple of minutes, then took a ruinously expensive taxi to the accommodation that VentaTech had booked.

Expenses. Lovely company expenses. I wouldn't get that luxury if I worked for myself.

He dumped his belongings in the smallish room on the 7th floor of a modest boutique hotel, dabbed on some aftershave—nine hours after shaving—and hit the boulevards.

He was torn between visiting different venues or remaining in one place, hoping destiny would land in his lap. Should he seek out the tourist hotspots, as he'd be more likely to bump into an English girl?

He wasn't fussed whether Miss Right was French or English, although if she was local, her English needed to be better than his French... which wouldn't be hard. If she was French, he'd consider relocating. Why not? The City of Love was ideal for a fledgling relationship. Work would be an issue, but he could pop across on weekends and holidays. Her too. When it came time to get a house together, she might move to the UK. Winchester was a nice place.

That was for the future. First, he had to meet her.

He bought a *thé noir* and a pastry at a café near the hotel, and stayed for an hour, surveying the scenery and the customers. It was a rare treat to spend more than five minutes without scrolling. He didn't want to scroll. He'd hate to miss The Moment.

The Moment didn't happen, though there was a chic mid-twenties girl reading some French novel. He considered saying hello, but then she moved to an outside table and lit up a cigarette. Some things would never pass his checklist.

He left, taking a long circular route via nowhere special, then selected a brasserie a few streets away from the hotel. He'd never meet The One *at* a hotel: that was too ordinary, unromantic. And, as he was only there three nights, the chances of taking her up to his room were minimal. That wasn't his style.

Two hours in the brasserie came and went. The waitress was cute, but he couldn't imagine dating a waitress. Still, it was heavenly to settle into the city's ambience. He returned to his hotel room, hopeful rather than dejected. This was merely Day 1.

In the morning, Sam took the Metro to a stop near the offices of Halva SARL, the small French software house that VentaTech were buying—or "merging with", to be deferential to his new European business partners. His childhood memories of the Metro were all noise and crowds and how different it was from the London Underground. Now? Much the same, but less overawing—especially the ticketing system.

Arriving early to avoid any travel snafus, he had half an hour to kill before the 10:00 meeting, so he went to the iconic Shakespeare & Company Café for a coffee and croissant... nicely supplementing the two coffees and three croissants he'd had at the hotel. Across the Seine sat Notre Dame. Boats plied the river. The morning rush on the pavements was abating, tourists replacing commuters. He sat on the terrace and imbibed every nuance. This was exactly where he needed to be. Exactly when.

He checked his watch: time to walk up to the Halva office.

Quick wee first.

As he headed inside the café, a siren sounded down the street. The iconic hee-haw sound was a throwback to his youth. Curious, he checked over his shoulder. A police car shot past. One step later, he crashed into something. Something soft. Something soft, feminine, and carrying a paper bag... which dropped to the floor, splitting open and splurging a custard tart across the tiled floor.

'Merde,' she said.

'Shit,' he exclaimed in unison.

Their eyes met.

'Sorry... er... *pardon*,' he added. 'Je m'excusez.'

Wrong verb form? Unlikely she'll care. I've killed her breakfast.

Annoyance on her face broke into amusement. 'No problem.'

Ah. She's English.

'Sorry... I'll...' He squatted down, endeavouring to corral the patisserie debris back into the torn bag. Behind, an arriving customer tutted in that particularly French way, then squeezed past.

The girl crouched. 'It's fine. Accidents happen.'

She wore a black trouser suit over a crisp white shirt. The latter was bloused by her pose, revealing a glimpse of bra strap. Her brown hair was cut in a shoulder-length bob, curtains on a pretty face with beautiful bone structure.

He swallowed hard. 'No. My fault. Let me get you another.'

'It's fine, really.'

They stood. 'It's the least I can do.'

She smiled. 'Okay, that's kind.'

He joined the short queue. She pulled out her phone. They exchanged embarrassed glances. You can take the Brit out of Britain, but you can't stop him, or her, being thoroughly British.

Soon, he handed over her replacement treat.

'Thanks,' she said. 'Look, I need to dash.'

'Me too. Sorry again.'

'No problem. Have a good day.'

'Thanks. You too.'

He watched her go. She had a great backside. And that attire... so hot.

Reminiscent of the first meeting with Beth, actually.

'Pardon!' someone said.

'Sorry.' He stepped aside, then went to the Gents, and successfully avoided cannoning anyone else on the way out.

He crossed the street as the pedestrian lights counted down 3...2...1..., then set off apace.

Ahead, he spotted a familiar figure.

Don't make eye contact. Too cringe.

He slowly caught up with the café girl. At the next pedestrian crossing, she looked across. He offered that "Oh, you again, how funny" nod. She reciprocated.

He let her get ahead, then kept pace a few yards behind. She didn't glance back, recognising, as did he, the mere coincidence that they were using the same city thoroughfare.

The Halva office came into view. He crossed the street onto the correct side. She carried on. He relaxed.

A hundred yards on, she crossed too. He'd nearly reached the office. Soon, the impromptu dance would be over. He slowed, checking the plaque on the building frontage. Correct place.

Ahead, she entered the tall glass double doors. He shook his head, amused. After pausing to avoid more awkwardness, he went inside. She'd bypassed the Reception desk and headed for the lifts.

He signed in and was directed to the 9th floor. In the lift, he checked his watch: all good. Bob had texted to say his train had arrived on time and he'd be in the office by 10:45.

At the Halva reception desk, he signed in *again* and was escorted to the pre-booked boardroom. He put his jacket on the back of a seat, then went to the full height windows. Inhaling contentedly, hands in pockets, he surveyed the iconic skyline.

Where are you? Where are you, my love?

'Hello,' came a voice.

He turned.

Oh. Crap.

Her face cracked into a grin. 'Well. There's a thing.'

'Um... yeah.' He stepped over.

She offered her hand. 'Sam?'

'Yes.' He shook, careful not to squash her hand like a custard tart.

'Hi. I'm Sandrine.'

'Nice to meet you, Sandrine. Again.'

Chapter Thirty-Seven

B eth's week at work was overshadowed by a non-business issue on Thursday morning. She arrived to find Eve dabbing her eyes with a tissue. In the bin were other scrunched parcels.

Beth scooped up her friend, led her to a small meeting room, and slid the Busy sign across.

Eve had broken up with Taylor. He'd wanted a statement of commitment, i.e. Eve selling her flat and moving in with him. Her polite refusal had been met with a lecture. She'd said that eight months was too short a time. He'd asked how long was suitable: *"Eight months and one day? Nine months? A year? Two years? How fucking long do you want?"* She'd decided that the pressure, too many spats, and his inability to watch Match Of The Day without calling *every single* referee a twat, were dealbreakers.

She and Beth talked it out, then went to Costa, devoured pastries, and reflected that love, like shares, can go down as well as up. Throughout, Beth's mind whirred. Could Sam ride to the rescue? She'd frequently thought of him, barely 250 miles away as the crow flies, yet in a different world. And, maybe, finding his destiny.

That evening, she focused on her upcoming date. Using the most recent app questionnaire, she completed a spreadsheet column for Adrian, based on everything she'd learned since he joined the company. Putting it alongside her profile, she used a rough approximation of the algorithm that Sam was constantly refining.

The match was promising: above 70%. Not a bad place to start.

On Friday night at seven, she met Adrian in a rural pub. She'd told him the place served great food, but it was also ideal for avoiding unwanted attention and interruptions.

They'd both gone home to get changed. She'd chosen smart jeans and a patterned top with a high V. He'd opted for a shirt and casual jacket, which accentuated his broad shoulders; he had the build of a rugby player—no giant, but arms she could get swept up in.

He wasn't presumptuous enough to greet her with a kiss, perhaps navigating—as she was—the odd feeling of "seeing" a coworker.

They ordered drinks at the bar, then sat. He politely suggested they go Dutch.

So far, so good.

Predictably, the conversation began with work stuff. Hardly an icebreaker, but safe ground. He talked about his clients and shared a couple of war stories. She gave him the app project headlines —but not the details of her working relationship with Sam, their fakery and the dates. He was intrigued, happy to join any pilot study or focus group.

Over dinner, they moved on to their dating experiences. Predictably, he'd had far fewer attempts than she, but still encountered a few disasters. Throughout it all, he was attentive, without anything creepy behind his eyes.

As two hours passed, she warmed to him. Still, there was scant laughter, no banter, no sparring, no warm feeling in her tummy—things she got from spending time with Sam.

Adrian asked about her date with Declan. She hesitated, not wanting to badmouth the guy excessively, then caved in. Adrian suggested that if the waters between her and the boss didn't calm, she should create a dating profile for Declan and run him through the algorithm. What better way to compensate for her rejection than by finding him a suitable partner, ideally a lasting one?

It was a decent idea, but she was wary of getting Declan too involved: he'd want to meet Sam and ask probing questions. As Sam was moonlighting, she wouldn't put it past Declan to stir things up. This would be self-defeating, because jeopardising the app would remove any chance of the investor getting their return. She certainly wouldn't reveal that she was pinning her own dating hopes on the app. He'd gladly pull the funding purely to deny her that opportunity to find someone. Someone who wasn't him.

Declan seemed the type to hold a grudge. He and Adrian had gone for a round of golf—a foursome, coincidentally—and Declan had tried to gloss over playing an illegal shot. Adrian had called him out, in front of the other players. Declan's face had thunder.

Beth was on Adrian's side. Nobody likes a cheater.

Adrian waved it away, asking to move off the subject. They discussed politics and global events. This was good in one sense—best to cover the big stuff early on. Sadly, she had to bite her tongue, as he was inexplicably dubious about man-made climate change. Very unexpected for such a smart guy—but no point in having a flaming row. So she smoothed over her prickles, conscious that this was merely one subject, and they had common ground on many other things. He also had looks on his side, good teeth, well-kept nails, a wide vocabulary, and didn't care for Harry Potter.

Overall, he was a solid 8/10.

When the meal was done, he asked, 'Where to now?'

After a misunderstanding—she worried that he was suggesting a nightclub or going back to her place—he said he wasn't looking for anything serious yet. Was this code for a fling, a series of flings, friends with benefits, or something else?

Did she want to invest time having fun with Adrian, in case his divorce had soured him to marriage? Had he swung in the opposite direction to her?

In the shingled car park, they parted with a warm embrace—perfect for the circumstance. She said she was happy to see him again, it had been a nice evening, thank you very much.

She drove home feeling positive. Despite a slow start, Number 34 showed potential. And 34 was also her age.

What a coincidence.

Was there a sense of... *destiny* about this?

Chapter Thirty-Eight

Throughout Thursday and Friday, Sandrine oozed a blend of nerdiness and cool. Sam admired her beauty, her exquisite fingers, and the way she slipped calmly into perfect French when needed. Her laugh was sometimes too girlish, but she smelled divine. Of all the people to meet in a riverside café in this glorious capital city, he'd stumbled—literally—into a very fine one. One who didn't mind him occasionally being an accident-prone, tongue-tied fool.

The hours passed quickly as they disappeared down rabbit holes, discussing technical details and the practicalities of bringing her projects under the VentaTech umbrella. While this was happening, Bob from the London office was in and out of meetings with various staff and execs. Probably taking notes on who'd be "let go" within a year of a buyout billed as "no redundancies, only synergies".

As Sam had, by necessity, monopolised Sandrine's time, Bob suggested the three go out for an early dinner on Friday, before he caught the 21:17 train to St Pancras. The guy was really putting in the hours... minus the one he got back due to the time difference.

At five p.m., Sam returned to the hotel, showered and changed, then strolled to the venue. It was a balmy evening, and he sensed love in the Parisian air... if he avoided another pastry-related snafu.

Bob was already at the restaurant, halfway into a glass of vino. Sam helped make a further dent in the bottle.

'So what do you think?' Bob asked.

'It's been a productive couple of days.'

Bob glanced at the door. 'I mean Sandrine. Gorgeous, isn't she?'

Sam didn't remind Bob about his marriage. 'She'll be a real asset at Winchester. Or are you having her in London?'

'Undecided. But I know which I'd prefer.'

'Me too,' Sam said.

Sandrine then arrived. She'd changed into something less businesslike, verging on flirty. Maybe she was going straight on for a late drink with her boyfriend...

Boyfriend! Shit. Surely she's seeing someone. Unless every man in Paris has gone blind.

He took a breath.

Or she's gay. In which case, the female population of the city hasn't gone blind.

Sandrine sat beside Bob and opposite Sam, and, with surprising speed, a waiter was on hand. Had she chosen the seat so as not to offer Bob a front row view of her modest but appealing cleavage? Perhaps he had a longstanding reputation as a sleaze? More likely, per the unwritten rule, she wanted to sit facing *into* the room. Sam had recently looked it up: social convention, rooted in chivalrous courtesy, always placed the female with the best view of the room or the door.

What happens when two girls dine together? Is there a fight for the best seat?

The chink of wine glasses jolted him from daydreaming. He joined the toast, "To new beginnings".

Was *his* new life dawning too?

Over dinner, the conversation moved from work to French politics, new developments within their technical arenas, the march of AI, and, perhaps predictably, Paris' horrendous traffic.

At seven thirty, and with a bottle of red inside him, Bob said goodbye: a handshake for Sam and a *slightly* overdone double kiss for Sandrine.

Sam hoped she hadn't been the victim of wandering hands. He imagined Beth in the pub with Adrian, and prayed that the guy hadn't taken advantage of such an eligible and adorable woman. Beth didn't need a bad experience to sour her recently upbeat view of the dating scene.

Sandrine exhaled heavily, as if the last two hours had been an ordeal, and drained the last inch of her glass. 'So Sam, tell me about yourself.'

Wow. We've drawn a real line between business and pleasure, huh?

He gave her the headlines: one sibling, parents alive, University, first job in IT at a bank, second job in software engineering at a vast conglomerate, redundancy due to Covid, current job at VentaTech.

They ate dessert.

He asked about her. English Dad, French Mum, both alive, one brother, Cambridge University, a brief spell as a singer in a band going nowhere, a year off in Paris to discover herself, current job at Halva for eight years. That led the conversation to work matters: favourite client, worst client, most embarrassing employee at the Christmas party, and whether he'd rather be doing something more exciting like driving an F1 car or hiking the Inca Trail.

His mantra was not to mention the app, his matchmaking talent, the fake dates, or Beth. Those were his personal domain; a silo, a world sandwiched between work, friends, and opportunity. Neither must he allude to his dream. Sandrine might feel like a fantasy ideal she felt pressure to live up to. He had to play it cool. Saying "You're the one I'm going to marry, it's written in the stars" is fine in movies, but in real life, she'd do more than give an insouciant shrug. Flag down a gendarme, perhaps. Plaster a custard tart in his face, then do a runner. Call him a *putain d'idiot*.

He had learned *some* French.

'So what about the future, Sam?'

'I can't imagine doing this forever. What about you? Are you happy about the merger?'

'Honestly, I can't wait to move back to the UK.'

'Really?'

'God, yes. This is the kick up the arse I needed. I'm fed up here. This "City of Love" thing is so overhyped. I've not found love. A few shags though.' She nudged him. The wine was starting to talk. 'People go gaga over the slightest suggestion of romance. It's like a bygone age of gushy crap like Casablanca, and noble acts, and people jumping on planes to chase a long-held crush and declare their true love.' She wrinkled her perfect nose, ruining it. 'Life isn't like that.'

'Oh. Right. What about... dating apps? You should try those.'

'Can't imagine anything worse. Too many charlatans and ugly people who can't get laid the old-fashioned way.' She gestured around. 'Out and about.'

'This is the city for it,' he suggested hopefully.

'If you like landmarks and art and stuff. But the nightlife's amazing.'

He sipped his wine, life force leaking away.

Hang on. As soon as she's back in the UK, her dim view of this fantastic city will fade. So she hankers for home? Great. Saves me relocating.

'That's nice,' he replied.

'And the pastries are delicious. Except when guys throw them on the floor.' She held his gaze. Whilst brown eyes were a big plus, Sandrine's didn't have Beth's natural warmth, vivaciousness.

'I was... enjoying the scenery,' he blustered. Which was partly true. Then and now. Definitely now.

'Hmm. Well, I'd invite you for a walk, but I don't fancy being accidentally knocked into the Seine.'

He shrugged. 'You could push *me* in. Then we'd be even.'

'But I'd have to dive in after you. Maybe get a mention in Le Monde. "Local girl saves tourist". Have to give you the kiss of life and all that, for the full effect.'

He swallowed. 'Sounds unusually... romantic for you.'

'I suppose. Cool, though. Providing I didn't get some deadly river disease.'

'Or me, in fact.'

'Definitely. Then you'd never speak to me again. Tough, if I end up in the Winchester office.'

'Yeah. But I *would* speak to you.'

She smiled. 'That's sweet. But let's not risk it, eh? Actually, I'm not that good a swimmer.'

'Maybe I'd have to save *you*.'

'Push me in first? Worth it for the kiss of life.' She pointed at the door. 'Wanna get some air?'

The sun was low and orange behind the tallest buildings, streetlamps flickering into life. The city buzzed around them as she led him down to the riverside path, Port de Montebello.

Iconic. Romantic. Perfect.

They walked. Sandrine had a purposeful gait, a tomboyish manner, rather than Beth's lithe locomotion. Her ears were triple-pierced, her shoes chunky. Yet her fabulous bone structure was undeniable, and her French accent was so sexy.

Now and again, when she glanced across, he sensed she wanted him to hold her hand, so he obliged. It felt... okay. Natural. Friendly.

She asked what Winchester was like. He considered offering his spare room in case she needed somewhere... but didn't. Wisely, as it turned out, because she was taking a few months abroad before the new start. Possibly Thailand. Or Ibiza. Live life. Live it large.

Gradually, the evening air dissipated the effects of six glasses of Chateau Somethingorother. The bells of Notre Dame struck ten. They paused, listening.

The fading light caught her just so. Their eyes locked.

'Sam?' she said softly.

'Yeah,' he murmured, feigning cool, his heart hammering.

'There's a brilliant club five minutes away. Wanna come?'

Chapter Thirty-Nine

B eth indulged in a Saturday morning lie-in. She curled up, pulled two pillows under her head, and replayed the Adrian date. Would she see him again? Definitely. She *had* to learn to give guys a real chance at being The One.

At nine o'clock, she succumbed to a desire for action, had breakfast, then went for a run. Then came time with Quincunx, a thorough clean of his cage, hoovering the house, lunch, ironing work shirts, and a catch-up with Eve to check she was okay.

Adrian hadn't been in touch, so to be courteous, she texted, thanking him again and wishing him a good weekend, see you Monday.

All this was nervous energy. Leon was coming round that evening.

At six o'clock, she stood at the wardrobe, hands on hips, seeking something not too slovenly, not too fancy, not too revealing, not too frumpy. She didn't want him to think their split had crushed her, emboldened her, impoverished her, or turned her into... a tart.

A warmth enveloped her.

Wonder how Sam is getting on?

The doorbell rang. He was early.

'Shit.' She quickly pulled something on and went downstairs.

She hadn't seen Leon, her *husband*, in nearly six weeks.

The first thing that struck her was the designer stubble. Then the jacket, sharper than he'd ever worn. He'd lost a few pounds, too. In his hand was an oversize plastic bag, one you might use to ferry a ton of wrapped pressies to Auntie's house for Christmas Day.

'Hi, Beth.' He leaned in for a kiss.

'Hi.' She let it slide onto her cheek.

Stubble graze. Yuk.

'Come in.' She backed up. It felt wrong to wave him through. This was *her* house. Or it would be soon.

In the living room, he set the big bag on the dining room table. A gift? Her birthday was weeks away. An anniversary present would be preposterous.

'Studmuffin,' squawked Quincunx.

'Ooh, observant,' Leon said.

'He says that to anyone,' she drawled.

'Bet you get into trouble with the plumber.'

'It hasn't got me laid *quite* yet.'

Leon winked. 'The night is young.'

'*Not* a good idea. We're getting divorced. Remember?'

'It's not a done deal.'

'And whose fault's *that*?' She shot him a glare.

'I don't want to fight, Beth. That's not us. We don't fight. We never did.'

'Hmm.' But he was spot-on. There were never snow-capped highs or murky depths. It was twelve years of... being okay. Being content.

'Look...' He opened his arms, coming in for a hug.

She backed off. 'What's in the bag? Wedding album? A bomb? A cat in a box, ready to spring out and eat Quin?'

'Like I'd do that.'

'So what's the big surprise? If it's a crazy, romantic gesture, you're too late.'

He sighed, fed up with her combative attitude. He had a point. She was raising the temperature in the room. 'It's the papers, okay?'

'Finally,' she breathed.

He went to the table, opened the plastic bag and pulled out a tall box. From beside it, he produced a sheaf of A4.

'You're kidding,' she said.

'Nope. Deadly serious.' He tapped the box. The picture on the side told the story. 'Either you sign, post the decree off, and turn your back on us... or you recognise that maybe we're being hasty, and you shred it.'

'Hasty?! It's been three years of a slow decline.' She snorted. 'And most of that was waiting for you to do the bloody paperwork.'

He looked hurt. 'I don't want to rush and make a mistake, that's all.'

'I wish we'd been that objective twelve years ago.'

'You don't mean that, Beth. You don't regret the whole *marriage*?'

She sank onto the sofa. 'No. But I think I'd regret it if we'd carried on as we were and not been adult and said stop.'

He sat beside her. 'We can carry on *differently*. A reset.'

She scrutinised his face. If there'd been a decline in his self-care—possibly due to the divorce proceedings—he'd arrested it.

Reversed it. Perhaps he was reinventing himself to be worthy of her, deserving of a second chance.

Yet they had evolved as people, realised they wanted different things, and weren't as compatible as they once were. Arguably, they'd carried on because it was the easy option. They'd let things slide. Now he was morphing from the tortoise into the hare, desperate to win the race in the last few yards.

She rubbed his knee. 'You deserve better than me, Leon.' That may or may not have been true, but it was something nice to say. Not antagonistic.

'I'm not sure I do. Actually, I wish we'd met for the first time now. You've never looked lovelier.' He reached towards her jawline. She let him stroke it for a second, then took his hand and placed it on the cushion.

'Look, I'm... kind of... seeing someone.' She didn't specify who, partially because she didn't know. Sam? Adrian? The perfect match, a man only an algorithm's 0.0001s runtime away?

'"Kind of"?'

'Yes. It's very early stages,' she said.

'Beth, you and I are *late* stages. We're *married*.'

'For now.'

A heavy silence. Then—

'Stuudmuufffiiin.'

He smiled wryly. 'I always liked your parrot stuff.'

'That is *such* a lie,' she said with dismissive good humour. 'You always thought it was immature.'

'Maybe. But that?' Leon pointed at the cage. 'It's brilliant.'

'*He's* good company.'

'So was I. Still am.'

'Let's not rake over it.'

He studied her face. 'Okay.'

The doorbell rang.

'Amazon?' Leon asked. 'Or Mr Early Stages?'

Yet she sensed he already knew the answer.

If this is a dozen red roses, a Mariachi band, or a 6-foot inflatable parrot, designed to win me back, you've wasted your money, mate.

She rose.

He sprang up. 'I'll get it.'

'But—'

'It's okay. Beth. Honestly.'

Nervous but compliant, she perched on the chair arm. The door opened, Leon said, "Forty-three", the door closed, and he reappeared with another plastic bag.

'Is this for *double* shredding?' she asked. 'To prove I'm serious about staying together.'

He laughed. 'No. It's dinner. Least I could do.' He unpacked the takeaway boxes.

She went to the dining table and read the receipt stapled to the bag. 'You ordered my favourite.'

'Well, picking something you hate would be stupid.'

'Ah. Currying favour?'

He held up a tub of chicken dopiaza. 'So it seems.'

'Do I get to keep the shredder, whatever I decide?'

'Yeah. More currying.'

She rolled her eyes. 'I'll get the plates. You want a beer with your currying?'

Chapter Forty

S am was back home at four thirty on Saturday afternoon.

His spirits were neither high nor low. Plenty of reasons to like Sandrine, to want to see her again, yet a niggling feeling of something missing. Yes, the first meeting was cute—if embarrassing—but that didn't mean his quest was over. They needed more time together, and luckily, he was returning to Paris in a couple of weeks. That, hopefully, would close the circle. Create a ring.

The ring that one day he'd place on her finger.

That evening, as he was mindlessly scrolling through TV channels in the faint hope of finding something watchable, his phone rang.

'So?' Elodie asked, cutting to the chase.

Earlier, Sam had sent his sister a picture from Paris. A deliberately cheesy one of him pointing at the Eiffel Tower, plus the group selfie that Bob had insisted on taking at dinner—possibly so he could squish up against a girl half his age.

'Wedding's next Saturday,' he replied, deadpan. 'You free?'

'How can you joke about something that's been the most serious thing in your life since, well, records began?'

'Because everyone else jokes about it?' he suggested.

'But have you proven us all wrong? I mean, she's very pretty. And nerdy, like you—'

'I'm not—'

Elodie chortled. 'I'm such a bad sister. All the same, spill.'

Sam took a deep breath and gave her the full works. She said it was a "top meet-cute, *very* Sam", but the Doc Martens and triple-pierced ears sounded *less* Sam. Which, he had to concur, was true.

'Still, another brunette. Definitely your M.O. And it's early days, right?'

It *was* early days. Things don't spark to life immediately. Except perhaps with Beth—but that was different. She was a friend. One who'd also been out with "someone from work".

Had Adrian succeeded where The Thirty-Three had failed? If so, would Beth still be as emotionally invested in getting the app to Go Live? Would she and Sam become merely account manager and client? He hoped not. He'd miss her vivacious, sassy... impossibleness.

Half an hour later, when the sibling chat ended, he texted Beth, keen to find out how *her* happy ever after was going. Fewer custard tart-themed slip-ups, he reckoned.

She replied quickly. "Catch-up? What u doing tomorrow?" "Supposed to hit shuttlecocks with George, but he got a better offer ;-)"

"Want to play? We did say..."

"Sure. Court booked for 10"
"CU then"

On Sunday, he reached the sports centre foyer at 09:50. Like him, Beth had arrived ready to play, sporting navy shorts and a white polo shirt, her hair tied in a scrunchie. An eye-opening look.

Is "legs" a criterion? Yeah. And you pass with flying colours, Beth. Rosettes and everything.

They exchanged a continental double cheek peck, and he pointed her towards the sports hall.

It was the oddest walk, a mix of tense silence, expectation, and glances at each other's physiques. They were sizing each other up, mentally and visually. He walked slightly ahead to avoid the temptation to watch her marvellous backside.

The cavernous room, all exposed breeze block and ceiling pipes, rang with the squeak of trainers, thwack of rackets, and assorted curses. They leaned on the wall at Court 5, waiting for the doubles game to finish.

Beth played with her hair. 'So what's her name?'

It was pointless to be coy or feign ignorance. 'Sandrine.'

'Ooh. She's French.'

'No, English, but with a French mum. A mum who calls the shots on names, clearly.'

'Is she pretty?'

'The mum?'

Beth whacked his arm with her racket. 'Sandrine. Dickhead.'

'Yes.'

She nodded slowly. 'Have you...?'

'No!' He poked her in the ribs. 'Of course we haven't. Have you and Adrian...?'

'No way.' She swallowed. 'Do you *want* to? With her?'

'Maybe. But I need to know there's something there.'

'So do I with Adrian.'

'Sure. But not a wipeout on first date?'

She pulled a face. 'No. And I get the implication, thank you *very* much.'

'Then I'm pleased, honestly.'

'Thanks.' She lifted one leg up behind her, grabbed her foot and stretched. 'Did you put Sandrine in the app?'

'Not yet.'

'Might be an idea. I know the fate aspect is important, but you also want something lasting. Wouldn't it be silly if this fantasy, even if it's happening now, was a short-lived romance? How would that feel?'

That smarted. 'Who says this meet is Miss Right? There could be other people later.'

'So how will you know which is the real one?'

He shrugged. 'I'll use my matchmaking skill to self-analyse.'

'Or the app, which will be working pretty soon.'

'You think it will be less fallible than me?'

She scoffed. 'I should hope so. Machines are supposed to *improve* on people.'

'If they're designed and programmed correctly.'

'So the pressure is on us to nail it. Your happiness, mine too, could be at stake.'

'Unless Adrian is your person.'

She waggled her head. 'Not sure.'

'So it's not goodbye to Number 34 yet?'

Her lips pursed. 'Technically, *you're* 34.'

'How?' He stretched his hamstrings.

'Err... we've been on dates.'

'Only for work, to make up numbers.'

Her mouth opened and closed. 'Yeah. It's just that every fake date feels like a real one.'

He levelled his racket at her. 'Remember the drill. No dates, only pretending.'

She used her racket to salute. 'Understood.'

He shook his head. 'Less than a week and I'd forgotten how impossible you are.'

She tapped the top of his head. 'Aw, you love it really.'

He pointed. 'Court's clear.'

They played. She was a decent stand-in for George, much less gobby and mocking. After fifteen minutes, they took a breather, had fluids, then swapped ends and resumed. The tempo was a nice balance between gamesmanship and fun.

They paused again after the next game, taking a five-minute break. Both their brows were glistening with perspiration, and her shirt had a translucency that hinted at the contours of her bra. He was pretty sure she didn't catch him looking, but was herself scrutinising his physique.

They resumed. Having narrowly won the first two games, he'd let her have the third. It might happen anyway, as Beth was on her toes, charging hard for every shot, determined to salvage some pride.

He flicked the shuttlecock, backhand, over the net towards the far corner of her court. She pushed off, pivoting, running back, lunging. Her foot slipped, sending her twisting, crashing to the wooden floor. Her knee rapped the ground, and she yelped.

He ducked under the net, dropping the racket as he knelt beside her. She clutched her left knee, grimacing in pain.

'Fuck, fuck, fuck,' she said through gritted teeth.

Helpless, he gauged her position and replayed the fall in his head. He didn't think she'd broken anything. Was this merely a knock, or something more serious?

'Where does it hurt?'

'My knee. Like I twisted it. Sheesh.'

'Ankle okay?'

'Yeah.' She rubbed the ligaments around her patella, wincing at tenderness.

'What can I do?'

She shot a pained smile. 'Concede the game?'

'Done.'

'Eleven-nil?'

'Don't get greedy. You want to stand up?'

'Maybe in a minute.' She tried to stretch her leg out. 'Ow.'

'We need to get ice on that.'

'Okay. I've got peas in the freezer.'

'No. Now.' His mind raced. 'Stay there.'

'I was planning to go for a quick half-marathon, but if you insist.'

He rolled his eyes. 'Back in a sec.'

He jogged across the hall, past two other courts, through the double doors, and down the corridor to the changing rooms. Outside was an ice machine.

Bingo.

Except he had no container. He reviewed the area, but came up empty, so he pulled off his polo shirt, laid it on the carpet tiles, and pressed the button on the machine. Ice cubes cascaded onto the dispenser shelf and then the floor. Rattle rattle rattle.

He scooped the scattered ice cubes into the centre of his shirt, folded the corners over to make a parcel, then trotted back to the sports hall. Beth had somehow made her way off the court. He wished she'd stayed put and not risked greater injury. As he approached, her eyes widened, mouth tweaking upwards. He knelt and held the impromptu ice pack to her knee.

'Ooh,' she peeped, startled by the cold.

So much for the fearless, snarky businesswoman.

She rested a hand on his, where he gripped the edges of the shirt fabric. They sat for a minute, she breathing deeply.

'Better?' he murmured.

'Yeah. My knight in shining armour.'

He glanced down. 'I had to take the chestplate off, but there we go. Hopefully, this'll ease the swelling. Ibuprofen when you get home.'

'Yes. *Doc.*' She grinned impishly.

He plucked out an ice cube. 'Want me to drop this down your top?'

'Not even *you* are that cruel. Or daring.'

That drew his attention to her cleavage. Briefly... though possibly not briefly enough? But she wasn't looking at him in disapproval. Instead, she touched a fingertip to the scar on his left pec.

'What's this?' she asked, concerned.

'Oh, some guy at Uni. Came at me with a penknife.'

Her mouth formed an O. 'Came at you? Looks like he *got* there.'

'It's fine. Few stitches. Overnight stay. No problem.'

'You could have *died*, Sam.'

He chuckled. 'Nah. Missed my heart by a mile. The dickhead.'

'Hardly a mile. I'm amazed he missed it at all. The heart is a *huge* part of you.' She traced her finger in a giant heart shape across, down, and around his chest.

His nerve endings crackled with her touch. For the first time, he wanted to kiss Beth Moore. Except it wasn't "needs must". And she deserved more than a poorly-judged gesture of affection.

She deserved Mr Right. The luckiest guy in the world.

Chapter Forty-One

B eth ached to kiss Sam. And wanted him to craft another makeshift ice pack, this time using his shorts.

But that was the pain talking, and the circumstance, and the spectacle of his gorgeous chest. If she kissed him now, their relationship would be in even more trouble than her knee.

Still, the fact that he'd been observing her legs, backside, and chest hadn't gone unnoticed. It wasn't the first time. Even if he refused to admit it to himself, or even recognise it, part of Sam Carter was interested in her.

She dismissed it.

'Wanna blow this joint?' he asked. A group of four had taken over their court. The hour was up.

That's not what I was hoping to blow, but...

'Yeah.'

Unbidden, he reached under her armpit and helped her up. She gripped his waist. Her knee throbbed as they gingerly went to the foyer. There, he sat her on a chair, said he was ordering an Uber because walking to the bus stop was needless. She bathed in his care and pragmatism.

In sickness and in health...

They gave up with the icepack, which had become a soggy shirt. Unable to put it back on, he stepped outside, wrung it out on the flowerbed, then slung it over his shoulder in a rope.

What's happened to the distant, affection-shy Sam? Perhaps Paris has changed him. He walks taller with Sandrine in his life. It suits him.

It suited Beth, too. A topless hunk ministering to her needs? That was worth an ouch.

'Five minutes,' he said, pocketing his phone. 'Let's wait outside.'

'You're a star, Sam.'

'Gotta keep the investor onside.' He winked.

He helped her hobble to the apron in front of the building. They perched on a low wall, taking the weight off her leg. She surreptitiously scoped his upper body, then focused on the beauty of life and nature: the flowers in bloom, the birds singing, a dad escorting his young daughter into the venue, maybe for a swimming lesson. And—

'Oh, shit.'

'What?' Sam asked, alarmed.

'Shit,' she hissed. 'Callum.'

'Who's—?'

'The guy trying to find me everywhere online.'

Callum was twenty yards away. He'd been aimlessly heading for the main entrance, sports bag in his hand, but his demeanour changed. He'd seen her.

Why the hell is he here, now?

Because this is a public place. And Callum was keen to point out that he could bench press his nephew.

If she'd kept her head down, Callum might not have noticed her, but a topless bloke hanging around outside the sports centre was something of a curiosity. Still, it was too late to curse herself for getting injured or wish Sam hadn't gallantly come to her aid.

Sam patted her arm. 'Don't worry.'

'Roll with it, okay?' she whispered, barely moving her lips.

Except they might not need to roll with it, if Callum decided it wasn't worth saying hello. If he got the "Stay Away" message she'd been radiating...

'Beth?' he said, stopping six feet away.

She looked up. Pointless to feign ignorance or deafness. She leaned on the wall, pushing herself up, internalising the knee pain, determined not to show physical or mental weakness. Sam clasped her arm in support. Immediately, she became happier, emboldened. Whilst she could handle Callum alone, Sam's presence provided a lifeline.

'Oh... hi.' She pretended to have only just recalled who he was.

'Hi, Beth. Small world. You okay?'

'Yeah. Banged my knee, that's all.'

Callum nodded, intrigued by the topless man beside her.

'Oh, sorry,' she added. 'This is my boyfriend, Sam.'

Sam put an arm around her, extending the other hand towards Callum. 'Alright. Sorry, I didn't get your name.'

Number 33 shook Sam's hand. 'Callum. Beth and I... met... a while back.'

'Oh, I see.'

Callum's attention darted between the girl who'd spurned him and this oddball hanger-on. His chest puffed, showing he was the alpha, the leaner and fitter. A sneer developed. She hoped Sam pretended to be a brain surgeon or something.

She held Sam's bare waist. 'We're waiting for a cab.'

'Yes,' he said with easy confidence. 'Get this lady home, rested up. She's too precious.'

She raised her face to his. 'Aww, you're the best.'

There was a gleam in his eye, an understanding. He was *loving* playing up to Callum's prickled demeanour.

So she kissed him, full on the lips, no hesitancy. He didn't flinch. Her heart skipped.

Mild distaste flickered on Callum's face.

'So is it squash, fitness stuff, or what?' she asked him.

'Gym.' He studied them both. 'Well... it's... good to see you persevered with dating. I got the impression you were giving up on apps. I certainly am.'

'Oh no. That's how we met.' She ruffled Sam's hair. 'They *can* come up with the goods.'

'Worth the wait.' Sam kissed her temple. Endorphins raced through her.

'So... which app was this? Just curious,' Callum asked.

She willed Sam to give a sensible answer. One which wouldn't drop them in it... or no *further* in it.

Sam flapped a hand. 'You wouldn't know it. It's only in the pilot phase. We were lucky enough to be asked and... here we are.' He beamed.

You are smashing this, mate. You fabulous man.

'Happy as happy can be.'

'You bet.' And he kissed her. On the lips.

Oh, Lord. More. More.

'Ah. Oh. I see,' Callum said, fake joy at the loving vibes they were frantically radiating.

'Yeah. A great app,' she added. 'And if it's this good already, imagine how life-changing it'll be when it's *live*.'

'I... suppose so.'

She rubbed Sam's nose with hers, inhaling his musk. 'It's the best. *He's* the best.'

'Would you... give me more details about it? When it's live?' Callum's demeanour had gone from superiority to plaintive in a heartbeat. Well, a few heartbeats, given how fast hers was thumping.

'Um, I—' Sam began.

'Definitely,' she said.

Over Number 33's shoulder, something taxi-like pulled up.

'Thanks,' Callum replied sincerely. 'That's very... understanding.'

'No problem,' she trilled. 'Anyway, this is our ride, so—'

'Oh, sure, yes. So... nice to see you again, Beth. Hope the knee is okay. And, um, good to meet you, Sam.' A smile was painted on. 'And... good luck.'

'Thanks. That means a lot.' She took Sam's hand. 'Come on, babe. My carriage awaits.'

Sam nodded at the latest guy to test their friendship. 'Cheers.'

And he led her to the kerb. She held on tightly... to stop herself from floating away.

He opened the rear door, and they climbed inside. The driver didn't bat an eyelid at Sam's partial undress, checked the name and destination, then pulled away.

She sank deeper into the seat. The tension of the encounter ebbed. Yet she didn't dare look at Sam. He was gazing out the window. The air was thick with unsaid words.

'Sorry,' she said into her chest.

He turned, smiling. 'No problem.'

'Yeah?' Her spirits lifted.

'Honestly, fine. Needs must. Absolutely. Worked, didn't it?' He thumbed over his shoulder.

'Looks like it.'

'He does seem like the kind of guy who'd hassle you. And I don't want that.'

A wave of affection and gratitude crashed over her. She took his hand. 'Thanks. You really... played the part.'

'Had to be convincing, so he'd back off. You were right, Beth. It's a great tool, used properly.'

'Was I... Did I jump the gun? About the app? I mean, I'm not sure we want people like that on it.' She shuddered.

'We want *everybody*. Don't hold a grudge. All of your castoffs can come.'

She shoved him. 'Snake.'

'I'm serious. Every user who signs up equals money. We need that word of mouth. We sold Callum on the brilliance of the app. We schmoozed him by schmoozing each other. Okay, it's a white lie, but what's a kiss between mates if it creates success?'

She patted his bare shoulder. 'See? A little sacrifice goes a long way.'

'Absolutely.'

It was no sacrifice at all. It was lovely. Bring on more.

They exchanged an expression which said, "So there we go".

Silence fell. The cab, a new electric one, whirred onwards.

Chapter Forty-Two

The atmosphere in the cab was odd. Undoubtedly, they'd done a brilliant tag-team job: not only warding off Callum, but also showcasing the app. All thanks to the stomach-knotting yet spine-tingling pretence.

What had begun as a social awkwardness, a misunderstanding, had become something of a game. A fun one. And one of the prizes was that he got to kiss a pretty woman. Without dating her. Without yeeting his dream future into the void. And they were handling this unexpected and unusual part of the project as superbly as the rest of it. They were building a halo around the product. A fake halo, but still.

He tried nonchalantly staring out the window, but his attention repeatedly wandered to Beth. Did she keep glancing at him? Yes. Probably because his shirt was in his hand and not on his body. If *her* shirt was off, he would find it difficult not to look.

She rubbed her knee.

'You okay?' he asked.

'Yeah. Great.' She brushed something from the seat, then angled her body towards him.

He sensed a revelation, a tricky conversation. 'What?'

'We should put kissing as one of the criteria.'

He laughed. 'That's pointless. Nobody will say they're *bad* at it. Even if the question is phrased "Would people say you're a good kisser?", users will lie. Nobody will *seek out* a bad kisser. Even if people were honest and say they're only middling or even *crap* at kissing, who'd want that? So it's a non-question.'

'Yeah. Stupid.'

He tapped her arm. 'No. There are no stupid ideas. Not with this. There's a *lot* to whittle down.'

'Definitely. Definitely.' She peered absentmindedly at the driver's satnav. 'What about...? Hmm.' She curtailed her notion.

'What?'

'What about French kissing?'

He swallowed. 'What about it?'

'Is there a question in that? Like... "When is too soon for tongues?" Date one, two, whatever.'

'Maybe. It could show a mismatch of expectations about how fast people want to move. But it depends on circumstances. It's instinct. There'll be that *feeling*.'

'Yeah, yeah, yeah.' Her eyes glazed over, as if daydreaming. 'But you're right. The "Are you a good kisser?" idea was a crap suggestion.'

'No problem... *darling*.' He grinned.

She picked at a thread in her shorts. 'So... how... would you score *me*? Hypothetically.' She glanced across.

He smoothed his chest. His exposed nipples had awoken. Caused by the car's aircon... maybe. 'Hypothetically?'

'Of course.'

'Okay. I mean, it's not an app question, is it? But if you *really* want a score...' His inflexion rose, showing how daft this was.

'Not to inflate my ego, of course. Curious, that's all.'

'Why? Have you had bad feedback before?'

She laughed. Deeper, sultrier than normal. 'No. *Hell*, no.'

'So "people" would say you're a good kisser?'

She poked his thigh. 'Yes. Just... interested if you belong in the data set of "people".'

'Ah.' He nodded sceptically. 'If it means *that* much, okay, you can put me under "people". I hope that's a good group to be in. I hope they're not all *arseholes*.'

'Some were, some weren't. Some were good kissers, some not.'

Mischief played on his lips. 'So you have your *own* data set?'

'Yes. Not on Excel, obviously. I'm not a geek like you.'

He slapped her thigh. 'I am not a geek!'

'Sam. You're a tech guy who is building an app.'

'It's a job. *Beanie.*'

'I am not a beanie!'

'Let's agree to disagree. Besides, we need each other.'

'Right.'

He nodded firmly. 'Right.'

The tyres hummed along the road. They'd be at her house soon.

'So.... want me to tell you what data set *you're* in?' she asked.

'Oh. So you want to put me in either your "Good kisser" or "Not" group?'

She looked away. 'I already have.'

Hell, she is flirting so hard. Maybe because I slapped her thigh. Was that too much?

'Okay, good.'

'Great.'

'Fine.' He folded his arms.

They took the third exit at a roundabout.

She massaged her knee. He peered over, seeking any signs of bruising. Then his attention wandered to her thigh—soft, tanned and inviting.

'Don't you want to know?' she said, jolting his reverie.

'Is it important? I'm *comfortable* with my ability. Your view could be an outlier. Edge of the bell curve. I'd discard that as statistically irrelevant.'

'So even if I said it was like kissing a warthog with halitosis, you wouldn't care?'

He shrugged, despite caring deeply. 'I mean, it'd hurt for a *while*, but I'd get over it. Couple of minutes, maybe.'

'Because you're not on a mission with me.'

'Exactly. If I got a slap back from someone I *wanted* to get serious with—'

'Sandrine,' she said.

'—perhaps, then it would kill the dream. But my *business partner*? No. It would be like... if my dad said he didn't like the way I danced.'

'Water off a duck's back,' she suggested.

'Yeah.'

Silence fell. She looked out the window. He did too.

He'd kissed Milly, his previous girlfriend, because she was pretty. That turned out to be a wild goose chase. Good kissing doesn't equal a blissful forever. With Beth, he wasn't in search of til-death-do-us-part. He was doing it in fun, for business reasons, and because they'd boxed themselves into something.

And he couldn't give Beth a score anyhow. That hadn't been a proper kiss. But if he *did* want to get serious with her—in a parallel universe where Paris wasn't a place and Sandrine wasn't a person—the kiss certainly wouldn't have *ruined* Beth's chances.

Chapter Forty-Three

Beth didn't pursue the discussion. Sam was an easy 9, but the kisses had been transactional, vanilla. Meagre portions, but all she'd get. The chat and the teasing gave her goosebumps. He'd been almost flirting.

Perhaps he could afford to, with Sandrine on the scene. When there's a deadline, you can measure your approach to it. When you have the stag do a week before the Big Day, it's alright to cut loose, because there's plenty of time to get back from Corfu or wherever, even if you've been tied up and eyebrow-shaved for a laugh.

Sam was letting her fool with him. And every minute of it was glorious.

He supported her waist as they walked up to her house. The pain had ebbed, but she needed to get anti-inflammatories inside her—realistically, the only thing which would end up inside her in the next ten minutes.

'Pay you back for the cab, okay?' she said.

'If we're getting picky, you owe me for half the court fee too.' He helped her to the sofa. 'Forget it. Coffee?'

'You asking or offering?'

'Stay off your feet. Trust me in the kitchen?'

'Implicitly. Stick your shirt in the tumble drier if you want.'

'Thanks.' He disappeared into the next room.

She closed her eyes, calming her fluttering heart. Across the room, hidden under the cover, feathers ruffled.

Sam poked his head around the door. 'Painkillers?'

'Upstairs bathroom.'

'Is it safe to go in?'

'That's very respectful. Thank you. Yes, it's safe.' He began to climb the stairs. Her lips broke into a mischievous smile. 'Because the vibrator's in my bedside drawer.'

His feet paused briefly, then continued their ascent. She sniggered. Teasing was her second-favourite thing to do with Sam Carter.

He returned, collected a glass of water from the kitchen and handed her the tablets. She swallowed them while he brought out the mugs of coffee. He noticed the sheaf of papers and the shredder on the dining table.

'Leon came round,' she explained.

He drank. 'Ah.'

She shuffled up the 3-seat sofa, legs outstretched along it, and Sam sat by her feet. 'He gave me a choice. Sign or shred.'

'Hmm. Still not decided, then?'

No. It's a huge moment. Much more than a simple signature.

She sipped her coffee. He'd made it perfectly. 'Procrastinating.'

'Well, it *is* a big decision. Whichever way. It's been a *lot* of your life, Beth.'

'True. So... any suggestions?'

'I can't give advice. I don't know you well enough.'

'Mate, you know me better than many.'

'All the same, it's not my call. But at least you get a shredder out of it.' He winked.

She wished he wouldn't wink like that. Especially topless. In her house. After running to her aid. And kissing her. 'Maybe we should put Leon and I in the app. That'll tell us.'

Sam waggled his head. 'It's still pretty rough. Might give the wrong answer.'

'But how would we know?'

He set down his mug. 'Easy. If it showed good compatibility, and you were *disappointed*, it means you hoped for *no* match, which implies you *don't* want to be with him. If we ran a match with, I dunno, Tom Hardy, and you came up 100%, you'd be dancing with glee.'

'Too bloody right. But we can't all have our dream person, can we?'

'Maybe not. We can only hope for the best *attainable* person. Hence the app.'

'Yeah. And how's it going?'

He gave her a rundown on progress. She wished he'd stroke her feet. He outlined the user options, the upsells. She wished he'd stroke her knee. He said he'd done a few test matches with dummy profiles. She wished he'd stroke her thigh.

He brewed another coffee. They shared biscuits. He asked how her knee was. She said it felt sore but okay. While he was up, she stretched it. She asked him to take Quin's cover off.

The bird clambered onto the cage wall and contemplated Sam beadily. 'Stuud-muffin.'

Sam did a little bow, then pulled an Atlas pose. Beth laughed, wishing he'd stroke her all over.

'Saaam's so hoooot,' Quin added.

Oh fuck.

Beth wanted the floor to swallow her up.

Sam coughed and shot a quizzical expression.

'I... um...' she fumbled.

'He's got a lot to say for himself recently.' Sam tapped the cage. 'Eh, buddy?'

'Saaam's so hoooot,' the parrot repeated.

Why now, Quin? Eh? Think I preferred you silent.

Sam eased onto the sofa beside her. His raised brow spoke volumes.

She cleared her throat. 'I... think that... he must have heard me mention the kiss.'

A smirk appeared. 'Ah. The kiss. Not today's, though. Too soon. So... the shuffleboard one?'

She quickly tied her hair up in a knot. Hot neck all of a sudden. 'Yeah, clearly.'

Amused by her transparent fibbing, he tapped his lips. 'Hmm.'

She shrugged hopefully. 'A kiss can be hot... right?'

'If that one, those *three*, are worth mentioning in front of pets, you have a *very* low bar for what's hot.'

It was time to stop digging. 'Personal preferences are allowed. Isn't that our *actual* raison d'être?' She folded her arms, desperate to shut this down.

He nodded deferentially... but with a glint in his eye. 'Absolutely.'

She swept up her mug, stared into it, and tried to remember what the hell they'd been talking about. 'We were discussing compatibility score, yeah?'

'We were. So... what kind of matchup percentage is necessary before you give long-term a chance?'

'Well, 100, but that's silly.'

'99?'

She sipped her coffee. 'Anything above 95 is good. It allows leeway for inaccuracies in the app, plus you can't look *forever* for a 100.

Couples can always work through the last 5 percent of relationship niggles.'

'Yeah.' His face fell. 'Paul and Lena prove there are always bumps to iron out.'

She bit her lip. 'Not sure I want big ones, though.'

'Me either. For any of us. Have you heard from her?'

'Not for a few days.'

'Paul's taking her away,' he said.

'Oh yeah?'

'Surprise anniversary trip.'

'Not a surprise to you,' she ventured.

'Actually, I suggested it. Romantic weekend away.'

She stroked her chin comedically. 'Let me guess where.'

'Was only an idea.'

'You think that city is the answer to *every*thing.'

'Not necessarily. It's the principle. An awayday. A treat. Space. A chance to speak.' He shrugged. 'Hopefully Lena will... unburden herself.'

'And if not?'

'Don't want to think about it. Move on?' he suggested.

'Sure.'

'I'm interested. Why are you looking for Mr Forever straight away? Why the pressure? Why not take a breather?'

Fair question.

'Because I have to believe it's possible. It's not *all* about my clock ticking, but I do want kids. All the same, I don't want to meet, marry and give birth within a year. I want time together. To grow and get to know each other. Kids are great, but they change the relationship dynamic. So I'm not in a *rush*, but I don't want to waste time on a non-starter. I don't want to look back and wish I'd met the man of my dreams earlier.'

'How about some "no strings" fun in the meantime?'

'I'm having that already, with you and these dates. Whilst a man *could* be round the corner, I'm not analysing every guy in the room at these venues, straining at the leash. In a way, you're *helping* me have a hiatus.'

'Glad to be of service. Relationship first aid as well as *actual* first aid,' he said.

'An ice pack and ibuprofen? Don't give up the day job.'

'Fine. Providing you rest up.'

'Will do.' She drank. 'Ooh, any dates on the horizon? Ideally not skiing or judo.'

'There's something on Friday if you're around. They were going solo, but if you don't mind the risk of line dancing, we can tag along. It's cocktails and cowboy stuff.'

'I do like a cocktail—'

'I'd noticed.'

'And I rock a Stetson.'

'I'll bet. So I'll drop you a text.' He stood. 'Okay if I head off?'

'Definitely. And thanks. *Doc.*'

He shook his head. She loved it when he found her "impossible".

He went to the kitchen, rescued his dried shirt and pulled it on. She hid her disappointment that the show was over. He bent down for a hug, insisting she didn't get up, then let himself out.

She lay her head against the sofa cushion. Contentment flooded her soul. Then an idea from earlier resurfaced, so she hobbled to the dining table, grabbed the laptop, and returned to the sofa. She sat with the computer on her lap, legs outstretched, feet on the coffee table.

Resting up, Doc. As instructed.

She accessed LinkedIn, searched for a "Sandrine", found someone who matched the location and company type, then cross-referenced with Facebook.

She closed the laptop lid. Sandrine was *beautiful*.

If there had been even a glimmer of hope for Beth's chances with Sam, it had vanished now.

Chapter Forty-Four

On Tuesday morning, Sam got a text from Paul with an invitation to dinner. The message was ominously brief and plain.

That afternoon, another worry appeared. Kristin, who he'd earmarked for the upcoming double date pairing, pulled out. It was a shame; she'd match well with James, a plainclothes colleague of Maya's.

He went to the office's swanky but soulless kitchen, making a builder's tea while he pondered the problem.

If only the app was live, or better populated with data. Opportunities were coming thick and fast, as if a love virus was circulating. It wasn't that. Dating apps were waning in popularity. Users, like Beth, were becoming disillusioned. Arguably, her company's investment was a gamble.

He texted Beth, asking if she knew anyone who wanted a night out, with a wildcard shot at romance. George and Maya were coming, making a nice group of six.

She replied with a potential candidate, so he agreed to stop by and discuss. By then, he'd know the Paul and Lena situation, and they could either fret together or share a sigh of relief.

He got to Paul and Lena's at six. His pulse was pounding, palms clammy. It was a world away from the high of last week, the moment the train pulled into Gare du Nord. Then, he'd sensed opportunity in the air, the world opening up like a giant flower. Now, there was a heaviness.

Paul opened the door. 'Come in, mate. Good to see you.'

'You too.' They embraced.

So far, so normal, so formal.

In the kitchen, Lena pulled him into an unusually tight hug—ominous, as if she'd had a bad diagnosis from a doctor.

She put her mouth to his ear. 'Thank you.'

Paul lifted a glass from the kitchen island and handed it over. Bubbles rose.

Sam took it, perplexed. 'Cheers.'

'It's been in the fridge for *ages*. We were saving it for our anniversary, but *someone* spoiled our plans.'

'But you got to drink champagne *at source*, as it were... right?' He held his breath.

Lena laughed. 'Oh, *so* much.'

He smiled nervously.

Paul laid a heavy palm on his shoulder. 'It's okay, mate. We're all sorted. I mean, it wasn't pretty for a couple of minutes, but she's

forgiven. I was scared shitless. I can't lose her. She's my *everything*.'
He took his wife's hand. 'This was my fault, not hers. Being selfish.'

She pulled him close. 'And I was stupid. I didn't want to ruin what we have. One or two kisses don't tell you who the best person is. Only a *connection* does that. Destiny. And this man is mine.'

Paul raised his glass. 'All thanks to you, buddy.'

Sam wanted to punch the air in elation and relief. His introduction *had* created a solid relationship.

Instead, he clinked glasses. 'I simply sow seeds. You two grew it.'

'Cheesy, but accurate,' Lena said. 'So you should know that... we're hoping to grow a seed pretty soon.'

Sam coughed. 'Well, that's... great news. But please, *don't* keep me updated on progress. Frequency. Ideal dates. Success rate. Stuff like that.'

'Promise.'

'So,' Paul said. 'How was *your* trip to Paris?'

'Much less sex, by the sounds of it.'

'But... any sex?' Lena asked mischievously.

Sam tutted. 'In the first three days? Come on, you know that's not my style.'

'Okay. Let me rephrase that. Any candidates? Any seeds sown that you want to grow?'

'Um... what's for dinner? I'm starved.'

She took his arm. 'Oh no. You don't get off that lightly. It's happened, hasn't it? You've found her?'

At eight o'clock, he said farewell to his dear friends and headed off, keen to tell Beth. He felt more upbeat than ever about the app.

In Beth's hallway, bursting with the good news, they shared a celebration hug, then she led him to the living room. Quincunx was perched on the sofa arm and greeted Sam with a familiar accolade.

For the first time, he stroked the parrot's feathers.

'You knee okay?' he asked.

'Yeah. Thanks for everything with that.'

He waved it away.

They sank onto the sofa, and she talked about Eve, who was the next date candidate. Beth had completed a profile on the spreadsheet, and Sam said he'd add her to the app database. Maya had provided a good outline of her colleague James, but whatever the result of the work-in-progress compatibility check, the date was happening. A good night out would even act as a celebration for Sam and Beth's renewed optimism.

'When are you seeing Adrian again?' he asked.

'Next week. He's away this week. You're going back to Paris?'

That filled his chest. 'Yeah. A couple more days, tie up the loose ends.'

'Tie up? Didn't know you were into that kind of thing.'

'There's a *lot* you don't know about me.'

She laughed. 'I find that hard to believe. But when you *finally* put your profile in the app, I get to discover all the dirty secrets.'

'Let's hope we're still speaking afterwards.'

'Yeah. Besides, you'll need the next tranche of funding soon. Then, nearer launch time, you'll need a ton more, or a lot of savvy moves to keep the wheels turning.'

'True,' he reflected. 'More users equals more revenue, but consumes a lot of cost. Server time is effing expensive. The build is the easy part. We need word of mouth and a financial backstop. Or I'll have to flog the house to keep the business afloat.'

She shook her head. 'That won't happen. And if it does, you'll find a way.'

'Thanks. Partner.'

The doorbell rang.

She rolled her eyes. 'Sorry. Give me a minute.'

'No problem.'

While she went to the front door, he ambled around the room, studying her decor, ornaments and parrot paraphernalia.

Voices drifted in from the hall. She sounded vexed.

Concerned, Sam hovered, unseen, near the lounge doorway.

'Beth,' a man was saying. 'You've been on at me for months to get my arse into gear, and suddenly *you're* on the fence. What's that about?'

'I'm busy, okay? You said this was important. I'm doing you and our marriage the courtesy of careful consideration.'

'Oh... then, if that's the case, why don't we go away for the weekend? Nothing seedy. I promise, Beth. Just... so we can chat like adults. Try to figure this out. Because I believe we *can*.'

Trembling slightly, Sam deliberately cleared his throat and strolled into the hallway like it was no big deal.

Beth's husband was tallish, quite lean, with short fair hair and stubble. His hand was on her arm—until he whipped it away.

She jolted. 'Sam.'

'Yeah. Sorry, I need to go. We... covered everything, didn't we?'

'Oh. Er. Yeah.'

The guy was eyeing him warily.

She coughed. 'Sorry. Sam, this is... this is my... This is Leon.'

Sam reached for a handshake. Businesslike yet excruciatingly awkward.

'Good to meet you, Sam.'

Everyone assessed the other.

'So I'll head off and speak... soon.' He shot Beth the most relaxed smile he could muster.

'Yeah, definitely. Thanks for popping over.'

'No problem. Thanks for that... data... for the project... and... see you around.'

'Will do.' She lightly touched his arm. 'Take it easy.'

He gave Leon a courteous nod and saw himself out.

Why is she reconsidering? Why all the dating if she's going to run back to something less than perfect?

At least I have the sense to wait for the right match.

Bring on Sandrine.

Chapter Forty-Five

I t was a week of inertia for Beth. Declan had the hump, wavering about releasing Sam's next round of funding. He protested that he had a lot on his plate, but that was probably code for the fact that she hadn't slept with him yet.

At home, she went back and forth over the meeting with Leon—mulling his suggestion, cringing at the unexpected encounter in the hall, and stupidly avoiding something that Sam would rightly mock her for. She needed to take her own advice.

So on Thursday evening, she set about the hateful task. If Sam had put Paul and Lena into the spreadsheet as a baseline test, shouldn't she put her own longstanding relationship on the line? Logically, for the app to indicate potential successes, it must also generate many mismatches. The question was whether her experience matched Sam's logic and their combined R&D efforts.

As she painstakingly filled in Leon's profile, her mind flip-flopped between hope and dread. If their match was awful, did that offer consolation? What if it was good—should she plug the shredder into the mains?

It was heading towards midnight when she totted up the score.

She decided not to burden Sam with the result. It wasn't *really* his business. This was already a momentous decision. Marriage had been than *one-third* of her life. She'd been Beth Moore for so long that she barely remembered her maiden name or who she was at age 21.

Plus, her version of the matching process lacked the finesse of Sam's algorithm. Spreadsheets only contained *data*. And, for a matter like her marriage, there was a lot to be said for gut feel.

On Friday, she pulled on tight jeans, soft shoes, and a favourite top. Nothing too flirty; she didn't want to steal this James guy away from Eve. Besides, policemen weren't her thing.

As Eve wasn't keen on a Western cocktail bar, they'd relocated the evening to the bowling alley. It wasn't original, but Beth had amused herself with thoughts of whipping Sam's ass in the bowling lane. She'd never mentioned her prowess.

She arrived to find Sam, George and Maya already at Lane 30, at the end of the alley. As they shared a hug, Eve walked up, and Beth introduced her to the group. A few minutes later, James arrived. The expression as he clocked Eve—flawless skin, flowing blonde hair, athletic frame—said everything.

Looks aren't everything, James. Sam doesn't put people together based on who they fancy, but who they match with at a more fundamental, lasting level.

Okay, he's not put us two together, but that's mitigating circumstances. He's an exception. There are always exceptions. The app won't be 100% infallible. Just a shame that the statistical error is such a perfect guy.

George volunteered to put names into the scoreboard. Beth chose "Annie", Eve's pet name for her, then explained its source.

Sam said, 'You learn something new every day', then asked to be listed as "Quin", also citing a private joke. Beth understood: he didn't want to publicly say "Studmuffin".

As the drink, bowling and conversation flowed, Beth grew unsettled. James wasn't following the script. He spent as much time talking to her as he did to Eve, who was visibly interested. It wouldn't be a problem if Beth fancied James, but he was too triangular in shape, overflowing with police anecdotes, and liked every TV show that she hated with a passion.

Sam, who'd also noticed, sidled over and laid a hand on her shoulder. She stroked it affectionately, aiming to give James sufficient signal to back off. Sure enough, his attention flitted between their faces and that touch.

Well done... babe. You hit the perfect note.

James's diatribe about paperwork ground to a halt. 'Oh. Oh, sorry, Beth, I didn't—'

George grimaced. 'Oh dear, mate. Don't try to break up the golden couple.'

Eve slipped her arm into James's. 'And you're a *detective*?'

He raised a hand. 'Aw, look, no hard feelings, okay?'

Maya slapped his back. 'Oh, sarge. No wonder you're single. Can't read the signs.'

He growled. 'Thank you, WPC Cole.'

'They are very cute together,' Maya added, moving to Beth's side. 'Come on then, what's his best feature? Other than the ones we can see.'

She met Sam's eye. 'The way he kisses.'

He nodded respectfully.

'What about you, Sam?' Maya asked.

'Her honesty.'

Eve laughed. 'Lame answer. Try again.'

'She's... very understanding of people's faults.'

'I am not!' Beth chuckled.

'Of mine you are.'

'Nobody's perfect, babe.' Their gazes locked, and she thought he'd drive home the point with a kiss, but he didn't. No need. George and Maya already knew the score, and James had got the message.

'Drink?' James asked Eve.

'Great.' She faced Beth. 'We'll sit out this game. See you for the third one, okay?'

'Have fun!' Maya chirped.

James put an arm around Eve's shoulder and escorted her towards the bar.

Sam indicated the computer. 'Set us up, Georgie boy.'

Beth sipped her cocktail while George typed in the four names. Maya stood at his shoulder, playing with his hair, then both excused themselves to the loo, promising to return with drinks for all.

Beth sighed contentedly. 'And then there were two.'

'What do you think?' Sam thumbed towards Eve and James.

'Better than fifty percent chance.'

'Then thanks for putting her forward.' He raised his glass.

They toasted. 'We're a love creation machine.'

'Love creation *facilitator*.'

'That's what I meant—' She gripped his arm. 'Oh *shit*.'

'What?' Alarm creased his face.

'Don't look, don't turn round, but *fuck*, it's Declan.' She angled her head, trying to hide in plain sight. 'What's *he* doing here? What are the *chances*?'

'Honestly? Firstly, it's a bowling alley. Also, the probability of meeting one man in this area is small, but you've met thirty-three, so...' Sam's eyes sparkled.

'Thanks. Snake.' She looked over his shoulder. Declan was wandering in their direction, but hadn't spotted her.

'I'm just saying—'

'Yeah, yeah. Seems like I'll be bumping into exes for the rest of my life.'

'I'm not sure they're exes if you only gave them two hours of your life.'

She poked out her tongue. 'No, and most won't remember me. But there are a couple I have to avoid, and Declan is one of them.'

'So do you hide behind the photocopier at work?'

'No, but I could use a photocopier right now.' She pressed into him.

He squeezed her hand. 'Better than that, you have me.'

She rotated him slightly. It was the tensest game of hide-and-seek, but luckily, her hiding place was a legend. 'You're my knight in shining armour, mate. Again.'

'What are friends for?'

She peered round his shoulder... at the instant Declan looked in their direction.

'Shit,' she whispered. 'He's coming.'

He cupped her waist. 'Hey,' he murmured. 'We're old hands at this. *Babe.*'

Her pulse pounded. Seconds crawled past. She daren't look. She willed Declan to pass by. His snide comments and probing questions could ruin the evening. They weren't in the office now; he was free to call her a bitch, and there would be no professional comeback. He might get a slap, though.

As they stood stock still, waltzers frozen as the band stopped playing, Declan entered her peripheral vision.

She grimaced, mouthing, 'Sorry.'

They exchanged a resigned look. He licked his lips and pressed them to hers.

I know what this is. A "please don't disturb us" pose. Like pretending to be asleep on the train so nobody asks you to move your bag. Well done, mate. Brilliant idea.

His lips moved across hers. She tilted her head, kissing with more intent. He kissed back.

Declan moved closer.

She put both arms around Sam's waist and sank into the kiss. Her body was on fire with the feel of him. In other circumstances, her eyes would be closed, revelling in this joy, but she kept them open. Sam was watching too. At such proximity, she couldn't glean his emotions, only that his gaze followed hers as she tracked their nemesis.

She looked at his lips on hers. He did likewise. Then she glanced left, hoping Declan, in the gloom and flashing lights of the bowling alley, couldn't see her pupils. Sam looked. Then he refocussed, drew her hip inwards, and kissed her—pretending, of course—more passionately.

Why don't you get the message and fuck off, Declan? I'm with my (fake) boyfriend and we're (fake) making out. Please leave us alone.

All the same, please stay. I want to keep kissing Sam for a week or so.

She lost track of time. It was probably only twenty seconds of uninterrupted lip-locking with the man of her dreams, but people need to breathe, and she didn't want her libido to go supernova, so she broke off.

Chapter Forty-Six

A *true* loving couple wouldn't stop cold, so when Beth's divine lips left his, he popped a kiss on her perfect nose. A sweet, cutesy touch to ram the message into Declan's skull that his subordinate was no longer available for dating, and he should avoid a scene in front of her new (fake) boyfriend.

But does the guy have any social graces at all?

Sam swallowed the lump in his throat. Blood coursed through every vein, supercharged by two pints of IPA and a gallon of manufactured desire. He hoped to hell he'd done the right thing.

This Declan git finally broke the sexual tension. 'Beth?'

Clearly. And you know it.

Sam observed him. About six feet, dark hair slicked back, strong jaw. A touch of Cary Grant, maybe.

'Oh, hi Declan,' she said. 'Fancy seeing you here.'

'Out for a bowling night?'

'Yep. Just waiting for our friends. Crack on with the next game.'

Sam noted she wasn't asking any questions: a clear "piss off" vibe. He took her hand.

'Come here much?' Declan asked.

'Now and then.'

Dickhead boss smiled thinly. 'Sorry, being rude, who's this?'

She squeezed Sam's hand tightly.

What is she signalling?

'Oh, sorry. Declan, this is... Max. We met through the app. You know? My project. Well, not the app, it's not live yet, but via Sam. The matchmaker. The client.'

'Ah, I see.'

Sam decided to offer his hand. 'Good to meet you. Declan, was it?'

The interloper shook. 'Yes. Beth's on my team. Think I remember the project. So... it's working out between you two?'

'Yes.' Beth lay her head on Sam's shoulder. 'I'm lucky that Sam introduced Max and me. You could say we're one of his... success stories.'

Declan took a half-step back. 'And you said you'd had *such* bad luck with men.' He smiled condescendingly.

Sam's bile rose.

Poor Beth.

But she returned fire. 'Yes, but perhaps I judge people harshly. I don't think I ever met a date that I wouldn't at least be civil to afterwards.'

Declan nodded patronisingly. 'Me too.'

You could cut the atmosphere with a knife. Sam begged the guy to go away, get back to bowling, or being slimy with a different woman, or *something*. He put his arm around Beth's waist, pulling her close, giving a signal so clear that even a blindfolded cretin could see it. For a split second, he was tempted to pat her bottom, but that wasn't "needs must".

Instead, someone slapped him on the back. 'Right! Let's get to it.'

Beth's eyes were saucers. She worried her lip. George and Maya were scrutinising the interloper.

Oh shit. Bigmouth George!

Beth was on it in a flash. For better or worse. 'Declan, this is Maya. Maya and... Sam.'

Declan's brow arched. 'Sam? The app guy?'

What are you doing, Beth?

Her expression said she'd done something idiotic or brilliant... and wasn't sure which. George looked at everyone and then, to Sam's relief, showed why he'd been captain of the debating team.

George's hand shot out. 'Declan? Good to meet you. Beth's a lifesaver. A real asset.'

Maya sipped her drink and looked away, possibly to chuckle or turn red.

'Thank you, Sam,' Declan replied. 'She was a big advocate for your app. How is the development going?'

George glanced at the real Sam. 'A lot of the back-end work is done. We're considering a focus group for the front end. A few select people, friends, some of the lucky folks who've benefitted already.'

'Like us, honey.' Beth raised her face to Sam, and they rubbed noses.

George nodded. 'Absolutely. I'm sure Maya will help too.'

The WPC beamed. She smooched George's neck. 'Yes. He... Sam, here, found me as part of the development process too, so, yes, if you need me for anything, maybe a testimonial, I'm there.'

'Well, this all sounds excellent,' Declan said. 'It's good to see your matchmaking skills in action, Sam.'

Hearing his name, Sam *almost* looked at the guy, which would have ruined things. Instead, he kissed Beth.

And Declan didn't say anything.

But George said, 'Thank you, Mr Black.'

'Okay, and I'll look at releasing the next round of funding.'

Beth was deep into the kiss, arm around Sam's waist. They could have stopped—the guy had got the message—but why offer wriggle room for more searching questions? The façade might crack at any second. And he *was* enjoying kissing her.

'I appreciate that,' George said.

'We should get back to our game, Sam,' Maya said, joining in the ruse.

Sam didn't flinch. He was too busy resisting the temptation to cup the back of Beth's head.

'Yes, sorry, me too,' Declan said.

Beth broke off. Sam licked his lips.

How lucky am I to have such a fantastic-tasting investment partner?

'See you at work, boss,' she said without irony or malice.

Declan coughed. 'Yes, have a good night.'

She winked at Sam. 'Oh, I intend to.'

Sam thrust out his hand. 'Good to meet you.'

Declan shook. 'You too, Max.' Then he nodded and, mercifully, *finally*, he buggered off.

All four exhaled in unison.

George slapped Sam's back. 'Well, *that* was a ride.'

Sam gripped his friend's shoulder. 'Legend.'

Maya laughed. 'Oscars all round.'

Definitely for me. I haven't kissed like that in too long. Still, it worked.

Beth hugged George. 'Thanks, mate.'

'No problem. Anything for Sam... sorry... *Max*.'

Sam poked her side. 'She likes getting into scrapes, don't you, honey?'

'All in fun. No harm done.'

George clapped his hands. 'So who's for some bowling? Or do you two want to get a room?'

Beth waved at the lane. 'Set them up, "Sam". I need a minute in the loo.'

'Ooh, me too,' Maya said. 'Nearly laughed myself into a pee.'

The girls linked arms and headed across the venue. Sam tracked them for a second, then sought out Eve and James.

'Looking for the newbies?' George asked.

'Yeah.'

'They bailed. Saw you two getting it on and reckoned that was it for the night.' He nudged Sam. 'Plus I think he wants to—'

'Take down her particulars, yeah, yeah.'

'Come on, let's get a beer while the ladies are in the bog, doing their lippy or whatever.'

This was a perfect plan. Sam needed a stiff drink—and to get his heart rate back down to normal. He couldn't believe they were getting away with this crazy ruse.

Chapter Forty-Seven

B eth closed the cubicle door and sat on the loo seat, regaining her composure. She was amazed by the passion in Sam's kiss. *Apparent* passion. The guy had really put on a show. And she'd had a front row seat. No—she'd been the co-star. And the role was *perfect*.

Shaking off the introspection, she joined the policewoman at the basins. One simple enquiry later, and they were chatting like longstanding girlfriends, hushing voices when others entered the washroom. More than once, Beth blushed. She played along with the woman's impression that the Sam relationship was real, but hoped George and Maya weren't drawn further into this game of pretend dating and impersonation.

Outside, they bought drinks and then joined the boys, who were waiting with barely concealed impatience.

Maya bowled first, then George. This gave Beth time to assess Sam's—the *real* Sam's—mood. Everything was fine: smooth waters, relief at their success, even a hint of amusement.

Happy, Beth relaxed into the game. Meaning she thrashed them.

Despite the departure of the date couple, the foursome decided to get their money's worth and have the prepaid third game, but George and Maya wanted five minutes' break to play a giant Space Invaders. Under the uniform, Maya was a real character, as the conversation in the loos had demonstrated.

Beth sat on Lane 30's bench. 'Sam?'

'Yeah?'

'We've had enough surprises for one day, so before either of those two tries to embarrass you even more than bloody Declan did, um, I may have spun Maya a few yarns.' She winced.

'Hmm. Have you been impossible? *Again.*'

Beth laughed nervously. Inside, she was gorgeously titillated. 'She asked about our sex life, and said she bet you were good in bed, and I said you are, and she asked whether you went down on me on, like, the third date, and I accidentally said yes.' She clasped his knee. 'Sorry.'

He looked deliberately unamused. 'Well, I *would*... I mean, I *might*, with the dream girl, in the proper circumstances.' He glanced around. 'Anyway, George asked me stuff about, like, what was your best feature?'

Her skin prickled. 'What did you say?'

'"Smile".'

'No way. I thought men would always say "Tits".'

'Well, I haven't seen them, but the smile is a winner anyway.' He winked.

She patted his hand. 'Ah, thanks. Anyway, glad it didn't get blokey and sordid.'

'Oh, he asked if you were okay with anal.'

'What?' She smoothed her throat. 'What did you say?'

'I said you're not that type of girl. Wild guess. Hopefully, that warns him off asking you out. I mean, if Maya doesn't last.'

'Thanks.'

'No problem.'

'If that's a criterion for *some* blokes, should we put it in the app?'

He grimaced. 'Feels wrong.'

'To you maybe, but the app is for *everyone*. "No anal" will be a dealbreaker for some people.'

'But if we're using our friends as test data, we'd have to ask *them* the question, which would be *really* awkward.'

'So get them to fill in the profile themselves. But we need to add Yes, No and Maybe as answers.'

'Okay.' He slugged from his beer bottle.

'You want my *real* answer?'

'No, thanks. Besides, if you *do* put a test profile on there, I'll see anyway.' He raised a hand. 'Not that I'll be interrogating it.'

'Because you won't be seeking a match.'

'No.' His eyes lit. 'But imagine if *you* matched one of the test people. That would be *mad*.'

'Stranger things have happened.'

The four played the final game. With a third cocktail inside her, Beth's form dipped, which was no bad thing, as she didn't want to embarrass the poor souls again.

George and Maya were smooching a little. Beth felt embarrassed and jealous. She should be grateful for what she'd already had—a spine-tingling minute with Sam's lips on hers.

Maya picked up her shoulder bag. 'We're heading off.'

There were hugs and kisses all round.

'Thanks, George,' Beth said. 'Let's hope Declan doesn't ask to meet "Sam" again.'

George's face fell. 'Oh, shit.'

Sam shrugged. 'Cross that bridge later.'

'I can bluster for you again, mate. Play the part.'

Beth hugged Sam's arm. '*Max* here is *brilliant* at playing along, aren't you, darling?'

'We make a good team.'

She looked up and was delighted to be rewarded with a kiss on the lips.

Maya tugged George's hand. 'Come on, Mister Speed Merchant. I want to take down your particulars.'

He shoved her. 'Hey, that's my line!'

Maya shook her head despairingly, then led George away.

Beth's shoulders relaxed.

'So how was that?' Sam asked.

A tipsy smile appeared. 'You mean the *quality*, or how brilliantly you read the situation?'

'I don't want marks!'

'Then well done for rolling with it. Yet again.'

'Thanks.'

She drained her drink. 'But a solid nine out of ten on the snogging.'

'Whatever. Just *please* don't offer pointers. Nobody needs to know I'm not the best you've ever had. They only need to believe we're dating. Right?'

She put an arm around his shoulders. 'Sam, my friend, I think we're smashing it.'

'Yeah. I do believe we are.'

She checked her watch. 'Head off?'

'Absolutely. Job done.'

'I'll change my shoes, meet you outside.'

'Great. I'll order the taxi.'

A couple of minutes later, she passed through the entrance doors and found Sam waiting.

'Five minutes,' he said. 'Okay to share? That's not weird, is it?'

'Not at all... *Max.*'

He poked her arm. 'Don't. *Stirrer.*'

She ushered him towards the wall. The warm night air and her modest but influential blood-alcohol level clouded her head for a second. Yet she was happy. Another couple created, another brilliant night. Not a date, but still. And, yes, the danger aspect, but that was oddly thrilling. Infinitely better than listening to Number 19 blather on about the "faked" moon landings. Yes, they could have done without bloody Declan's appearance, but shit happens.

Around them, singles, couples and party groups came and went. A hen do, which had luckily been at the far end of the venue, tottered out and headed down the street. Sam angled his head at them and shot Beth the expression of a disapproving parent. She giggled.

Then a lone figure exited the doors.

Shit.

She pulled Sam's hand, manoeuvring him like a barrier. Again.

His shoulders fell. 'Oh, no.'

'Yeah. Mr No Social Graces is still here.'

She pressed tight into Sam. It was pointless. Declan knew what Sam—Max—looked like. But surely even *he* wouldn't want another thorny conversation?

Declan gazed around, no doubt seeking out his cab.

She held the back of Sam's neck. 'It's a good job you're a 9,' she whispered. 'And that I like you.'

Their lips met. She rotated their bodies for a better view of Declan's impatient striding. He checked his watch.

Whose cab will come first? No point in wondering.

She closed her eyes and drifted off. For a few seconds, the kiss was an echo from earlier, tinged with panic and tension. Then, loosened by good spirits, Sam let go. Their mouths moved together, moist and supple.

Oh, man.

He gently broke off and tried to assess the situation, but had his back to the road.

'Still there?' he murmured.

She manoeuvred him. Declan was at the pavement edge, looking up the road, first away, then in their direction.

She tensed. 'Yeah.'

'Good job I like you, mate.' He winked *sooo* tenderly. 'And that you're a 9 too.'

A million butterflies danced in her belly. 'Ta.'

He put a hand in the small of her back, eased in and kissed her.

This is a drug. Think about Emma Watson if you need to, Sam. Think about Sandrine. I'll be whoever you want for the next minute or so.

He appeared to do exactly that, because the kiss blossomed. Driven by libido and instinct, her fingers stroked the nape of his neck. He responded by bringing the other arm around her, locking them in a lovers' embrace. A few seconds of heaven, and he broke off.

'Let me know, okay?' he breathed.

She assumed he meant notice of Declan's departure, not that he'd hit 9.5 on her kissing scale. She peeked over his shoulder. Declan was watching them.

'Will do.'

Then she drew his head down and kissed him with unrestrained desire. Quickly, he was giving equal quarter. Pretty soon, her watch would beep with an Elevated Heart Rate warning. She ached to grab his bum, kiss his neck, feel their groins ease together.

If this is acting, mate, then the Bafta goes to Max... whatever Max's surname is. Studmuffin, probably.

And then his tongue was in her mouth, hers in his. She let out an involuntary low moan, snogging harder, deeper, rotating him bodily. The train was running away. Now he was against the wall, and however hungrily she kissed him, he took it all in his stride.

If you want a show, Declan, you slimebag, this is Drury fucking Lane.

And then Sam broke off. If it even *was* Sam. More like Max, a raffish playboy younger brother.

Without meeting her eye, he looked for their spectator.

'Night, Beth. Night, Max,' called her boss.

Unbelievable.

She tossed a hand up in silent, dismissive farewell, then cupped Sam's jaw and kissed him. No tongues this time, but he responded with a languid tenderness.

A car door slammed.

Chest heaving, she held her forehead to his, as Sam's eyes tracked something, moving, moving, gone. And she eased back. Despite euphoria, her stomach was heavy. What would he do, say? Was this the end?

She was about to ask when he spotted something.

Oh crap, Declan's forgotten his wallet or whatever. Seconds out, Round 3...

But Sam encouraged her away from the wall. 'Ours is here.'

She sank gratefully into the cab's back seat. Sam closed the door, and the car pulled away. There was no point in tenterhooks, in delaying the inevitable Morning After discussion.

'Are we still okay?'

'Yeah,' he said softly.

'Sure?'

'Yes, Beth. Really. It worked, didn't it?'

'Yeah.' She gripped his hand. 'Thanks.'

'It's to both our advantage. Professionally and personally. And I've had worse evenings.' His wink spoke volumes.

Every muscle relaxed. 'Me too. So... we're going back to my place?'

'*You* are. Max might, too, but I won't.'

She frowned, amused. 'What's the difference?'

'I'm pretty sure he'd want to... take down your particulars. I get the impression Beth and Max are at it like rabbits.'

'Why?'

'Well, if they kiss like that in public, imagine what they get up to in *private*.'

She laughed, welcome levity. '*All* the positions.'

And their gazes locked. That spark, the invisible connection, the one that had been there since the picnic. Even without an audience, she wanted more.

Come on, mate. Be Max. Be Max for a night.

Chapter Forty-Eight

Sam's poor soul. Beth was an intelligent, vibrant, attractive woman, and the snog had generated a maelstrom of endorphins. They'd joked about Max, but he was in there, busting to get out. He would have unclipped her bra without hesitation.

Maybe not in public, but here, now, in the cab? Max is undoubtedly less rusty at the casual, one-handed clasp release than I am...

Get real.

Even if she was interested, they couldn't *actually* date, not while working together. Plus, he'd never have a fling, a stopgap, until destiny arrived. That would be caddish, unconscionable, cruel. Beth meant so much—as a friend, a sparring partner, a business mentor, a source of career change—yet she wasn't the dream.

He was *so close* to destiny. To throw it away at the eleventh hour would be absurd. And he was less rusty at the whole dating game, thanks to Beth, which was a win.

The evening had been full of wins: for teamwork, for the app, for Eve, for James, for many things.

'Tonight was good, right?' he said.

'*Weird*... but good.'

'Was I a bit full-on?'

'I mean... I'd have settled for having my neck nuzzled or my arse groped.'

'I'm *not* groping your arse just for show.'

But another minute, and it might have happened, eh, Max?

'Okay.' She glanced out the window. 'But... the neck thing?'

'Are you *coaching* me on how to fake date you?!'

'No!'

He poked her thigh. 'Good.'

'You have most of it down pat.'

'Err... thanks.'

'I meant that if you don't want to French kiss, you could smooch me here.' She touched a spot behind her ear. A soft, inviting spot.

'You are, once again, impossible. And the *queen* of digging us deeper.'

She whacked his arm, eyes wide in mock offence. 'I could hardly introduce you as Sam, could I? Not after he'd seen us snog. There would be serious questions about the wisdom, hell, the impropriety of getting involved with a client.' Her expression grew serious. 'We're bloody lucky that Declan hadn't met you before. That's probably his one redeeming quality. He trusts me with clients. He's a box ticker. It's not about the person, only the financial return.'

'Or... he's giving you enough rope to hang yourself. I bet he'd laugh at the irony if a dating app brought you down.'

She grimaced. 'Yeah.' She waved a hand. 'Anyway, George was a star. Declan seemed to buy it.'

'Well, if you get sacked on Monday, we'll have our answer.'

She massaged her cheeks. 'That is not at all funny.'

He put an arm around her shoulder. 'Gallows humour. And look at it this way. If it's contractually forbidden to have office relationships, too, Declan would be silly to chase you.'

She beamed. 'That would be a brilliant upside!' She winced. 'But for completeness, I'll check the rules to see if it's allowed for you and me to date... *pretend* date... You know what I mean.'

'I do. And if it's forbidden, dump me. We can say it *was* true love, and the app does work, but we can't date due to the conflict of interest.'

They high-fived. 'Or... you ask for a different account manager. Great idea! In Declan's mind, Sam is being handled by someone else. Even make it a bloke, and *they* can do the admin and mentoring stuff, or "pretend to" if I have a word with them.' She patted her thighs, excited like a girl. 'Then you and I can work on the project behind the scenes, and keep dating.'

He coughed. 'Beth?'

'What? It's an excellent plan!'

'We aren't *actually* dating. Remember that *tiny* detail?'

Her cheeriness vanished. 'Oh. Yeah. But let's keep everything crossed this facade doesn't blow up.'

He nodded hard. 'Especially as you're the person inside the company who *believes* in this app, and we can't have the funding cancelled, not when things are going this well.'

She scoffed. 'Declan would pull it in a heartbeat purely to spite me.'

'Doubt it. Not if he realises we're onto a winner.'

'True. And Max has shown him that.'

They high-fived again.

A couple of minutes later, the car pulled up outside her house, and he hopped out.

An invisible shiver went down his spine. A memory. Walking Milly to her front door, that first kiss, going inside, to the sofa... and more.

This felt more like a date than any recent dates. Probably because he'd had a delightful snog with a woman he was escorting home. Yet there was no continental music, no moonlight shimmering on the Seine, no vast iconic metal tower. No unidentifiable... *magic* in the air. If there had been, he would definitely have ensured Beth got to bed safely...

She joined him on the pavement. 'Sam?'

'Yeah?'

'I'm a grown woman, and I'm pretty sober now, and this is a safe neighbourhood, so I don't need walking to the door. But will you anyway?'

'What are friends for?'

She actually led the way, and an automatic outdoor light came on as they stopped at the door.

She pulled him into a parting hug, one of companionship. One that said, "We've been through the wars and emerged unscathed."

Then she looked him straight. 'Thanks for tonight. And good luck with Sandrine.'

'Cheers. Good luck with Adrian. Or Leon.'

'Thanks. I'll keep you posted.'

He nodded. Still, something nibbled at his gut. 'But promise me something.'

'Anything.'

'If there *is* a sniff of problems at work, with Declan, whether because of tonight or not, if he sees through this circus, let me know, okay? Early doors. I'll do what I can, fall on my sword if necessary.'

Her jaw dropped. 'To save my job?'

'Yeah.'

'Why would you *do* that?'

'Because you put up with a *lot* in me. And you went out on a limb at the *exact* time you should have taken a safe bet project. Especially not one which is a red flag to Declan.'

She rubbed his shoulder. 'I don't regret a second of it, Sam. In fact, I wish I'd met you months ago.'

'To save The Thirty-Three?'

'Yeah. And it would have been better for you too.'

He frowned. 'Why?'

'I wouldn't have met Callum or Declan, meaning they wouldn't be a factor, and you wouldn't have the ignominy and shock of your platonic business partner sticking her tongue in your mouth.'

He was pretty sure that *he'd* initiated the French kissing. Odd that it had happened in England and not, as he'd anticipated, in France. Odder still that it was with her. Or perhaps not? Circumstance had demanded it... though it was an easy demand to bow to.

He winked. 'True. Let's hope I'm not mentally scarred for life.'

'Me either.'

He took her hand in both his. 'Don't worry. We're good, Beth. We're all good.'

'Great. Onwards?'

'Onwards.'

Chapter Forty-Nine

Beth's Sunday was quiet, reflective. The marathon kissing session with Sam felt like a hollow victory, a last meal for the condemned woman. With Sandrine on the scene, he'd surely say that this pretence had to stop.

Although Beth hated this, it was for the best. She had to let go of Sam. It was a waste of time and energy to wish things were different. She needed to get real, not fixated. She had to accept him for who he was, and have faith in his ability to help *other* people—like her. Undoubtedly, recent experiences had made her more self-aware and ready to start again. He'd been a huge force for good in her life.

At work that week, Declan's demeanour was different, as if he saw her in a new light, perhaps wary, disgusted, intrigued? They had a civil conversation about Saturday's happenstance meeting at the bowling alley. She almost put her foot in it, but managed to maintain the "Max" charade.

Declan's body language around Adrian had changed, too. It seemed the two had buried the hatchet. Maybe they'd gone golfing again, and Adrian had let the cheating slimebag claim 18 holes-in-one.

The men hadn't discussed the Beth and Max situation. She knew this because Adrian didn't storm up to her desk and say something like, "What are you trying to do, two-time?" That would be a kick in the gut—Declan ruining her chances with Adrian.

Instead, Adrian arrived for Thursday's date as agreed. He'd changed and shaved—for a second time that day. He was turning up the wick, signposted by a peck on the cheek as a greeting.

After a pleasant drink in a bar, they went on to the restaurant. Hardly original date fare, but she'd been spoiled recently.

As the evening went on, she remained alert for The Thing. The dealbreaker, a warning sign, something which set her teeth on edge, the red card for a potential future together.

It didn't come. Perhaps Adrian *had* turned on the charm, but it suited him. He wasn't obsequious. They hit it off. True, he glanced at his phone too much, and the spiteful belittlement of his ex-wife was damn uncomfortable, but otherwise, they had a lovely evening. More than once, he touched her hand where it rested on the table. When he tried to play footsie under the table, she pulled back, then relented—it wasn't excessive.

Outside the restaurant, she let him kiss her. For the first two seconds, it was romantic and enjoyable. Then, when she reciprocated, he ramped up the intensity—vertically. Even her snog with Sam was more well-judged—and that was acting!

He held her head tightly, kissing violently, his other hand wantonly squeezing her bum. Fearing a grope of her chest, she pulled away, struggling to breathe.

She shot him the evils. 'What the hell was that?'

'That was a kiss. People do them. On dates,' he said patronisingly.

She shook her head. 'No. No, you crossed a line. You need to slow the hell down, Adrian.'

His nose wrinkled in disdain. 'Is that so?'

She folded her arms. 'Yes.'

Resignation flooded his face. 'Sorry.' He reached out. 'Look, Beth—'

She stepped back. 'No. Some people would call that assault. We're not doing this. Goodnight.' She strode away.

'Maybe Declan has a point,' he called.

She stopped, swivelled, and marched back. 'We have to *work* together, Adrian. You made a mistake.' She curled her lip. 'I'd had a *nice* time tonight. *You* caused this. Not me. I'll see you tomorrow. And if the word around the office is suddenly how much of a bitch I am, it'll be clear who's the *real* villain.' She took a deep breath. 'Night.'

Adrian, sensibly, didn't follow her.

Still, it was a broken night's sleep.

As she headed to work on Friday morning, Beth struggled to suppress ridiculous nerves. She'd done nothing wrong, yet worried about what the atmosphere at the office would be. She hadn't considered the downsides of a workplace relationship that went sour. The Declan situation already hung over her like the sword of Damocles.

Adrian arrived and blanked her. This was to be expected, though she didn't regret issuing his marching orders.

As the day wore on, she noticed Adrian conversing with Declan in his office. Probably trading notes about Ms Undateable. She went to the Ladies for a few minutes, working things through, hoping to gain perspective.

As she passed Adrian on the way back to her desk, he looked up from his computer to sneer, like she was dogshit on the sole of his shoe. She lifted her chin.

I will not be cowed by you and your new buddy.

She sat, pulling her keyboard close.

Someone came to stand at her shoulder. 'Do you have a minute, Bethany?'

Her jaw clenched. Why was Declan calling her "Bethany"? That was the name Mum and Dad used when she was in trouble. Normally, it was "Beth", "Daughter" or "Darling".

She glanced at Adrian and got a thin smile in return.

Oh shit.

'Yes, sure,' she replied.

Declan led her into his office and closed the door. She sank into the seat in front of his desk, her stomach boiling with the most awful feeling.

He showed her the PC screen—Sam's LinkedIn page... with his profile picture.

Oh fuck.

'So what's the story, Bethany? Impropriety with a client? And you lied to hide it?'

'We're not dating. It was... a silly lapse.'

'It damn well looked like you two are an item. You were certainly being *very* friendly. *Getting off* with him. And that's the beginning of a relationship. Even I know that.' His tone was patronising, cocky, a victor crowing from the podium.

'But—'

'And you said you met through his app. If you *didn't*, that was a lie, so why should I believe he has the requisite skills, or that this product will ever find a market?' He leaned over the desk. 'You even had his friends cover up for the two of you. How deep *is* this deception, Bethany?'

'Mr Black—'

'Is there even an app? Perhaps you're simply stealing money from this company for your boyfriend.'

'Sam Carter is a *legitimate* software engineer.'

Declan tapped the screen. 'Oh, I can see that. And I'll be making his employer aware of all this.'

Quaking, she held back tears. 'I can *explain*.'

'It had better be the best explanation ever heard on this planet, Bethany. I want the truth in writing.' He steepled his fingers. 'You're on unpaid leave as of now. I'm freezing the funding. If there's no satisfactory explanation, and either or both of you are in breach of contract, Sam Carter's account is terminated. All monies to be returned.'

'I... understand,' she sputtered.

'And I'll review whether your employment here should continue. You've breached confidence and protocols. I'm not an *idiot*, Bethany. I know you're not thrilled to be working for me. But if there's any spite in this, any personal animosity, you've made a *fatal* misjudgement.'

Never had a bigger pot called a kettle more black.

Black. The irony.

Her mind whirled. She wanted to throw something, to bludgeon the vindictive tosspot with a paperweight. However, thanks to the stupid march of progress, paperweights weren't a thing anymore.

Never a heavy, blunt object nearby when you need one.

She opted for a response that wouldn't further jeopardise her career. 'There isn't any spite. But I can... appreciate your perspective.' She stood, jelly-legged. 'I'll head home. Thank you for... leaving things open. I'm sorry for what happened at the bowling alley.' She forced a smile. 'Have a good weekend.'

She, however, would not have a good weekend. There would be crying, and wine, and pizza. And Quincunx would learn a lot of interesting new words.

Chapter Fifty

All day Sunday, Sam worked on the app. Partly it was necessity and impatience; the James/Eve hookup had given him renewed confidence. Partly it was to occupy his mind, which might otherwise get stuck in a replay loop. Beth truly was a 9.5 on the kissing scale. However, those kisses were nothing more than a dry run for the real deal.

The week flew by. Two projects at work reached Go-Live. In the evenings, he laboured until midnight on the app database, algorithm, and rough designs for the UX.

On Thursday, he boarded the 14:01 Eurostar to Paris. He'd asked to take the meetings on Friday so he could spend the weekend sightseeing. He hadn't specified the sights he wanted to see, namely Sandrine... in daylight, moonlight, and possibly by bedside light.

Friday morning was spent alongside Sandrine. She was as chic as he remembered, now with an office-appropriate playfulness to her demeanour.

At lunchtime, they went to a bistro down the street. He talked about the bowling evening and Beth's badminton injury, always referring to her as a friend. Nevertheless, Sandrine was intrigued, openly asking if he was single. He said he was waiting for the right person, without intimating that it might be her.

Walking back to the office, she asked whether he was busy that night, suggesting they start with dinner and see how things went.

Could a guy get any luckier?

That afternoon, as Sam was pondering how to phrase "I told you so" to everyone back home, his mobile rang. It was the boss. He excused himself from Sandrine's desk and went into a small meeting room.

The call wasn't to check on progress with project handover technicalities. Nor was it to ask about the weather. Not even to warn him off dating a future colleague.

It was to metaphorically kick him in the nuts with a hobnail boot.

He listened, quaking, sinking into a chair, as the charges were outlined. Breach of employment terms, using company resources for personal gain, and deception. He was to come into the office on Monday with a full explanation, and should consider his position fragile at best.

He mustered a plaintive response, an acceptance of the terms of surrender, and hung up.

The River Seine was probably lukewarm at this time in July. He pondered what it would feel like to jump off the Pont au Change. With any luck, a passing barge would knock him unconscious, and he'd sink to the bottom, drowning painlessly rather than thrashing around and then being rescued by a misguided passerby—Sandrine, knowing his luck, because he'd have to explain the source of his malaise. They might laugh about how they'd laughed about this exact scenario. Maybe he *would* get mentioned in Le Monde: "Local girl saves tourist". Perhaps he'd get the kiss of life she'd promised.

Sure, his life would be screwed, but a snog from a French beauty would take the edge off.

He examined his life choices. There had been mistakes, chiefly in the "Breaking company policy" area. However, the company had only discovered the moonlighting because his boss had received a call from a guy called Declan Black.

Sam didn't like the direction his logic was taking him.

The call was surely caused by the chip on Declan's shoulder about his date with Beth. Which was caused by the woman's insistence on having a drink with—and then rudely casting aside—half the county. If she hadn't gone hell-for-leather at the dating game, she wouldn't have alienated Declan. Or been so desperate for a successful love story that she'd leapt on Sam's app idea with all her weight. Or leapt on *him* with all her weight... and tongue... and wandering hands.

And she had mocked his cautious, organic, single-minded approach to finding a dream partner. That was worth an unvarnished, "I told you so". He'd show Beth who was the fool. And he hoped she'd feel guilty as hell for triggering this entire shitshow.

He stared at his phone, dearly wanting to give her a piece of his mind.

No. He'd have the good grace to say it in person. In the meantime, he was going to get shitfaced.

The restaurant was an out-of-the-way place, not on the tourist drag. It was busy, yet a diner didn't have to raise their voice above a hundred others in seventeen languages.

He liked it. Typically Parisian but not very Sandrine. He suspected she'd chosen it for intimacy. Since receiving the catastrophic phone call, he'd put on a poker face, but she sensed something was up. Initially, he glossed over it. At this point, the first bottle of red they'd chosen was too dry for his taste, so she picked out something more rounded, and they chugged that while devouring a baguette's worth of pre-dinner bread basket.

During the starter, he alluded to a problem at work. They finished the second bottle of red. By the main course—a gorgeous beef dish—he'd revealed his matchmaking ability, the dating app, and the moonlighting as CarterSoft. Laudably, whilst having a few kilos of squashed Bordeaux grapes sloshing around his system, he didn't mention the Beth part. Sandrine was looking unbearably lovely, and it was a bad idea to give the impression that he had another woman on the go. Beth was a friend. Sandrine was his destiny.

By the time dessert landed—a fat slice of rich chocolate cake, plus a half-bottle of sweet wine to share—the topics had become even more personal. Intimate. Enlightening. Unlike him and Beth, Sandrine *had* had a threesome. Four times. She highly recommended it. He hoped she didn't wheel out a surprise guest for the end of the evening. That wasn't what he'd envisaged for his first time with Mademoiselle Right.

He paid the bill, praying that the dent in his bank balance would be filled by a wage packet next month. That forlorn hope accompanied him as they emerged into a sultry city night. His face must have shown it, because Sandrine took his hand and escorted him—her swaying less than he—to the riverside. They were apparently en route to her flat, and he hadn't yet cried or puked, so the evening was going pretty swimmingly, all things considered.

A full moon was reflected on the rippling waters of the Seine. Opera drifted down from somebody's window. The buzz of traffic, the sounds of impatient horns. A skein of geese in the navy sky. And he was on the arm of a single, attractive, intelligent woman he'd met in Paris.

They'd stopped. And he was struggling to recall *exactly* when they'd decided to go back to her place and not his hotel, or even say goodnight outside the restaurant.

And then she kissed him. And suddenly life didn't seem like such a shitshow after all.

Chapter Fifty-One

B eth trudged home from work. It was four miles, but she didn't care. If she rushed, she'd get to the wine faster and be talking to the toilet bowl by nine o'clock. This way, fresh air calmed her, allowing her to gain some perspective.

On the way, she texted Eve and Danni, but neither was free for the evening. Quin would have to suffice as a feathery shoulder to lean on.

She ordered fish and chips, which arrived five minutes after she got home. She slathered it in salt and vinegar, opened a bottle of Chardonnay, and filled her empty soul with calories.

Then she took Quin out of his cage, retired to the sofa, and fussed him.

'I can't wait to finish this sodding app. If I can't have Sam, it'll be a relief to say goodbye.'

'Stud-mu-ffin,' the parrot deduced brilliantly.

She scoffed. 'Yeah, and that's the problem. Why the fuck couldn't I be working with Quasimodo?' She stroked plumage. 'Ha ha! Quasimodo. The Paris connection. Get it?'

'Stud-mu-ffin.'

She looked into his beady eyes. 'Please stop saying that, mate. I'm trying to forget that part. It's his bloody fault. If he wasn't gorgeous and perfect and fun to be with and chivalrous and giving and funny and smart and...' She tossed her head back and growled. 'I wouldn't have kissed him, and none of this would have happened.'

Quincunx cooed and rubbed his head against hers.

'What the hell am I going to do?'

'Fuck-in Deeecclan,' the bird squawked.

'Too bloody right.' She held in laughter: this wasn't a remotely funny subject.

Was it better to resign? If she wasn't pushed, should she jump? No more days sharing an office with Declan... or Adrian. The app was—or possibly *had been*—the project she'd enjoyed the most. How could any other client provide as much excitement, nourish her so well?

She sipped the second, large glass of wine.

Without more funding, the app would stall. Sam, unless he'd been keeping his cards unbelievably close to his irresistible chest, didn't have six figures sloshing around his bank account. He might complete the build, but things would go no further. Would this give him enough satisfaction? If he perfected the algorithm, filled the database, and even knocked up a functional front end, he could prove it was *possible* to codify his matchmaking skill. If he ran a few names through the app, it might even confirm that the existing couples *did* statistically match.

Even better if Sam proved that her marriage was doomed from the outset.

No, not *better*. Sadder.

She sought solace in her brother. The time difference to Australia was ideal; he and Alyssa would be waking up, having a perfect couple-y Saturday morning.

She told him The Paperwork Decision. He was relieved. More than that, he had a crazy idea. The timing was perfect. This would be a hell of a tonic: get out of Dodge. If she could arrange parrot-sitting, the plan was a go.

Whatever happened next week, life couldn't carry on as it had been. Even if Beth wasn't in charge of her *career*, she could take *love* by the scruff of the neck. It would be good to have some distance from Sam, too. How could their friendship survive this? It didn't bear thinking about. Then she remembered him saying that if things went tits up at work, she should call, and he'd do his best.

She checked the clock: 22:17. An hour later in France. Unkind to ring now. Knowing her luck, she'd call just as he was taking Sandrine in his arms for the first time. Beth couldn't sabotage that. She'd already done enough harm. Whatever else, Sam deserved love. A forever love. Besides, if he returned home with a girlfriend, he'd be in a better mood to deal with the fallout.

Beth wouldn't.

She slammed a fist into the sofa cushion.

Fuck my life.

She'd gone into this project with high hopes, with everything to gain. She'd met the best man, had the best time, and it had cost her job. She'd met the *wrong* man, someone she could never truly have had. Maybe *she'd* been the one living in a dream world. Perhaps this *wasn't* what true love felt like.

Have I deluded myself? Have I put Sam through all this embarrassment and jeopardy for nothing?

What have I done?

Before any tears came, she finished the wine, switched off the lights, went upstairs and ran a bath, in the forlorn hope it would relax her. She stripped off and examined her figure in the full-length mirror.

Tan lines from the picnic showed the margin between work and fun. Fun with Sam. Even better with Max...

There'll be more fun next weekend. Can't wait for quality time with Leon.

She rummaged around in a seldom-used drawer and pulled out some beachwear, holding it up to her body. There was plenty of time to pack... particularly if Declan threw her under a bus.

She sank under the bubbles and rested her head on the end of the tub. The rising heat brought perspiration to her face, and when she wiped it away a few minutes later, there were tears mixed in.

Everything was so clear now. This was all her fault. The ceaseless dating, trying to shake off the self-loathing of the divorce. Throwing herself at an unavailable man on the pretence of a game. How stupid—the woman who was always quick to see the tiniest faults and reject men immediately, why the hell hadn't she taken heed of Sam's glaring obstacle and given up the chase?

Now, she'd cost herself a job, a friend, and the golden opportunity for thousands of other people to find love.

What a stupid, selfish cow.

Chapter Fifty-Two

S am's mind stuttered into life like an irascible generator on a winter's morning.

The hotel room was a lot smaller than he remembered. This was because it wasn't his hotel room. It was somebody else's hotel room.

No, not hotel room. Bedroom.

A shiver of realisation wracked his body. The room was warm, a window cracked open to let the Parisian air and noise bleed in. Faint pastry smells drifted past his nostrils. He wiped sleep from heavy eyelids.

'Bonjour.'

He jolted, a reflexive, 'Fuck' spitting from his lips.

Pieces of the puzzle—the corners and edges, anyway—assembled with remarkable speed.

'Are you okay?' Sandrine asked.

Surreptitiously, under the too-hot duvet, he ran a hand over his body.

Not dressed. Just boxers. Of course. That happens when you have sex with a beautiful French—well, half-French—woman. After drinking the European wine lake.

But how the fuck did I...?

She turned his face towards her. 'Not a wine guy, are you, Sam?'

He cleared cobwebs, rubble and fur from his mouth. 'Not so much.'

'I'll get you a glass of water.' She slid from the bed and left the room.

She wore navy pyjamas with three-quarter bottoms. The short-sleeve top was fastened with two buttons. He attempted to recall whether he'd seen what lay underneath. And how he'd got here. And into bed. And whether they'd lain awake chatting. Or had been awake for other reasons.

His ardour stirred.

She perched at his waist and offered the glass. He drank. The water was as reinvigorating as a skinny dip in the Norwegian Sea. His mind blazed. Sandrine—leaning forward, stroking his forehead—deserved The Morning After Conversation.

'Um, sorry, but can you... like... fill me in on... things?' Hardly ideal that his memory of the perfect first night of love and romance would be second-hand news.

She giggled. 'It's not War and Peace. The kiss by the river was *very* nice, then things went downhill. The kiss here was okay, but you were flagging. I was a little. We got as far as underwear, then I needed the loo, so you had a lie down. When I came out, you were dead to the world.'

He winced. 'Sorry.'

'You had a bad day yesterday, didn't you?'

He laughed, hollow. 'You could say that.'

'Shame it didn't end with a bang.' She winked.

He propped himself up. 'You deserve better than the state I was in.'

'Yeah, that's what I thought. So I hopped in and turned out the light.'

He stroked her leg. 'Sorry.'

'It's okay. Besides, it's the weekend. Pronounced "long and lazy".' She kissed him and stood. 'I'm having a shower. Then I'll run out for breakfast.'

'Er... okay.'

The bathroom door closed. He slumped into the bed. This wasn't how it was supposed to be. What a way to make an entrance. At least he hadn't fallen in the river or woken up underneath a roadsweeper... which would be extremely on-brand. Beth would laugh like a drain at his haplessness.

The shower ran. He tried again to piece together the evening, but only succeeded in replaying the afternoon. The call from work. The catalyst for a first romantic date which had been wasted because he was wasted.

The shower finished. Somewhere in the high-ceilinged, one-level, four-room apartment... possibly... a phone rang. And rang. And ceased.

Sandrine entered, towelling her hair. Now, he was sure they *hadn't* got beyond the underwear stage. Because she was naked. He shifted position, creating a wave in the duvet to hide his arousal.

She was lithe, with bonier shoulders than he liked, and an outie. On her hip was a discernible mark which, on scrutiny, appeared to be a small tattoo.

Hmm. Not a fan of tattoos, but this is tolerable.

She pointed towards the shower. 'You want to go in?'

'Great, thanks.' After his hard-on subsided. 'Gimme a minute.'

'Okay.' She went to the wardrobe.

His heart sank. Occupying half of Sandrine's back was a vast tattoo.

He rolled over.

Is this really the dream? Is she truly The One?

'Sam?'

He jolted.

She was assessing him, brow knit, curious. Naked. Desirable... and clearly desirous. She didn't *need* to parade around, showing what he'd missed out on. Or perhaps this was who Sandrine was: comfortable in her own skin, in her own home, in the company of a guy she'd spent the night with.

Either way, it was a slam dunk to have sex with her. For one, he was at full sail. For two, if she was lying down, he wouldn't have to look at the dragon-mermaid-sword-skull thing decorating what was probably a lovely back. For three, she was up for it. But that wasn't the turn-on it appeared. This *come-hither* vibe didn't sit well with him.

Beth had judged it better over the last few weeks. Their evolution towards kissing had been more organic, more honest... and that was only *acting*.

Still, and he'd learned this from Beth, he had a natural guardedness that needed to be shaken off. Hell, Sandrine had wined and dined him, shown him the City of Love, and taken him under her wing.

So he threw back the duvet and went to her. She surveyed his body.

He laid a cheek against hers. 'Breakfast sounds good.'

She clasped his backside. 'And afterwards, maybe come back in here.'

He kissed her temple. 'Yeah. Maybe.'

The shower woke him up. Putting on yesterday's underwear sobered him up. Breakfast filled him up. Sandrine cheered him up... to an extent.

She picked at croissant crumbs. 'This was a mistake, wasn't it?'

He sipped the industrial-strength coffee. 'Which part?'

'The third bottle. Bringing you home. You're not that guy, are you, Sam?'

Getting sad drunk and shagging on the first date certainly wasn't how he'd envisaged destiny unfolding.

'Are you that *girl*?'

She pursed her pretty lips. 'A bit. But for the right guy, I'll stick, not twist.'

'And who's the right guy?'

'Remains to be seen. But if you want to carry on from where we left off...' She glanced at the bedroom.

He took her hand. 'Whatever the French equivalent of "rain check" is, how about that? I *could* stay here all day, and it is *really* tempting, but my life is waiting for me to fix it. My work life, anyway. And a friendship.' His shoulders fell. 'If I still have one.'

She frowned. 'With me?'

'Oh, no. Someone else.'

She smiled weakly. 'I see.'

'I still have it with you, don't I?'

'Yes.'

That was a relief. 'Good. So... okay if I head off?'

'If you think that's best. If not, stay for some fun?'

That was Sandrine. Fun. Yes, he wanted fun, but their versions of fun didn't align. Of course, when she moved back to the UK, her "living it large in a foreign city" crusade might evaporate. Things could morph into the kind of easy-going, tease-and-banter-filled good times he'd had with Beth.

Sandrine could still be The One. The first box was ticked: meet, and fall for, in Paris. He'd never known how the journey would unfold from there. Sensible: Beth had mocked him enough for mapping out the exactitudes of the fantasy meet-cute; to have

295

itemised the next forty years would have been anal. And Beth hated anal. Yet she'd have to concede that the notion of encountering a beautiful, cosmopolitan, vibrant woman in this city hadn't been so ridiculous all along.

And although he wanted to sleep with this woman, it could wait. Circumstances would be better next time. A visit with more... romance. More *feeling*. He needed convincing that she wasn't seeking merely a boyfriend, but something more. Their goals had to align. The dream was of forever, not a fling.

So he told Sandrine thanks but no thanks, she was a sexy woman, and he'd had a memorable evening—the parts he *could* remember. He went to the bedroom and pulled on his remaining clothes, ready to brave a bustling midsummer Saturday on the Metro. Whilst hungover and a bit regretful.

In the apartment, that phone rang again.

It's mine!

He yanked on the second sock and darted into the kitchen-diner.

'...yes, this is Sam's phone,' Sandrine was saying. 'He's in the... oh, here he is.'

Sam froze, throat drying. Was this the boss, bearing an olive branch?

'I'm Sandrine. No, it's fine. We were awake. I'll put him on.' She tendered the phone.

He pressed it to his ear, excitement balancing dread. 'Hello?'

The line was dead.

He stared at the screen, then went to the caller list. He sighed with relief: only Beth. He tapped her number. It rang twice, then went to voicemail. He hung up.

'Okay?' Sandrine asked.

'Yeah. Got cut off.'

'Oh.' She looked at him with resignation. 'You run along, then. I hope things work out. Really.'

'Thanks.'

She drew his head down to hers. The kiss was intense but brief. Then she showed him out.

As he rode the hot, packed tube train to his hotel, one thought occupied his mind.

Have I made a colossal mistake?

Chapter Fifty-Three

As a distraction from the maelstrom that was his love life and employment situation, Sam focused on one thing he could control: the app.

He spent Saturday in his room, finessing the matching algorithm, pausing occasionally to gaze out across the city skyline. A huge early lunch made him feel almost human again. He rang Beth a couple of times, but it went to voicemail. Was she *blanking* him? Had he done something wrong? *He* was the one who'd lost his job.

There had to be another explanation. He'd find out when he saw her.

He ate dinner in the hotel, then crashed out at half nine.

By noon on Sunday, he was back in London. The crazy adventure was over—but he was walking into a storm. Possibly more than one.

As the train whisked him down to Winchester, he felt held by two pieces of elastic; one attached to Paris, egging him to explore a future with Sandrine. Another pulled him, like a necktie caught in a waste disposal unit, towards the wreckage of his life in the UK.

He couldn't move on until he'd faced the music; music which began, like the portentous opening chords of Beethoven's Fifth, at VentaTech the following morning.

He dumped his suitcase at home, had a second shower, then went to George's house. Someone neutral had to weigh in on this debacle.

His friend was hoovering. *Hoovering.* He'd never seen George hoover. Or dust.

The cause was obvious. Sam was happy that George seemed about six months shy of weekend IKEA visits, dinner parties, and buying a puppy, but that didn't need discussing. Fixing.

As Sam's world *did* need fixing, or certainly analysing, he gave his friend chapter and verse. The real, *platonic* relationship with Beth. The fakery. The work meltdown. Sandrine.

As George hadn't completely changed his spots, he wanted details about Sandrine. Sam told him everything. The moonlight kiss, crashing out, the tattoo, her eagerness, the feeling that reality wasn't living up to the dream. Six weeks ago, George would have called Sam a dickhead for turning down morning sex—or any sex. Now, he barely batted an eyelid.

'This whole bloody thing's a crossroads, mate,' he said. 'Sandrine? She'll wait, right? She needs to. Priorities.' He pulled two bottles from the fridge, cracked them open, and handed one across. It was barely four o'clock, but this wasn't a "cup of tea and everything will seem better" conversation.

They plopped onto the sofa. 'I can't give up on the app.'

'No,' George insisted. 'You won't. Not with all the grief it's caused. I mean, how can things get *worse*?'

'They can't.'

'Exactly. There's opportunity in every crisis. Look at me and Maya.'

'True. Now there's at least *one* copper in the city who won't ticket you.'

George gave Sam the finger. 'What I reckon is this.' He glugged the beer. 'The universe is sending you a sign that the app is going to change your life.'

Sam scoffed. '"The universe"? Who are you and what have you done with George?'

'It's a Maya thing. Don't ask. Point is, everything happens for a reason. Paul and Lena's wobble. Me getting pulled over. Having Beth as your VC bod—'

'Which will either make me or ruin me.'

George grabbed Sam's leg, matey and supportive. 'Ask yourself this. How much do you *really* want to hang onto your job?'

'Why, you reckon I'm already screwed?'

'I'm saying it's only a disaster if you want it to be. The *real* tragedy is keeping a job you don't give a shit about, but tossing the app on the fire.' George shrugged. 'That's how I see it.'

'But working with Beth is going to be impossible.' He shook his head. 'If we don't thrash this out, things are over, and nobody else at her company will ever be as good to work with, or enthusiastic—'

'Or kiss like she does.'

Sam thumped him. 'The kissing is what bloody well started this.' He necked half his beer.

'Then go solo. You're a good enough developer. You already have CarterSoft. Most of the work is done. And we'll all support you, advocate for the app.'

'Support isn't the problem, Georgie boy. It's money. If Declan Black knows about all this, he'll pull the funding. Then I'm buggered.

The app goes nowhere without more investment.' He put his head in his hands. 'Which I can't provide if I lose my job.'

'But you have to at least get a working beta version, even if the Beth situation is a casualty. You have a business inside you, mate.'

Sam slouched back. George was right. Appy Ever After was so close. Even if the app failed to find an audience, it would still be a valuable learning experience that he could take forward to whatever came next.

He chuckled. What irony if he let dating—fake dating—kill a dating app.

'Okay, mate. But to prove the algorithm works on a few... guinea pigs... I need more data. Soon as.'

'I'm on it. Send me the mahoosive spreadsheet and I'll get everyone to fill in a proper profile. Flesh out your... starter pack. I get your logic, absolutely. You want to put all the couples in there and get great percentage matches. Rob would love that. I certainly would.' He glanced around, as if concerned his character metamorphosis would be discovered. 'I think Maya's the real deal, mate.'

Sam nodded. George was stating the bleeding obvious. Proof that sometimes love can come from many unexpected sources, and when you're least expecting it. Sometimes, trying too hard, pursuing a path you foolishly believe is correct, leads to disappointment.

Which turned his thoughts to Beth. How she'd almost, if not completely, brought down the house of cards. The woman who desperately wanted a perfect dating app had put the skids under it.

That hurt.

But he didn't want to spend the evening on George's sofa, drinking his beer, railing against Declan and tearing strips off Beth, so he headed home, ready to drink his *own* beer and work out what to say to her. How not to let the whole matter go nuclear. Or *more* nuclear.

He unpacked the suitcase, tossing the dirties in the half-full washing basket, ready to launder a load. When he tipped the basket into the washing machine, a single blade of grass fluttered to the kitchen floor.

Huh? Who's been putting grass in my clothes?

He sank to his haunches, the realisation dawning. He ran the grass through his fingertips. It was a legacy from the picnic, the day when he'd realised that Beth was impossible... in the best way. Her intentions were only ever good, her attitude always supportive or curious.

It was cruel to blame her for this shitshow. He couldn't chastise her for all those prior dates—she deserved a second chance at forever love. Why not blame *himself* for agreeing to go ahead with his friends' suggestion about the app in the first place? *That's* what had triggered the lunch with Beth. Even so, meeting her wasn't the problem.

What had *actually* caused things to go off the rails? Bad luck. Nothing more, nothing less. Coincidence. Probability in action.

In that case, did he regret the fake dating? No, because if that were all undone, it would also erase the positives: winning over Callum and Rob, the removal of constant nagging to forget Paris and *find someone*, let alone the pleasure of kissing a smart, beautiful, funny woman.

They had gone into this with eyes open. There had been no accident, no haste and regret, no stringing along. They were *unlucky* to meet Declan. Simple as that.

Just a shame that it had such ripples.

Weeks ago, he'd had a choice. He could have told Beth, "I don't think we should kiss any more", but the big prize—and his libido—had won out.

Sometimes life is unfair. You try to do the right thing, but get rewarded with a kick in the head. They were on a mission of love, for heaven's sake, and the world had thanked them with one catastrophic wrong turn. There were always going to be setbacks with the app—all projects have that—but this was an emotional hit, not a technical one.

Technical issues are easy to fix. Saving his job, the friendship with Beth, and his future career?

That seemed like a mountain to climb. Yet he had to try.

Chapter Fifty-Four

B eth only slept because she took a herbal sleeping pill to quiet the maelstrom in her head.

It was bitchy to be screening Sam's calls, but she couldn't get over the fact that he'd snared his dream woman, while she'd self-sabotaged their friendship and her career.

There was something else, too. A thunderbolt of realisation that perhaps she'd taken something for granted. She woke in a cold sweat at five a.m. and couldn't get back to sleep.

Maybe Sam's reticence all along was simply because he didn't fancy her. Why had she assumed he did? She wasn't vain. Not everyone liked her look or personality or whatever. Perhaps the private joke about her being "impossible" was no joke. Perhaps Sam's banter was merely his good nature and a way of maintaining a pleasant working relationship.

And the kissing? It was *acting*. There was intensity but no… passion or feeling.

She lay there, reliving every breathtaking sensation. The snog outside the bowling alley was *faked* lust. Yes, she'd had to set aside the inclination to kiss him *properly,* but when they stopped, he moved on like it was no big deal. True, he'd scored her a 9, but that was to avoid hurting her feelings, wasn't it? The experience hadn't delivered him an epiphany.

Worse still, kisses that meant nothing had affected *everything.* The fake dating—her idea—was about to ruin their lives. Except Sam would have Sandrine, and she had nobody.

She was back to square one.

Fuelled by coffee, she spent the day doing chores, trying—and failing—to keep her mind off the myriad issues. How to say sorry? How to rescue things? Had she been too hasty and final with Adrian? Was it worth fighting Declan, or should she move on to pastures new anyway?

At five o'clock, during a cuppa-and-cake break, the doorbell rang. She frowned. Amazon weren't due.

Curious and a mite nervous, she went to the door.

It was Sam. Her pulse spiked. She took a step back.

'Hey,' she said, quiet, nervous.

'Hey.' He held up his phone. 'Why did you call? And then blank me? Is everything okay?'

She put a hand on the door, ostensibly nonchalant, actually for support. Her mind spun, stomach roiled.

'What do you reckon?'

'I... don't know. That's why I came. Plus, I wanted you to know that I'm probably getting fired. Thanks to Declan squealing to my boss.'

That was a piledriver to her chest. 'What the *fuck*?'

He fell dejected. 'Yeah. Our little act, our apparently brilliant name-swapping game, didn't work.'

Her head drooped. 'I know. I'm on the ropes too.'

He leaned against the porch wall. 'Shit,' he breathed.

They mentally circled each other.

Her hand quivered. 'I'm suspended. Declan has me over a barrel. And it's all my fault. I'm sorry, Sam. I'm so fucking sorry.'

'Shit,' he repeated.

She looked at him with hooded eyes. He moved closer, half-reaching towards her. Two souls cast adrift. Two souls who needed a soothing hug from a friend. Life would feel a bit less shit if she got her friend, her fake date, her playmate back.

She clenched a fist. *Damn all this.*

'No, it's okay, Beth, really. I fucked up too. If I get sacked, it's for what I did at work, not what I did with you.'

'All the same...' She shrugged limply.

He nodded sadly. 'If Declan hadn't called my boss, maybe I'd have sneaked under the radar.'

'If I hadn't tried to date him, he wouldn't be on me like a fly on shit.'

Sam frowned. 'That makes *him* the fly, which isn't fair on you. Let's say he was... a wasp at a picnic.'

'On a cherry tomato.'

'Or a pork pie.'

She moistened her dry lips. 'He wants to break us up. And kill the dating app, as well as our careers.'

Sam jammed his hands in his pockets. 'Might already have done.'

'Hmm. Might have.'

A squadron of swallows raced past.

Sam shifted on his feet. 'Maybe this is a sign. Maybe this... whatever we have... isn't everything it appeared. Maybe you and I *aren't* supposed to work together.' His smile was forlorn.

She took a deep breath. 'So we could shake hands and say "Thanks for everything", or... you're welcome to come in and we can try to rescue this. I have tea. Or whisky. Depending on your current outlook on life.'

'That sounds... good.'

'Be warned, I've been in my PJs all day, and haven't had a shower.'

He grimaced excessively, a spark of the real Sam. 'Then that's a hard pass on sex tonight.'

She turned away before she blushed, then led him inside. They were in the living room for less than five seconds before,

'Stuudmuufffiiin.'

She dashed to the cage and hauled up the cover. 'Fuck off, Quin.'

'Fuuuck off,' the parrot squawked.

Sam corpsed, then held up a defensive hand. 'Sorry, I shouldn't.'

She chuckled, the embarrassment and tension broken by his good humour. 'What a mess.'

'Yeah.' He sank onto the sofa.

'Drink?'

'Beer, if you have it.'

She grabbed two bottles and returned. He was watching her thoughtfully.

'What?' she asked.

He explained how he'd broken his employment contract and used company software. The prognosis wasn't good, but it wouldn't help if she ran, begging, to his boss, and she sure as shit wasn't begging Declan. Still, she could support Sam emotionally and help with the app... if he even wanted that. He had to do what was best for *his* life and career, as she did with hers.

Perhaps this situation was a positive catalyst for change? Sam had the drive to succeed in his business, and was now in a better position, in control of his destiny. Working freelance meant the freedom to travel. To France. He'd obviously found love with Sandrine—that's why Beth had hung up. It was too in-your-face to actually *talk* to Sam's girlfriend the morning after they'd...

Beth shook it off. 'So what's the plan?'

'With the app? That depends. Should we bin it, or what?'

She analysed his body language. 'Don't throw the baby out with the bathwater. Don't give Declan the satisfaction of killing your project. If you need a hand getting it over the line, I'm here.' She chuckled. 'And if I get the boot at work, I'll have a *lot* of free time.'

He raised his bottle and they chinked. 'Ditto.'

'So where are you up to?'

He gave her a summary. They needed more users. Beth had an idea. They required one dummy profile for every possible combination of answers on the questionnaire. This was a BIG number, but creating the data was simply a spreadsheet and formula exercise.

And she was the queen of spreadsheets.

Sam shrugged. 'If you want to be the data guru, great. Drop me the file this week.'

'Cool.' She fingered the condensation on her bottle. 'Something to distract me from real life.'

He moved along the sofa and laid a hand on her knee. Absent of a hug, that was a huge tonic.

'That sucks, Beth. Looks like we're both in shock. One minute, life is dates and finance and opportunities. Next minute, the roof's come down.'

She squeezed his hand. 'You're a wise man, Sam Carter.'

'I simply want people to be happy. Us too, in our own way.' He took a breath. 'So... are we okay?'

'Collectively? I think so. Individually? We'll see what washes out.'

'Should I come to your office and throw myself on my sword? Tell Declan I was the instigator of all the lies, the fake PR story? Say I took my business partner for granted. Took advantage of her.'

Her chest tightened. 'No. It was nobody's fault. Just the universe, and probability, giving us a reality check.'

He picked at the beer bottle's label. 'Yeah. That's what I thought. Odds catch up with you sooner or later. Like George and speeding.' He chuckled sadly. 'Except when he got caught, it turned out well. Us being caught in a lie is unlikely to create a dream finish.'

She rubbed his arm. 'Don't give up, okay?'

'No. And I am serious about taking the blame for this.'

She shook her head. Inside, she melted. 'You are the sweetest guy, Sam, but no. Pointless. Declan isn't the best at listening to reason. So... let's... take a few days. We've got a lot to think about. Work out where our lives are heading, and how the app moves forward.'

'You're a wise woman, Beth Moore.'

'Thanks.'

And, oddly, the mention of her name, her married name, stirred something inside. A realisation that this week, her love life was changing. And what better time to reboot her career, too?

Next weekend was a watershed. She was so excited.

Chapter Fifty-Five

Was there ever a Monday more Monday-ish?

Sam sat in his boss's office, slowly hunching lower in the seat, shoulders collapsing in tune with his life, as the charges against him were read out.

No good deed goes unpunished. You try to do right by the world, help out your mates, have a bit of a kiss with a fantastic woman, and the world shits in your kettle.

Still, he was culpable. Pointless to argue the circumstance, say it was bad judgment, not evil intent. Better to take it like a man. As George had said, perhaps this was one door closing and another opening.

An innocent man who loved his job would be furious at the impending termination of his employment. Even a guilty man, desperate to stay, would try to talk himself out of a hole.

Sam was neither. He accepted the four weeks' paid garden leave, went to his desk, and cleared out his things. Sacked for love. Kind of.

There were two choices for that lunchtime, that day, that week. Sit in the pub and wallow, or seize the opportunity within the crisis.

So he went home, changed, drove to the supermarket and did a huge shop, then settled down at the laptop.

On Tuesday evening, he went to George's and recounted what had happened.

Wednesday was Paul and Lena's turn.

On Thursday, Beth sent over the database of a million entries, and he loaded it into Appy Ever After.

Time for the ultimate road test.

There was only one place to start. The origin story. His first matchmake. His best friend. This was the acid test of the profiles and the algorithm. Real life had shown that Lena and Paul were a brilliant match. If the computer said NO, the app needed more work. Alternatively, his friends' blip was more than that—it was a portent of doom.

Heart pounding, Sam closed his eyes and pressed Enter.

Half a minute later, he dared to look.

Paul + Lena = 96%.

He leapt from the chair, cracking his knee on the underside of the table and swearing like a navvy. It was a good thing he didn't own a parrot.

The clock said 15:38.

Sod it.

He took a beer from the fridge and drank deeply.

An hour later, when he'd calmed down, he put another pair into the algorithm.

George + Maya = 92%.

He punched the air, picked up his phone, and was about to text his friend when a message arrived.

Sandrine wanted to know how things had gone at work.

His chest filled.

She cares.

He told her he'd got the boot, but was upbeat about the future.

She replied, "If you want to pop over, we can hang out. Plus, you have a lot of free time now, right? ;-)"

He leant back in the chair, pondering. Then he pulled up the Eurostar timetable and cross-referenced it with his sparsely populated calendar. He retrieved his wallet, pulled out the debit card, and began typing the numbers into the Payment screen.

A pop-up appeared from another open application: "Run another match?"

His fingers froze. A tiny voice entered his head. A female voice of reason. Something about an inventor being brave enough to try his own product.

He put down the debit card and tabbed to the app browser. It was time for the ultimate test.

He typed Sandrine's name, hit Enter and held his breath. Two seconds later, the results came back. The top spot was held by User192809 with a 100% match. This was logical: as every combination existed in the database, there had to be a perfect answer. It simply wasn't Sam Carter.

So he scrolled down a little. Then a bit more. And more.

A minute's scrolling later, there he was.

Sandrine + Sam Carter = 65%

He slouched against the chair.

Holy shit.

He cleared the results and reran the query. Same outcome.

Catatonically, he slid the debit card back into his wallet. He closed the Eurostar booking tab. His mouth gaped. Either the app was a pile of dogshit, or his Paris dream was in tatters.

This can't be happening.

Or can it? Did Sandrine ever feel like The One? Honestly?

65% laughed at him from the screen. Yet it was nothing more than he knew, deep down, to be true.

Shaking his head, he pressed knuckles into his eyes.

He'd been pursuing a storybook fiction, not attending to facts, observations and preferences. How could he ever admit that his friends were right to mock a dream future that read like a Hollywood rom-com script?

The cursor blinked.

It could be even worse. What if, besides treading water for years, he'd unwittingly passed up a golden chance? How galling if, throughout his matchmaking, during all those double dates, he'd been in the same room as his perfect life partner?

For one, Danni had been all over him. Eve, too, was good-looking, smart and funny.

What's that phrase? Charity begins at home.

He certainly wouldn't be setting up any more couples without running the girl through the app, checking to see if she wasn't a match for him.

Have I already missed the boat?

His fingers hovered over the keyboard.

One way to find out.

He typed "Sam Carter" and hit Enter.

Chapter Fifty-Six

He stared, heart trying to escape his ribcage.

It can't be.

He ran the search query again.

It was.

With a shaking hand, he picked up his phone and dialled. It went to voicemail.

Shit.

He paced the lounge.

Think, think!

She'll be at home.

He pulled on presentable clothes and ran to the car.

He had to find her. She needed to know. Unless she already knew? Maybe it had been clear as day, and only *he* was walking through life with blinkers, or cataracts, or another brilliant metaphor for his inability to see what was staring him in the face.

Her house was in darkness, but he rang the bell. Twice. Three times. He knocked. He looked for movement at the upstairs windows.

Nothing. He tried her mobile. Voicemail.

Shit shit shit.

Was she at *work*? It would mean she hadn't been fired. Which would be utterly brilliant.

Filled with joy and hope, he zipped into town. He'd never visited her office, but this was the time. Even if Declan was there too, surely he'd be in a good mood. If he'd given Beth her job back, perhaps it would be rainbows and unicorns between the three of them.

Sam didn't care. If necessary, he'd bodily march her out the door and tell her what he'd discovered. Was this her last day? If so, he might save her at the eleventh hour. Proof of the app's effectiveness *had* to be music to Declan's ears.

Filled with even greater hope and joy, he hurried to the foyer reception, signed in, and was directed to the 3rd floor. Entering the company's office, he bumped into Eve, who was leaving for the day.

'Oh. Sam? Funny seeing you.'

'Yeah, yeah.' No time for pleasantries. 'Is Beth still here?'

'Beth? No. You mean working here, or—'

'Is she here right now?' he asked impatiently.

Eve frowned. 'No. She's away. A long weekend.' She smiled. 'Celebrating a new start. Such good news.'

'Do you know where she's gone?'

'A place in the Bahamas. Built by some squillionaire. Private villas, sun, sand. No mobile reception. And she's excited to spend time with Leon—'

Sam's bowels loosened.

This is crazy. She couldn't. She wouldn't dare.

'What's the name of the resort?' he asked.

'Err... "Lifetimes"... or something like that. Why?'

'Never mind. Thanks, Eve. You're a star.'

'No, you are. James is a *dream*.' Her pupils dilated.

'I'm pleased. Honestly. But I *have* to go. Dating emergency.'

'Ooh, sounds exciting.'

'It is. Thanks. Bye!'

He fled.

It *was* an emergency. It *was* exciting. It was also scary as hell, mad, and heartbreaking.

As he jogged to the car, he called Beth. Voicemail. Again.

Shit. "Desert island. No mobile reception".

He sat in the driver's seat, chest heaving.

She absolutely had to know the facts. See the proof. Nobody ranked higher in her matches than him. Not even Leon. History alone had proven that.

Nevertheless, it seemed they were trying to rekindle something. Sam couldn't let her embark on more years of okayness. Even if she told Sam to take a long walk off a short, idyllic, rustic pier into sun-dappled, crystal-clear Caribbean waters, he'd have done his best to show her where the ideal future lay.

If he could get there in time.

He drove home.

The first task was to locate the resort website. Easy. Next, flights. A nice selection. Only one with availability. Leaving Heathrow in four hours.

Shit.

Gritting his teeth, he booked, paid—this was credit card territory—and sat back in the chair, wondering what the hell he was doing.

But he *was* doing it.

Upstairs, he threw things into a suitcase whilst calculating the chances of reaching the airport in time. And whether he could survive the flight without vomiting. And what charger adaptors to bring.

The doorbell rang.

'Aaargh!'

He pounded down the stairs and opened the door.

'Are you alright, mate?' George asked, seeing the stress and thunder on Sam's face.

'You did say six o'clock?' Maya added.

'Shit. Shit. Completely forgot.' They'd arranged to go out for a drink.

'What's up?' George asked.

Sam beckoned hurriedly. 'Come in.'

Almost without taking breath, he explained the last two hours, then showed them the laptop screen.

George beamed. 'Mate, that's brilliant!'

'Is it rude to say it was pretty obvious to all and sundry?' Maya asked.

'Yeah, yeah, I've been a dick, I know.' Sam raised both palms. 'But that doesn't get me on the plane, so can we postpone?'

George slapped his back. 'Of course. Want a lift?' He looked at Maya.

She folded her arms. 'You mean blues-and-twos him up the motorway?'

Sam's fingertips crackled at the anticipation of a mercy dash thrill-ride.

'Yeah,' George replied, eyes wide, eager to travel even faster than usual—but legally.

Maya grabbed his chin. 'I love you, pookie, and I'm quite fond of Sam too, but using a police vehicle for personal business? I'd get

suspended for a stunt like that. This isn't *Hollywood*. It's Winchester.'
She faced Sam. 'Just get an Uber.'

He got to Check-In with five minutes to spare. Half an hour later, he boarded.

He sat in Economy, his stomach roiling, remembering those halcyon days when creating a dating app was the craziest thing he had ever done.

He wished he'd taken sleeping pills or had time for a triple whisky in Departures. The best he could do to counteract the hatred of flying was to grip the armrests, focus on his breathing, and plan what the hell to say to Beth. Assuming she was where he expected.

'Shit,' he breathed.

Why didn't I ring the resort and ask for her?

His shoulders collapsed in self-defeat.

I suppose this is a romantic way of doing it. And she likes romance, doesn't she? If not, I'm out of options, because Beth Moore is the Number 1 match in the entire country.

Well, not technically out of options. Numbers 2 to 1000 might be acceptable.

But he hadn't met those women. He'd met Beth.

The plane rolled into motion, engines building to a crescendo.

Even if she says no, I get a few days in the sun.

The choice of in-flight movies was terrible, so he sought solace on his laptop.

He ran profile match queries for Maddy & Ian, Anna & Mark, James & Eve, and Rob & Danni. They all came out above 90%.

He tried Beth & Adrian. 56%

Beth & Declan. 44%.

Then, taking a deep breath, he ran a query on Beth & Leon. 82%.

A decent result, Mr Moore, but I still beat you hands down, so I hope you'll step aside when you hear the game's up. You've had twelve years, and it didn't work out.

So why the hell did Leon think it would work now? Was whisking Beth away for a dirty weekend his last throw of the dice, an attempt at an eleventh-hour divorce reprieve?

Sam sipped his fourth tiny cup of tea. Wasn't it pretty ironic to question the guy's motives?

After all, here I am, flying all this way, like some misguided Benjamin Braddock, to intervene in Beth's life. I've blown a ton of cash on something even more fantastical than expecting love to blossom under a French moonrise.

Unable to stop second-guessing himself, he went through his and Beth's profiles, line by line. Occasionally, he paused to reminisce about their time together, recalling their conversations, validating that the data was based on reality and not purely hope.

Yet data was merely part of the story. As the images burned brighter in his mind's eye, a pattern formed, one of a vibrant, beautiful, *sexy* woman. The loveliest, most life-affirming person. Someone he felt utterly at home with. Belonged with. Desired.

As the plane touched down in Nassau, something had become abundantly clear.

He was head over heels in love with her.

Chapter Fifty-Seven

T he wallowing, air-conditioned cab trundled towards the resort.

Sam couldn't fathom his jitteriness. Surely this was meant to be? A slam dunk. The more he'd examined the last few weeks, the clearer it became... and the more awful and idiotic he felt.

Then he put his finger on it. The nervousness of standing at a precipice. A readiness to embrace a dream future, tempered by the possibility that now wasn't the time. Plus, he was riven with excitement, jet lag, a feeling of not being in control, and a realisation that *this* was the thread the app hung from. If Beth didn't see things the same way the algorithm did, the whole project was worthless. What if the fake dating, the pretend kissing, the superficial gestures of affection were nothing more than that?

What if Beth wasn't, in fact, in love with him?

Soon find out.

The cab wafted to a halt outside a whitewashed building surrounded by palm trees. It was like something from a reality TV show. A dating show.

Beth and I are contestants. Whatever happens, this is a ratings winner. Either she laughs in my face and it's the story of a hapless, deluded goon who reckoned he was good at matchmaking, or we'll be in the papers, a PR story about the app creators—the story we already lied was happening.

He hauled his case from the boot, paid with a handful of notes he'd hastily grabbed at the Foreign Exchange in Terminal 5, and went to the Reception desk.

The walls were decked with pictures of iconic locations. On the ceiling, an old-timey fan rotated. The place oozed class and antiquity.

The clerk rose from his seat. 'Good afternoon, sir.'

'Good afternoon. Which lodge is Beth Moore in, please?'

'And you are...?'

'I... am... her colleague.' Sam tapped his suitcase. 'She left some important contract papers behind. Asked me to bring them over ASAP.' His fingers twitched.

Come on, mate. Don't kibosh this crazy plan. There may be only minutes to save her from a terrible future.

The clerk scrutinised Sam. 'Beth...?' He ran his finger down the register. 'Ah, Parris.'

Sam frowned. 'Paris?'

'Yes. It's that way, sir.' The clerk extended an arm.

'What is?'

'Paris, sir.'

Sam blinked, bemused by the geography lesson. 'Right. Okay. Sorry, I think there's been a misunderstanding. I'm looking for Beth Moore.'

'Yes, I believe you mean Beth Parris. There's no Miss or Mrs Moore staying with us at present. But we do have a Beth Parris and a Leon Parris.'

Sam leant on the counter and ran sweaty hands through his hair.

It's the heat. I'm going mad.

He put on a non-confrontational expression. 'Fine. Thank you. And where is Beth...?' He swallowed hard. 'And *Leon*.'

'In Paris, sir.'

Sam's mouth moved. 'No... but... you said she was *here*.'

The clerk smiled in the way one does to an imbecile. 'Indeed she is, sir. In Paris lodge.'

'Lodge.'

A sweep of the clerk's arm took in the framed pictures. 'The architect of the resort constructed twenty lodges, all named after cities that hold a certain significance in his life. San Francisco for the founding of his first business, London for the place of his first wedding, Paris for the location of his most iconic creation, etcetera, etcetera.'

'I... Ah... Okay.'

This is a mindfuck.

'Turn left outside the main door, sir, and follow the path to Paris lodge.'

'Thank you. Sorry for... the confusion.'

'Not at all, sir.'

Sam's roller case bumped along the flagstone path that weaved between manicured lawns, widely spaced chalets and frankly awful modern art sculptures. Water sprinklers hissed. Parrots squawked.

We'll always have parrots.

He stopped on the steps of a small veranda. A wooden sign on the pillar read "Paris". He glanced around. The nearby lodge was "Marrakech".

What are the chances?

He took a deep breath, determined not to spoil this idyll by creating a scene with Beth's husband, and knocked on the door.

It was answered by an unfamiliar face. Either this sun-drenched paradise had remarkably transformative properties, or this wasn't Leon. Or Adrian. Was Beth shagging someone she'd picked up during the last week? Or someone she'd hooked up with at the resort?

Ah. Wrong lodge.

'Hello?' said the guy. 'Can I help?'

Sam glanced around. 'Er... sorry, I'm trying to find Beth. Bethany. I'm a... friend.'

The guy warily looked him up and down. 'Beth, yeah?'

'Yes, Reception said she was in Paris. This... is Paris?' The train wreck of this visit was now in slow motion.

The guy called over his shoulder, 'Some... guy for you, Beth.'

'Sam,' Sam blustered.

Beth's roommate suddenly got it. 'Oh, *you're* Sam. But aren't you—'

She appeared in the doorway. Breath caught in Sam's throat. A tidal wave of relief swept his body.

'*Sam*?' she gasped.

'Yeah. How's... things?' His brain was too occupied with other matters to form useful sentences.

She eased the guy aside. 'What the hell are you doing here?'

How to articulate that?

He pulled out his phone and scrolled to a picture of a computer screen. The most important message on any computer screen he'd ever seen or was likely to see. He showed her.

A myriad of expressions vied for space on her gorgeous face. 'Wow,' she whispered.

The roommate eyed them both. 'I... think I'll give you two some space.'

She roused herself. 'Yeah, thanks, Lee. Oh, Sam, this is my brother, Leon.'

Brother. Leon. Brother Leon.

Of course. Why wouldn't it be? Things have all been so humdrum these last few days. Life needed a bit of fucking pep.

Brother Leon extended his hand. 'Good to meet you.'

Sam shook. 'Er... yeah. Same.'

'See you later, sis,' Leon said.

'Great, thanks.'

'I'll go for a snorkel or something. For a few hours.' He winked, then wandered across the road to Marrakech and went inside.

Sam stepped closer to Beth.

'Do you want to explain?' she said softly.

Now *Sam* shook himself. The phone was a deadweight in his hand, like he'd been carrying his entire being.

He admired the vision in the doorway. The bikini's pattern was tough to make out beneath a half-buttoned white linen shirt and navy calf-length sarong skirt whose slit ran up to her thigh. She looked like a Bond girl in an iconically Bond location. Heart-stoppingly lovely.

He licked his dry lips. 'You see, I'm working on this app, and—'

She swatted his shoulder. 'You flew here because of this?'

Best not to reveal the bit about believing she was getting back with her husband. Things are embarrassing enough.

'Well... yeah.'

A familiar, uplifting smile appeared. 'Better late than never, though.'

That was a kick in the teeth and a shot in the arm. 'You *knew*, didn't you?'

She nibbled her lip. 'Yes. Sorry. I didn't need a *number*. But *you* did, and that's okay. Really. Nothing worth having comes easy.'

He couldn't comprehend how much pain and frustration he'd put her through. After months of dating unsuccessfully, she'd met her

324

perfect match, only to find out he wasn't interested. She must have despaired.

His head fell. 'I'm so sorry, Beth. I treated you awfully.'

With a finger, she lifted his chin. 'Forgiven. You had *les blinkers de la France* on. The question is whether you believe it now.'

'You did come out top.'

She grinned. 'Only 99% though. You came here on rubbish odds like that? I mean, why don't I get 100%?'

'It's probably the interval between our kids we disagree on.'

'Or you don't like parrots.'

He stepped close. 'Why not? They say nice things.'

'Quin has a sixth sense about people.'

'I've been the blind one, haven't I?'

She pointed at the lodge. 'Maybe not. You always believed you'd find your true love in *Paris*, right?'

'Hmm. I think that absolves me of all blame in this matter.'

Her eyebrow cocked. 'Does it really?'

He put a hand on her waist. 'If we're going to fight, get that 1% out of our systems, let's do it inside. If not, let's go inside anyway.'

She pressed a gentle kiss to his lips. 'Sounds good.'

Chapter Fifty-Eight

He parked his roller case inside and closed the door. The living area was beautifully appointed.

'Do you want the tour... *mate*?' She waggled her eyebrows.

'Definitely. *Babe*.'

She led him to the kitchen, then bathroom, then bedroom, whose centrepiece was a four-poster bed. Diaphanous drapes hung from every side. A slatted blind covered a large window.

Why ever Beth had come here, with her brother, she'd certainly taken a high-end spa break from the rigours of being trampled on by life.

He stood close, beholding the personification of destiny, exploring every inch of her face with a fingertip.

'I... can't believe I didn't realise. I... should have said. Told you.' His words were virtually a whisper.

'What?' she breathed, trying to look into his soul.

'That you are the most amazing, beautiful woman I've ever met.'

She swallowed, licked her lips. 'Same for you. But "man".' She ran soft knuckles across his cheek.

He stroked the open collar of her shirt. 'There's only one thing I don't know about you, Beth, and it's important... no, it's *vital*, so I can be sure that you truly are the perfect person for me.'

'What?'

His finger traced down the margin of her shirt to the first button. He eased it open. Then the second. Third.

She watched him work.

He drew the shirt from her shoulders and tossed it onto a wicker armchair nearby. His pulse quickened. He investigated the waistband of her skirt, located the single button, unfastened it, and let the material drop into his hand. He shook it into rough shape, loosely folded it, and placed it on the chair. His mouth dried.

The pattern on the bikini was, yes, parrots. What they were guarding put a crease in his trousers.

He cupped her chin and laid a long, soft kiss on her lips. He could have kissed her for hours, but they'd already had a head start on that.

Instead, he took her shoulders and turned her around. Then he carefully, teasingly, un-knotted the tie on her bikini top, slid it off and threw it in the direction of the chair. Lastly, he released the bow on her bikini bottoms and cast them aside.

He spun her to face him.

I matched this woman? Holy moly.

Her expression was one of gentle, amused enquiry.

He sighed hard. 'Oh well, never mind.' He turned to go.

She held in a laugh.

You are impossible too, mate. Babe. Darling man.

She grabbed his hand, restraining Sam's faked departure. 'Hang on a sec. Don't *I* get a vote on this partnership?'

'I suppose.'

So she stripped him. Languidly, savouring the reveal of every muscle, ripple... and bulge.

The ludicrous transatlantic dash was the icing on the cake of his perfection. Now, she had the cherry on top.

She pulled a face. 'Hmm. Close but no cigar.'

'It was fun while it lasted.'

'Yeah.' She stroked his pecs.

'Besides, this would be sex on the *zeroth* date, which is a hell of an achievement. Very *not* Beth.'

'Who are you kidding? We've had a ton of amazing dates.'

He ran gentle fingertips over her perfect backside, raising goosebumps. 'True. But sex on the zeroth date has a nice ring to it, don't you think?'

'Definitely a story to tell the kids.'

'One of each, right?'

'Absolutely. With an *exact* two-year and four-month interval between them.' She pressed her nose to his. 'Give or take whatever the hell you want. My love.'

He leaned into a kiss. The nape of her neck prickled with desire.

He broke off, holding her gaze for a beautiful eternity. Then he backed away, opened the front door a crack, moved the Do Not Disturb sign to the outside handle, and locked it.

Her attention didn't leave his physique, his broad shoulders, his fabulous backside, and his rampant desire. He stopped a yard away, surveying her body, visibly controlling his breathing. Then he pulled her into an embrace.

Finally. Good things come to those who wait.

Impish, she offered her neck.

'Ah,' he said. 'Want to coach me on how to kiss you? A smooch here? A squeeze of the bum? Any requests?'

He pressed his lips to her neck and took her gorgeous backside in both hands.

She nuzzled his ear. 'You go for your life. Just three things.'

'What?' He kissed her so softly she might explode.

'I'm not in any rush. The dirty talk can wait.' She met his eye. 'And missionary first, because I want to look at the guy I'm in love with.'

Chapter Fifty-Nine

S am was woken by movement.

She's getting up, his brain said. *Beth. Your girlfriend.*

He decided to await her return. Life was too perfect to be ruined by leaving the bed.

A noise. The front door being opened. Voices. Laughter.

He peered over the duvet.

She was at the doorway, talking to someone. Her brother. The man from Marrakech. The man who'd left them alone all night. Who'd now come to check whether his sister had been seduced by their unexpected visitor, or murdered.

Sam strained to hear.

'But you're okay?' Leon asked.

'I'm more than okay, Lee. I've found the man I want to spend the rest of my life with.'

Sam's chest filled with something he'd never experienced.

In the living room, a phone rang. The lodge's landline or satellite phone, or whatever. The number Sam *could* have rung to tell

Beth that they were destined to be together... swiftly followed by pleading with her to abandon the dirty weekend with her possibly-not-ex-husband. The dirty weekend that had all been in Sam's stupid imagination.

Of course, if he'd rung, he'd still be in Winchester and not the Bahamas. And he wouldn't have been able to make love to her. Twice.

Beth dashed off a farewell to Leon and answered the phone. 'Oh, hi, George. Is there a problem?'

Silence while she listened. Sam tried to peer around the partition door. Her shadow approached. He snapped his eyes closed and settled into the pillow.

'Yes, he found me okay,' she said. 'Yes, I let him have sex with me. Worst experience of my life, but I'm stuck here with him now. What're you gonna do, eh?'

Sam feigned waking, a throaty moan followed by eyes fluttering open.

She was at the foot of the bed, dressed in the complimentary white towelling robe, looking down at his spreadeagled form under the thin duvet.

He made a heart shape with his hands. She blew a silent kiss.

'Yeah, he's here. Actually, he's gesturing. Either he reckons you're a tosser, or he wants hand relief.'

'Both,' Sam mouthed.

'I reckon so,' she said to George. 'That's why he and I are such a good match. I think you're a tosser too.'

She used her shoulder to hold the handset to her ear, untied the robe and let it fall to the floor. She laughed at whatever George's comeback was, never taking her attention off Sam as he gazed on.

Her expression fell more sombre as she listened. Then intrigued, surprised, excited.

'Do you want me to put him on, George, or shall I tell him?' She listened. 'No, I don't think he does. He's giving you the finger. But tell Rob we'll meet up next week.' She perched naked on the bed, tantalisingly beyond Sam's outstretched hand. 'Okay, I need to go. Sam will asphyxiate if I don't take this rubber mask off him. Love to Maya. Thanks for calling.' She thumbed a button and slid the handset onto the ottoman at the foot of the bed.

'Declan?' he asked.

She gave a Bafta-winning eye-roll, then slid under the cover. It had only been a few hours since he'd felt her warm skin under his fingers, but that was too long.

'Good morning, Studmuffin,' she cooed.

He stroked her breast. 'I see Quin has been teaching *you* to talk.'

She slid a hand between his thighs. 'Fuck off,' she squawked.

He pulled her leg across his. 'What did the speed demon want?'

'He told Rob what happened with us.'

'Even the part where you got cramp during the second time and I had to massage your calf for a bit before we carried on?'

She grabbed his attention. He winced.

'Rob wanted to arrange a thank-you drink for setting him up with Danni. When he couldn't get hold of you, he called George, who gave him the whole "Sam got the heave-ho" story.'

Sam pressed his head deep into the pillow. Being on an island paradise, in bed with the most beautiful, sexy, adorable, smart, sassy, funny, caring person was priceless, but it didn't change cold, hard facts.

'Yeah,' he sighed.

She stroked his forehead. 'Sorry, babe. I didn't mean to make light of it. But we *should* talk about what we're going home to.'

He lolled his head. 'Easy. You're going home to a parrot with keen eyesight and a minuscule vocabulary, and I'm going home to the dole.'

She nipped his backside. 'I meant a *serious* discussion. Serious in a good way, rather than "fuck my life".'

'You want to tell me?'

She told him.

Then, after sex, they ordered room service for breakfast.

They sat up in bed and ate. She explained her weekend getaway, which, to a panicked idiot chasing around Winchester on a Friday evening, had seemed ridiculous but was nothing of the sort.

Her brother was heading from Australia to the US for a meeting and had planned a stopover with his girlfriend, but she'd picked up a persistent stomach bug and couldn't come. When Beth told Leon that her divorce had come through, he suggested she celebrate by coming along instead. It was a great chance for the siblings to catch up for the first time in three years.

When they arrived, her original lodge, Phuket, had suffered a catastrophic plumbing issue, and the resort had been forced to relocate her to Paris.

'So you're definitely, one hundred percent, single?' he asked.

'After last night, I'd hope not.'

'Does this mean our fake relationship is over?'

'Definitely. You're dumped, Sam Carter.' She pinched his jaw. 'Now, will you go out with me?'

'Not a chance in hell.'

They spent the afternoon with Leon, and Sam got on famously with the guy.

In the evening, he and Beth had dinner in the resort restaurant and retired to the lodge's veranda to sip cocktails and watch the sun go down.

'So,' she said, 'What do you think of your future brother-in-law?'

A jet of alcohol spurted from Sam's lips.

She chuckled. 'The most romantic man in the world. The man with a knack for creating forevers. Mr 99% match. How can commitment *possibly* scare you?'

She couldn't be more wrong. The prospect of a life with her was incredible, but there'd been enough impulsive actions already this week. At this rate, he'd wind up on the beach tomorrow with a hastily assembled motley gathering, an internet-accredited priest, and a ring-pull in his hand, ready to slip it onto her third finger.

He laid his forehead against hers. 'You, Beth *Parris*, are certifiably impossible.'

'Hmm. I know that's code.'

'What for?'

She put her lips to his ear. 'It's code for the same thing it's always been, Sam. Right from the start.'

The final penny dropped. 'Yes. I've been in love with you the whole time.'

She stood, taking his hand. 'So how about you spend some more time in Parris?'

Chapter Sixty

Beth fiddled with the ring on her left hand. Public speaking didn't usually hold much fear, but today the stakes were enormous.

The media were here. Today marked the beginning of a PR circus. The BBC researcher had said hello in person, following up on the previous week's Zoom call. Beth had joked with Sam that the girl was sizing up whether the couple was suitable for the Breakfast sofa. It was an eye-catching story—"Dating app founders find love".

About a hundred people were milling around the large, swanky London conference suite that Rob had hired. He'd asked for their input, of course. Rob, unlike Declan, wasn't an arsehole to work for. Leaving the VC firm was a blessing.

It had been a whirlwind three months.

The long, lazy Bahama weekend had felt as much like a honeymoon as was possible for two people who'd only recently discovered their love.

A few days later, they'd caught up with Rob. He'd split from his company, sold his shares, made seven figures, and started a tech development business. This new company needed a software engineer and a business development manager. Rob suggested that Sam keep CarterSoft as a safety net and work for him on a consultancy basis. Additionally, Rob did a Dragon's Den deal, taking a thirty percent share in the dating app for an investment of a hundred grand. Appy Ever After was secure... for now. The build needed to be completed, followed by user testing, focus groups, marketing, and launch. Then it needed to scale.

Over the following weeks, it *had* scaled, partially thanks to Rob's enthusiasm and his girlfriend Danni's input. Danni, with tech experience, a keen mind, and having had enough of massage, was a co-director of Rob's business. They matched perfectly at work and at home. Another stellar success story for Sam and the app. CarterSoft also had two additional clients in the works.

Other matchmaking success stories were in the room, including the OGs Lena and Paul.

Sam walked over. He looked dapper, and gorgeous as ever.

'Okay, muffin?' she asked. He'd conceded to that nickname as a halfway house.

'Yes, babe. Rob's going to kick off now.'

Rob stepped onto the small stage, took the mic from its stand and addressed the room. He introduced himself, thanked everyone for coming, gave Danni a shout-out, then asked Beth to come up.

Deep breath.

She met Sam's gaze, which made everything fine. Nothing could go wrong now that he was in her life.

Most people in the room knew the app's story and her relationship with Sam, but she wasn't addressing them; she was doing a PR job. She was championing Sam's skills and the app's potential, as she had done from day one.

The product worked—that was the key message. She omitted the details, the fake dating, Callum, Declan, and her and Sam's ejection from corporate life. Nobody wanted that crap. They wanted the romance of it. The mad Caribbean dash to confirm the algorithm had proven what they'd known for weeks—total long-term compatibility.

She concluded by thanking Lena for the introduction to Sam, then announced that the app had signed up its 10,000th user. Not bad for a first month on sale.

She left the stage to applause. Sam blew kisses. Her heart was ready to explode. With the speech done, she could relax, so snaffled a full champagne flute from a nearby waiter.

Lena pulled her into a hug. 'Thank you, hon.'

'Oh no. *You're* the one who made the best introduction of all. Ever considered an app for *business* matchups?'

Lena laughed. Beth lifted a second glass from the tray and offered it to her friend.

Lena raised a hand. 'No, thanks. I'm on the wagon.'

Beth frowned. 'Everything okay?'

'More than okay. I'm just taking a break for... seven months or so.'

Beth hopped up and down. 'Ohmygod, ohmygod, ohmygod.'

'Chill, hon. This is *your* party.'

Beth hauled Sam over, whispered in his ear, and the trio embraced. Someone coughed.

Beth turned to see George and Maya, and was forced to explain the group hug.

'Sounds like there'll be more celebrations in the weeks ahead,' George said.

'We must all go out,' Maya added. 'Quadruple date or whatever.'

'No hangers-on this time,' Beth said.

George slapped Sam's shoulder. 'You know, mate, I considered stealing the limelight today. Hop up on stage, grab the mic, ask this lady a question.' He pulled Maya close. 'Then I realised I had a reputation to maintain, so I'll give it a few more months.' He winked.

'You're a rapscallion, George Linley,' Maya said. 'But I'll wait. You get time off for good behaviour.'

Sam was also getting time off for good behaviour. The diamond ring was only a symbol of intent; no date was set. Life was too crazy to plan a wedding. For now, they were living under her roof, which hadn't ruffled any feathers, including Quin's.

Paul, Rob and Danni wandered over.

'Sunday Times are interested in a feature on you two,' Rob said.

Beth took Sam's hand. 'Sounds good.'

George flagged down a passing waiter, handed Lena an orange juice, then made sure everyone else had a champagne flute. He ushered them into a circle and raised his glass.

Seven other glasses were held aloft and chinked.

'To you, and all our futures,' George said.

Beth met Sam's eye. 'Appy Ever After,' they chorused.

THE END

Acknowledgements

It continues to be a pleasure to work with my editors Becca & Ellie, and my valued author friend and critique partner Elizabeth Holland. Thanks to all three for your input and wisdom.

I'm indebted to Dr Kate Morgan for help with research on apps and software engineering, Pandora Yates for a perspective on the thirtysomething dating scene (!) and my advance reader Sarah Saya.

Last but by no means least, huge thanks to Alex Allden for another brilliant cover design.

Also by the Author

The Cathedral City Comedies – a rom-com series

"Floored"
"Appy Ever After"
Book 3 – Autumn 2026

Touchline Girls – a sports rom-com series

"Match Daze"
Book 2 – TBC
Book 3 – TBC

Pavilion Girls – a women's cricket rom-com series

"Wicket Maiden"
Book 2 – Spring 2026
Book 3 – Spring 2027

Also from the Publisher

Here's the complete list of books from Valericain Press.

Whether your reading taste includes sci-fi, romance, comedy, or something quirkier, there may be a story here for you.

Romantic Comedy   **Historical Romance**

 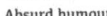   

Absurd humour   **Quirky romantic comedy / cosy mystery**   **Post-apocalyptic**

Near future sci-fi adventure   **Space opera**

CHRISSIE HARRISON

About the Author

Writing romcoms is my happy place. After working in other genres for many years, I couldn't resist the pull towards comedy and romance. I have a soft spot for stories with strong women, nice guys, and a touch of the bittersweet. I like the connection between my protagonists to be more than physical – a bond that helps solve their problems. Often I shine a light on mental health issues, especially neurodiversity, which is close to my heart.

Fundamentally, I try to write the books I like to read – those with wit, heart and intelligence.

Away from the writing desk, I enjoy great scenery, a relaxing train ride, delicious coffee and cake, and catching up with friends and fellow authors.

Chrissie Harrison is a pen name.

To get early notice of future releases, free excerpts and more, join my Readers' Circle at https://www.chrissieharrison.co.uk/newsletter/

Find me on social media @AuthorChrissieHarrison